W9-BVZ-608

The 13th Target

Books by Mark de Castrique

The Buryin' Barry Series
Dangerous Undertaking
Grave Undertaking
Foolish Undertaking
Final Undertaking
Fatal Undertaking

The Sam Blackman Series
Blackman's Coffin
The Fitzgerald Ruse
The Sandburg Connection

Other Novels
The 13th Target

The 13th Target

Mark de Castrique

Poisoned Pen Press

Copyright © 2012 by Mark de Castrique

First Edition 2012

10 9 8 7 6 5 4 3 2 1

Library of Congress Catalog Card Number: 2011942737

ISBN: 9781590586150   Hardcover
      9781590586174   Trade Paperback

Poisoned Pen Press
6962 E. First Ave., Ste. 103
Scottsdale, AZ 85251
www.poisonedpenpress.com
info@poisonedpenpress.com

Printed in the United States of America

For Linda, once again

Prologue

They never called each other by name, although they knew one another like family. In the large, oak-paneled room, two of the three sat in leather armchairs by a draped window and spoke in whispers.

The third stood apart. As the youngest, in his mid-forties, he was assigned the task of showing the DVD. A monitor and playback machine rested on a silver cart. Neither had ever been used before. He thumbed through an operating manual, studied the remote control, and strained to catch snatches of his colleagues' conversation.

Rain beating against the window obliterated not only the words but the language. At times he thought they were speaking German; at other times, French. Occasionally Arabic laced the phrases. The woman's voice was higher pitched and more difficult to discern.

The man holding the remote read the manual's instructions in Spanish, but only because it had opened to that section. A faint squeal of a dry hinge came from the single door to the room. The man looked up from the manual and saw a thin, stooped figure slip inside. Stronger light from the hallway haloed his gray hair, turning him into an ancient angel. He clutched a black leather briefcase in his right hand, closed the door behind him, and stepped slowly, steadily, and silently across the Persian carpet.

"Sorry I'm late," he said in a voice surprisingly loud. "The weather delayed my landing and then the hassle with customs."

The others laughed, knowing his private jet touched down at a private airstrip and no customs officials had a clue he had returned. He set the briefcase on a side table and thumbed its dual combination locks. "Is the TV hooked up?"

The man with the remote laid the manual on the DVD player. "Yes." Evidently the meeting would be conducted in English, fitting since the topic focused on the pending elections in the United States.

"Good. Let's get started. I need to be in a cabinet meeting in less than two hours." He motioned them to four chairs set in a semicircle in front of the television. While the others sat, he passed out printed information collected in briefing packets. "The DVD is in the inside pocket of yours," he told the man with the remote. "But I have a few things to say first."

The others gave him their full attention, keeping the binders unopened in their laps.

His posture straightened as energy overcame age, fueled by the passion of his commitment to the task at hand. "As I told our full group last year, it is my belief that the Republican candidate for president will win the election in the fall, regardless of whether Senator Brighton or Governor Nelson secures the nomination. Given that likely scenario, I'm working to develop ties and assets with both. I've drawn up a list of potential problems either of the two might present to us and what we should do to apply the proper leverage."

He paused, letting his audience of three absorb his prediction. Each of them glanced down at the briefing papers, anxious to see the data for themselves.

"Yes, you'll find impact assessments with strategic and tactical modifications that must be considered in light of the coming political shift. But those will be minor in the immediate future and can be viewed as opportunities to be studied and exploited."

A murmur of agreement affirmed his analysis.

"But the real challenge continues to be the domestic economy of the United States. No question the out-of-control real estate speculation and undisciplined greed of the financial sectors is headed over the top. Yes, we moved our money out, but a meltdown is coming and the American public's confidence in their institutions will plummet. Those morons are bringing it on themselves, unaware or unconcerned they're killing the geese laying golden eggs."

"But we'll ride it out," the woman said. "Our European central banks will be safe havens."

The old man shook his head. "Not without an infusion of American dollars. The economic collapse will generate internal unrest within the United States which, in turn, could encourage attacks by groups from without, some of which we barely know." He cleared his throat. "But those are just problems to be addressed and turned to our advantage." He nodded to the man with the remote. "There is something else festering that will gain momentum if the U.S. economy unravels. Something with far more serious consequences."

The younger man pulled the DVD from the sleeve in his packet. He stood and walked to the machine, waiting for the cue to insert the disk.

The older man continued. "What you're about to see happened last month at Vanderbilt University during a debate featuring the Republican primary hopefuls."

The machine swallowed the DVD and then whirred softly. A picture glowed on the screen, unrecognizable at first as the camera struggled to focus in dim light. Somewhere offscreen a man's garbled words echoed through a PA system.

"The students are outside of the packed auditorium, listening to the debate over loudspeakers. Watch the group of students in the upper right."

The cameraman tilted up, evidently attracted by a small ball of fire. Then more flames erupted, flaring briefly before burning out. Some drifted upward, borne on a light breeze.

"What are they burning?" asked the man still standing beside the DVD player.

As if in answer to his question, the camera zoomed in. The circle of flames grew larger. A chant drowned out the PA, swelling like the roar of a wave rolling into shore. "Burn the Fed! Burn the Fed! Burn the Fed!"

"Mein Gott, they're burning money." The woman's voice cracked in disbelief.

"Dollar bills." The man who brought the video turned to the woman beside him. "Showing their contempt for the words Federal Reserve Note inscribed on the currency and for the institution they believe is leading them to ruin."

"That's madness," said the man on the other side of the woman. "Those candidates have got to be stopped."

The younger man standing by the television shook his head. "The candidates didn't start it, did they? That's the problem."

The man running the meeting smiled coldly. "Exactly. You're watching a spontaneous event, unorganized and unplanned. Not at Berkeley or NYU. These are students in Nashville, Tennessee, the home of the Grand Ole Opry, for God's sake. Students not yet vested in the system. Students whose mothers and fathers effectively changed the course of the war in Vietnam and demonstrated how a groundswell could engulf a nation."

"But no one's getting killed," the woman said. "Won't they burn out just like the dollar bills?"

The man shrugged. "Where this goes, especially given the hard times on the horizon, is anybody's guess. But, like I said, our European banks will need an infusion of U.S. dollars. Our source is the Fed. No one else has the power to increase the money supply."

The woman grasped their dilemma. "You think the Fed will curtail foreign lending?"

"The Fed is likely to become the whipping boy for these students who will find no jobs when they graduate. The issue will move into mainstream politics within two years." He paused a second. "Or the anger against the Fed could be picked up internationally by those groups always looking for any excuse to blame capitalism, international financiers, or the Jews. Either way, the Fed will come under increased pressure, and that will have consequences worldwide. At the very least, consequences of disclosure and transparency which will cripple the Fed's lending policies. At the worst, the dismantling of the Federal Reserve System or violent attacks like the Oklahoma City bombing of 1995. All are consequences we cannot tolerate, or the world economy and our interests are at risk." He looked at the man by the television. "You head the media interests. What's the best way to control a story?"

The man holding the remote smiled. "Create the story."

"Exactly. We don't have much time. Between this election and the next, things could turn ugly." He pointed a gnarled finger toward the younger man. "Show us you have what it takes to replace me. I suggest you begin constructing that story now. Just be damn sure it ends the way we want it to end."

The four looked back at the monitor where burning bills danced like fireflies against the night sky.

Part One
The Set-Up

Chapter One

Four years later—

"Rusty. Have you got any money on you?" Paul Luguire caught his driver's eye in the rearview mirror.

"I'm not sure. Maybe forty dollars." Russell Mullins looked ahead at the traffic clogging the 14th Street Bridge headed out of Washington, D.C. "I can check."

Luguire laid the papers he'd been reading in the open briefcase on the seat beside him. "Don't bother. I'd rather you keep your hands on the wheel. Swing through the BB&T off Washington Boulevard and I'll use the ATM. I'm meeting the grandkids for ice cream and I believe it's irresponsible to use a credit card for something that melts."

Mullins laughed. "I wondered where the term economic meltdown came from."

"Not funny, Rusty."

Mullins laughed again, only this time silently. He knew Luguire liked his pun but the economy was a sore subject. It was also funny that the man most responsible for printing U.S. currency didn't have any of his own. "Old Greenbacks" was the name Mullins called Luguire for the duty roster.

Having a code name for your charge was a habit he'd kept from his Secret Service days. He'd done a stint with "Rawhide" former President Reagan and "Timberwolf" former President

George H. W. Bush. His active presidents had been "Eagle" Bill Clinton and "Trailblazer" George W. Bush. Then when his wife Laurie got sick, Mullins put in for a desk job in counterfeiting and settled for a schedule that gave him more time to care for her. That had been the toughest assignment of all. And he'd lost her. The worst thing that can happen to a Secret Service agent, lose the life you're trying to protect.

Mullins shook his head, flinging off thoughts from the past. He glanced back in the mirror at his present charge. They'd been together almost a year. Mullins noticed how much the gray hairline had receded, the circles grown darker under the blue eyes. Luguire was about ten years older than him. Fifty-eight. But Mullins had watched the man age five years during the past eleven months. He felt sorry for Luguire. A decent man trying to navigate a floundering economy while under attack both literally and figuratively by forces opposing his efforts.

Mullins turned on his signal for the exit off I-395. He knew the bank branch Luguire meant and it would only be a slight delay to the high-rise in Clarendon where Luguire had a luxury apartment.

"You want me to hang with you during your ice cream outing?" Mullins asked.

"No. Margie's bringing the twins by after T-ball practice. She can pick me up in the underground garage. And I doubt if anyone is staking out Ben and Jerry's."

"I don't know. That Cherry Garcia's a pretty radical flavor."

"I was thinking of something stronger. Like Rusty Nails."

Mullins shot a quick glance in the mirror. Luguire smiled, knowing he'd surprised his bodyguard.

"Who have you been talking to?"

For the first time since Luguire got in the black Mercedes, he relaxed. "Today a little bird who knows her history told me Rusty's not your only nickname. Rusty Nails. How'd you get named after a damn drink?"

"The Secret Service. They thrive on nicknames. I already had Rusty for Russell. But that wasn't good enough. So, I made the mistake of having a couple Rusty Nails one night when some of us were off-duty, and the name Nails stuck. At least within the presidential protection detail."

"Well, you're tough as nails in my book. Or maybe Tough-Ass Nails is even better."

"Don't go saying that. Somebody will latch onto it and I'll be cursed with Tough-Ass the rest of my life."

"Like Old Greenbacks?"

Again, Mullins' eyes shot to the mirror. He felt his face redden.

Luguire laughed. "Don't worry. I like it. Did you ever make up any nicknames for a president?"

"Actually code names come from the White House Communications Agency. Back in the day, they were supposed to be secret. Now everything's so encrypted it doesn't matter."

"Do you know President Brighton's?"

"Orca."

"Killer whale," Luguire mused. "Good choice. How about the first lady?"

"Opal. The first family's code names usually start with the same letter."

"And code names were the only names you used?"

"Well, we did tend to generate our own off-the-record names as we got to know them."

"Such as?"

"Such as I'd sooner give up our nuclear launch codes." Mullins swung the Mercedes into the drive-through lane for the ATM.

Luguire laughed. "Then I'll definitely settle for Old Greenbacks." He reached in his suit coat for his wallet and looked at the briefcase next to him. "I'm spread out back here. Would you do the transaction?"

Mullins rolled down his window and pulled the car close to the ATM. Luguire handed his debit card over the seat.

"How much do you want?" Mullins asked.

"Better get a hundred. You need the PIN?"

"Yeah. I make a point of forgetting it."

"Liar. You don't forget anything. Give it a shot."

"The machine might eat your card."

"If I'm trusting my life to your brain, I can certainly trust my card."

Mullins punched in the four digits. The ATM screen presented withdrawal and deposit options. Mullins selected Fast-Cash for a hundred dollars. He passed the five new twenties and the card back to Luguire. "You must have ordered these this morning."

Luguire separated the bills, crinkling them so they wouldn't stick together. "You're right. The ink's still wet."

Mullins laughed and eased the car back onto Washington Boulevard. It was nearly six and traffic thinned slightly. "How do the twins like T-ball?"

"Okay. They like the uniforms. Margie says Lenny spends most of his time drawing in the dirt in the outfield. Lanny wants to be pitcher because on TV the pitcher's always shown in a close-up. He doesn't understand why T-ball doesn't need a pitcher."

"Have you been to a game?"

"Not yet. They've only had a few practices. The first one's this Saturday."

"Let me know where and when," Mullins said.

"Are you working?"

"No, I'm off-duty. But I'm babysitting Josh. Never too young to teach a boy the great American pastime."

"I'd like that. I'd like to meet your grandson. The game's at the field by William Ramsay Elementary. I'll let you know the details tomorrow."

When he reached the high-rise, Mullins drove into the underground garage, entered the security code, and dropped Luguire at the elevator. "Eight?" Mullins asked, as Luguire closed his briefcase and slid out of the backseat.

"Right. Have a good night, Nails."

"You too, Old Greenbacks."

Chapter Two

Fares Khoury steered the silver Ford 150 pickup along the leaf-covered lane. The truck's shocks rode so low that every root and rut sent a jolt up his spine. He took comfort knowing his part of the mission was nearly complete. The last haul of fertilizer bags lay in the bed behind him, the final purchase of the quantities he'd assembled from feed-and-seed stores across five Virginia counties. Because of federal regulations and purchasing paperwork, many gardening and farm suppliers no longer carried ammonia-nitrate fertilizer, but his contact had given him accurate source information, and his photo ID and background story passed scrutiny.

Khoury swung the truck around the small clapboard house and parked in front of the shed. The rough plank walls were weather-beaten and the tin roof rusty, but the wood was still solid and the shiny padlock on the door would require a heavy-duty hacksaw to dismantle. Two days before, a heating oil supplier had filled the tank on the back wall of Khoury's rented house. Then Khoury had siphoned that oil into ten-gallon drums now safely locked in the shed with the fertilizer.

He still hadn't gotten used to sleeping in the house. There were no streetlights or traffic noise, only pitch black nights and cries from wild animals Khoury imagined lurked just outside his door. As a native of Miami and son of Lebanese immigrants, he had no experience living off a dirt road in an isolated mountain valley. His four weeks in this alien landscape had passed with the speed of a prison sentence. Only the thought of returning to his wife and four-year-old daughter gave him comfort. He didn't like that they'd been taken from their home. For their protection, he'd been told.

The most nerve-racking event had been dealing with the bank. Bankers had ruined his life and to walk into their den, play the role of a businessman, and smile as he opened the new account pushed him to the limit. He kept thinking of the end game and how those responsible would pay. Now the need for the bank was behind him, although it seemed like a lot of trouble to net a thousand dollars. His contact had said transactions over ten thousand dollars drew the jackals' attention so he did what he was told. He wondered if the banks had also cheated the rest of the chosen.

Although the evening temperature began to cool, Khoury became drenched with sweat as he transferred his cargo from the pickup to the shed. When he finished, he fastened the new padlock, locked the truck out of habit learned in Miami, and went into the house. The place had come furnished, but the few chairs, rickety table, and moth-eaten sofa looked like rejects from a yard sale. The box springs of the bed were so shot that Khoury had pulled the mattress onto the floor. He shuddered at the thought of what kind of vermin slept with him.

He took a quick shower because the water heater's recovery rate meant only four minutes before the temperature dropped to that of the well. Then he sat in his underwear at the kitchen table and wrote down the day's activities: the cost of the fertilizer and the gasoline for the truck were entered in a ledger and a short narrative of his actions went in his journal.

His contact stressed that both records be carefully maintained. Khoury would hand them over to the man who would replace him, the man who would convert the resources he'd gathered into a lethal bomb and then give it to those who would deliver it to the target and destroy the evil enslaving them all.

Khoury finished writing. He felt weak. He drank a glass of orange juice and got the kit for his injection. He'd pick up a prescription refill on Saturday that would carry him through the mission. Khoury had been instructed to wait patiently. The man would come. Any delay wasn't to be questioned because the man was overseeing everything and he had his own target, the thirteenth. Khoury was curious as to what that thirteenth target could be. But he wouldn't ask. He would wait. He would wait for the man called Russell Mullins to come to him.

Chapter Three

Mullins poured himself a Scotch and sat in his easy chair. He checked the TV listings to see if the Washington Nationals had an evening game. Not finding one, he flipped through mindless sitcoms and indignant talk show guests until he gave up and turned the set off. Maybe later he'd find one of the British cop shows. They were more realistic than their American counterparts.

He took a sip of his drink, and then picked up the phone. His daughter answered just as he thought he was headed for voicemail.

She spoke a breathy, "Hi, Dad."

"Kayli, have I caught you at a bad time?"

Her voice brightened. "No. I was changing Josh. Yet again. I've plopped him back in front of the potty training video."

"He's only two. I'm sure he'll be housebroken by first grade."

Kayli laughed. "Housebroken? What? Should I make him go on the paper?"

"Whatever works."

"You can try that with him at your place."

"What time did you need me to come by Saturday?"

"My haircut's at eleven. Anytime before ten-thirty."

"Good. I might take him to a T-ball game if it fits your schedule."

Kayli laughed again. "T-ball? Who's the one pushing him now? He's a little young for centerfield and not housebroken."

"Just to watch. Paul Luguire told me his grandsons have a game."

Kayli's voice sobered. "Is it dangerous? I thought there were threats on his life."

"Yes, technically. I'm more of a precaution. But I'm off-duty. Somebody else will be assigned to him."

"Sure, if you think it's okay."

Mullins took a sip of Scotch in victory. "What's the word from Allen?"

"We talked earlier. He's still off the coast of Somalia."

"Does Naval Intelligence let him use a webcam?"

"No. We exchange video DVDs, but that's by mail. There's no Skype. Everything's done to protect the security of his location. I'm grateful his rank lets him use a POTS."

"What's that?"

Kayli laughed. "A highly classified acronym. Plain Old Telephone System."

"Got to be tough for both of you."

"I'm pretty lucky, Dad. If he were on the ground somewhere, I'd be worried sick. But on a ship, he's reachable. I don't take that for granted."

"Never do."

Kayli heard the sadness in the words. "Well, should I buy Josh a glove for Saturday?"

"No. But pack his Nationals cap. And some extra diapers."

Mullins hung up, warmth from the Scotch and warmth from the call mingling together. "We've got a good daughter and grandson, Laurie."

He found himself talking to his dead wife more and more frequently. Comforting in the lonely evenings and he saw nothing alarming about it. Laurie wasn't talking back. Yet.

Mullins checked his email and sent most of the messages to the trash. He refilled his drink and headed for his easy chair. He stopped, then retraced his steps to the kitchen and pulled a dusty bottle of Drambuie down from a cabinet. He estimated half an ounce and mixed it with the Scotch. He held the glass up to the light. "To baseball and grandkids." He took a sip of the Rusty Nail, trying to remember when he'd last had one. Then he watched an episode of Inspector Lewis he hadn't seen. Shortly after ten, he went to bed.

The cellphone on his nightstand jarred him awake. His inner clock told him it was too early for the programmed alarm. A glance at the time confirmed his intuition. Two-forty. His heart started pounding. No good news came at two-forty in the morning. Kayli. Josh. Or maybe his son-in-law, Lieutenant Commander Allen Woodson, tracking pirates and flying drones from the Indian Ocean.

"Hello," he whispered anxiously.

"Russell Mullins?" The man's voice was clear and calm.

"Yes. What is it?"

"Are you the Russell Mullins with Prime Protection?"

"Yes. What is it?" he asked more urgently.

"I'm Detective Robert Sullivan with the Arlington Police Department."

"My daughter. Has something happened to my daughter?"

"No, sir. I'm calling about Paul Luguire. He's been shot."

Mullins stood, his bare feet slapping the hardwood floor. "How badly?"

"I'm afraid he's dead. Mr. Mullins, we need to talk."

Chapter Four

Detective Robert Sullivan bent over the table, his eyes focused on the single, blood-splattered sheet of typing paper, his mind ignoring the body slumped in the chair next to him.

A uniformed police officer stuck his head in the kitchen. "Rob, that Mullins guy's in the lobby."

Sullivan straightened his back and groaned. "I told him to go to the station."

"Well, he didn't listen."

"Of course he didn't listen. Once a fed always a fed." Sullivan rolled off his latex gloves and dropped them in his suit pocket. Three-fifteen in the morning. He should be home in bed with his wife instead of here with some banker who couldn't take the pressure. Sullivan had pressure too. Luguire was evidently a big-shot and the media would be crawling all over each other for information. He hoped the statement "apparent suicide" would send them scurrying for titillating gossip and leave him clear to finish the investigation. This case looked routine, but Sullivan had been on the force long enough to know that as soon as you started treating something as routine it would bite you in the ass.

"What do you want to do?" the uniformed officer asked.

"Bring him up. The crime lab's cleared the living room. I'll talk to him in there." Sullivan took a seat in a teal chintz chair that might have cost as much as he made in a month. He didn't begrudge Luguire his fine possessions. How could he? What did Luguire have now? Sullivan felt sorry for him. And for the man's daughter. No child should see a father with the side of his head blown off.

Sullivan heard footsteps in the hall. A second uniformed officer ushered in a man whose thinning red hair looked like it had been styled by a hand dryer in a public bathroom. He wore rumpled tan slacks, a wrinkled white shirt, and a blue sport coat that bulged slightly under the left arm. Probably a Glock, Sullivan thought. He might have dressed in the middle of the night, but he'd sooner forget his shoes than his semi-automatic. The man swept the room with a turn of his head. Any trace of sleep was gone from his piercing brown eyes. They settled on the detective.

"You Sullivan?" Mullins didn't wait for an introduction.

Sullivan stood. "My name's not important. The fact that I told you to go to the station is." Sullivan strode forward. "I thought you'd respect law enforcement, Mr. Mullins."

Mullins kept his eyes locked on the detective, ceding no ground as the other man walked into his space. He studied him carefully before replying. "Paul Luguire was my charge. I'm not cooling my heels at the station while some murderer walks the streets. There's a job to do."

Sullivan eased back a step but kept the edge in his voice. "It's a little late for you to start doing your job now."

Mullins' jaw clenched. He fought the urge to deck the guy. But Sullivan was a head shorter and twenty pounds overweight. Assaulting a police detective wouldn't solve anything. "I didn't say it was my job."

Sullivan saw the restraint win out. He'd baited Mullins but the man kept his cool, if barely. "And I didn't say it was murder."

Mullins shook his head. "It was murder. You can take that to the bank. I don't care if you found a videotape of him putting a gun in his mouth and pulling the trigger, Paul Luguire didn't kill himself."

"You haven't examined the crime scene."

"Then show me."

Metal clanked as a gurney rolled through the front door. Two techs looked at Sullivan. The nearer said, "We were told we're clear to take the body."

Sullivan held up his hand. "Wait a moment." He turned to Mullins. "You're a civilian. You know I can't do that. I cut you slack bringing you this far into the apartment."

"If it's suicide, then what's the problem?" Mullins asked.

"If it's not, then I can't have you contaminating the murder scene." Sullivan smiled. "You see your murder premise keeps you out."

Mullins glanced at the gurney. "Looks like you're through with the scene."

"We might have missed something. I'll do a final sweep when Luguire's been removed. I don't want a trace of you showing up in that kitchen."

For the first time, Mullins looked surprised. He understood the implications. "I'm a suspect?"

"You were the last person to see him alive. A defense attorney would claim any DNA or fiber evidence against you came from your tour of the scene."

"What about his daughter? His grandkids?"

"What about them?"

"He was meeting them for ice cream. You don't share a sundae and then blow your brains out."

"No," Sullivan agreed. "They never got together. His daughter got a text at practice that something had come up."

"What time was this?"

"About six-thirty. She was supposed to pick him up here."

"I dropped him off at six-ten. What could have happened in twenty minutes to cause him to kill himself?"

Sullivan shrugged. "You tell me. Maybe he never intended to go for ice cream."

Mullins thought better when he moved. He stepped around Sullivan and paced back and forth across the living room. "Then why did he make me stop at an ATM? Why get a hundred dollars? Even if he intended to meet the grandkids for one last time, that's a hell of a lot of ice cream. No. He was looking beyond last night. I was coming to see his grandsons play T-ball Saturday. We made that plan just before he left the car." Mullins stopped pacing and stared at Sullivan. "So, you tell me."

"I see where you're coming from," Sullivan admitted. "But Luguire left a note. We're pretty sure it's in his handwriting and written with his fountain pen. There are ink smears on the right edge of his palm and a slight smudge on one of the lines where he must have brushed across it."

"What's the note say?"

"We don't make those things public."

Mullins threw up his hands. "Do I look like the damn public? Come on, Detective, has nothing I've said given you pause in your rush to judgment?"

Sullivan flushed. The points made by Mullins did make him reassess the case. And he had been ready to dismiss the ex-Secret Service agent as someone trying to cover his own ass. He turned to the men by the gurney. "Follow me." He pointed a finger at Mullins. "You. Stay where you are. Don't sit. Don't touch anything."

Rusty Mullins fumed. He wanted to see the crime scene. Faking a suicide was difficult, but not impossible. However, evidence was only as good as the person interpreting it and Mullins had never worked with Sullivan before. He could be Sherlock Holmes or Inspector Clouseau.

Sullivan returned carrying a clear evidence bag. Mullins saw blue ink and red smears on a white sheet of paper. Sullivan didn't look at him. "Let's walk."

Mullins followed the detective down the hall and into the elevator. Neither man spoke until they reached the lobby door.

"I've got an unmarked at the curb," Sullivan said.

"Are you taking me to the station?"

"I'm not taking you anywhere. Now get in the passenger's seat."

The passenger's seat meant Mullins wasn't being placed under arrest or treated with hostility. He ratcheted down his attitude a notch and slid into the bucket seat. "You got a partner?"

Sullivan laid the evidence bag on the dash and closed the driver's door. "Yeah, but he went home sick an hour before we got the call. You're lucky. I'm the one with the sparkling personality." He pulled a thermos and two cups from the floorboard underneath his seat. "Here." He handed Mullins a cup. "Run your fingers around the inside to clean out the debris. My wife's coffee will kill any serious germs."

"Thanks." Mullins held the chipped cup steady while Sullivan poured. "How many years have you been a detective?"

"Fifteen. Ten in homicide. So this isn't my first time to a barbecue."

"I didn't think so." Mullins sipped the coffee. The scorched taste brought back nights with the Secret Service, waiting for a president to arrive or depart.

Sullivan poured himself a cup. "But I admit my experience is nothing like the boys in the district. Corpses in D.C. have to take a number to see a detective."

Mullins didn't laugh, but he appreciated the bridge Sullivan was trying to build. "I got assigned to Luguire about a year ago. I was really a glorified chauffeur. Resentment and opposition to the Federal Reserve had created an atmosphere of personal threats and the Federal Reserve Chairman wanted protection for key personnel."

"But you're private now. Why didn't the government take care of it?"

"Because the Federal Reserve System isn't really a federal agency. It's operation is independent of the government. Most people don't know the Federal Reserve Regional Banks are privately held by commercial banks. Yes, the president appoints the Board of Governors, designating the chairman and vice chairman. And the Senate confirms. But Congress has limited operational oversight, and some say there's less transparency than with the CIA."

"Well, I know it says Federal Reserve on our money. You'd think it was a government agency."

"Is Federal Express a government agency?"

"No." Sullivan laughed. "They're too damn efficient."

"As I understand, the Federal Reserve tells Treasury to print more money or simply creates it on its balance sheet by buying Treasury bonds with its own Federal Reserve Notes. Money flows into the financial system and commercial banks charge you interest. As a taxpayer, you're also on the hook for the Treasury bonds purchased to back the currency. A growing number of people think that's a raw deal, even unconstitutional. They think the U.S. government should be directly responsible and accountable for the country's money."

"What do you think?"

"The argument's above my pay grade. Like most things, there are probably points on both sides. I do know disagreement doesn't give anyone the right to assassination."

"Did you make Luguire's security arrangements?"

"Hell, no." Mullins waved to the building in front of them. "Do you think I'd have him in an apartment building accessible with a keypad? Luguire conceded to the bare minimum of having an armed escort when working. And we provided protection if he attended some big event on his own time. He stayed here because it was close to his grandkids."

"What was his job?"

"He was the guy who interfaced with Treasury. He made sure enough money flowed into the banking system."

"His daughter said you were his main bodyguard."

Mullins caught his breath. "Did she find him?"

"Yes. She got the text that he was tied up. Then, after practice, when she and her sons got to their car, they found a flat tire. She had to call her husband to put on the spare. They didn't get home till after eight. She tried her father several times, but he never answered. She got a funny feeling. Even if he was busy, he'd always text her during a break. She was afraid he'd fallen, or maybe had a heart attack. She drove over after eleven, leaving her husband with the kids."

"She found him by herself?"

"Yeah. You can imagine the shock."

Mullins sighed. "No, I can't."

The two men drank their coffee in silence for a moment. Then Mullins gestured to the evidence bag on the dash. "Did he leave the note for his daughter?"

"I guess. And the rest of the world. He wrote, 'I'm sorry. I want to be with Elaine. I'm not as tough as I thought I'd be. Please understand.' His daughter said Elaine was her mother."

"Yeah. She was killed in a car wreck three years ago. He'd talk about her sometimes."

"Did you get the impression he'd die to be with her?"

"No. Not a chance. The fact that he was hurting would keep him from doing something so stupid. He would never pass that kind of pain along to his family."

Sullivan studied the other man over the rim of his coffee. "You liked him, didn't you?"

"Yeah. We kinda hit it off. We found we had things in common. My wife died about the same time as his. My daughter lives close by. I've got a two-year-old grandson who means the world to me."

"What happened to your wife?"

"Ovarian cancer. Laurie thought she had the flu. The cancer that whispers, they call it. When the symptoms arise, it's in the late stages." He paused as the remembered horror of the diagnosis flowed over him. "Laurie showed me how to die with dignity."

"I'm sorry," Sullivan said.

"I am too. And so was Luguire about his wife. But Paul Luguire would also die with dignity. Not as a bloody mess for his daughter to discover."

"I saw powder burns on his hand and on his temple."

"He didn't swallow his gun?"

"No. I know. That's the way most people do it so they can't jerk the gun away at the last second."

"It doesn't make sense."

"What bank did he use for the ATM?"

"The BB&T in Clarendon."

"That is odd, and that he'd set up the Saturday T-ball date."

"Did you check his phone to see if he got any calls after I left him?"

"Yes. Nothing. We saw the text he sent to his daughter. We'll review the records from his cell service as well."

Mullins eyed the evidence bag again. "You brought that with you. Can I take a look?"

Sullivan switched on the courtesy light. "You should be able to read it through the plastic."

Mullins angled the bag toward the light. A few bloody spots stained the right edge of the paper. Maybe blowback from the head wound. The letters were written with shaky cursive script in royal blue ink. He read the words Sullivan had told him. Then he re-read it. This time one phrase stopped him cold. "It's a double s," he whispered.

"What?" Sullivan leaned over to see.

"Here." Mullins touched the protective cover. "It's not 'as tough as I thought I'd be,' it's 'as tough ass.' Luguire learned Rusty wasn't my only nickname. Some of my Secret Service colleagues call me Rusty Nails. Luguire teased me in the car yesterday, calling me 'tough-ass Nails.' He didn't write this note to his daughter. He didn't write it to the world. He wrote it to me."

Chapter Five

Amanda Church maneuvered her black BMW convertible off Connecticut Avenue and down Tilden to Rock Creek Parkway. The woodland road was her favorite route into the heart of D.C., and with the morning traffic pattern turning both lanes inbound, it was also her fastest.

At seven, the June humidity had yet to build to smothering oppression. The car's open top allowed the cool air to flow over Amanda like an invigorating stream, energizing her for the challenges of the day. As she neared the Kennedy Center for the Performing Arts, she cranked up the all-news radio station to catch the morning headlines. The lead for the local news grabbed her attention.

"The Arlington Police have reported the death of Federal Reserve executive Paul Luguire. Mr. Luguire's body was discovered by his daughter late last night at his residence in Clarendon. Preliminary evidence suggests Mr. Luguire took his own life. A statement is expected later this morning by Federal Reserve Chairman Hugh Radcliffe. Financial markets are expected to pay close attention, and it is anticipated Chairman Radcliffe will speak prior to the opening of the New York Stock Exchange in an effort to alleviate any investor jitters. Unofficial sources say Mr. Luguire had suffered bouts of depression since the death of his wife."

Amanda clicked off the radio. Yeah, she thought, that's what they would say. Anything to divert concerns away from the

Federal Reserve. The day would become a zoo at the office. At least she was in Federal Reserve security and not public relations, but something this big would affect all departments.

She wanted to call her husband Curtis. He'd taken the previous night's last red-eye from Dulles to Paris where he was researching his new thriller. He'd crash at his usual hotel, the Odéon Saint-Germain on the Left Bank, and though it was early afternoon in France, he probably wouldn't be up till supper. Curtis claimed he wrote best at night. Amanda now felt like a character worthy of one of his intricate plots.

She wanted to wake him up and tell him what the newscast reported. She wanted to review her options. But that might put both of them in danger, as much danger as Luguire had encountered.

No, she'd head straight to her office and act the way she'd be expected to act if she didn't know there was more to the story.

There was only one person she would tell, one person she felt confident would believe her. She had to arrange a meeting as soon as possible. No one else could be trusted. Now everything depended upon Rusty Mullins.

◇◇◇

Over 3800 miles away, Amanda's husband wasn't asleep. Instead, Curtis Jordan sat alone at a table in Aux deux Oliviers and finished a light lunch of an assortment of cheeses, a baguette, and a half bottle of Tavel Rosé. Since the restaurant was across the street from the Luxembourg Gardens, he planned a short stroll and counted on the wine and exercise to relax him enough that he'd catch up on his sleep during the afternoon. He wanted to be well rested before facing the task of reining his story into the structure that would create a satisfying conclusion.

Gimmicks like coincidence or the introduction of last-minute characters who provided solutions weren't the trademarks of a consummate craftsman. Curtis Jordan prided himself on developing stories whose endings weren't predictable but were inevitable. The conclusion was the only one possible and every brick, every stone of the story had been chosen and constructed to provide the climax and resolution.

Sometimes minor characters would take over or events cause unintended consequences that propelled the story in a new direction. Jordan liked that part of the creative process as long as he controlled the final destination.

He signaled the waiter for his bill and pulled his iPad from the small briefcase he always carried. The Coach-leather satchel also held his fountain pen and writing journal—a spectrum of technology spanning centuries. Jordan neither wrote nor surfed the Internet during a meal, but while the waiter brought his check, he logged on to his home page, the website of the *International Herald Tribune.*

The headline on the lower lefthand column read "Federal Reserve executive found dead." Jordan enlarged the font to avoid pulling his reading glasses from his pocket. The story was rudimentary coverage: Paul Luguire's daughter discovering his body, Chairman Radcliffe planning to make an announcement, an anonymous police quote of suspected suicide, and the link to Luguire's possible depression. Jordan exited the page and dropped the electronic tablet back in his briefcase.

He understood his wife's morning had just been shot to hell. He thought about calling her, but at this point he had nothing to offer. She'd reach him if she needed him. The Fed would circle the wagons, its security department would react to Luguire's death as a threat until proven otherwise, and Amanda would rely on her old Secret Service confidant, Russell Mullins, the man Jordan suspected would do everything in his power to discover the truth of what happened to Paul Luguire.

Jordan left eight Euros for the waiter, exited the restaurant, and started walking through Luxembourg Gardens. He blended in with the Parisians, trim and fit, not like so many of the fast-food-fed Americans swarming over the tourist sites. His good looks and charm even drew the attraction of French women. As a class, Jordan considered them the most beautiful in the world.

But Amanda was now the most important character in his life and he wouldn't screw that up over something as mundane as an affair. That might work in fiction, but Curtis Jordan knew the line between fantasy and reality was one he never crossed.

Chapter Six

Rusty Mullins splashed cold water on his face and stared into the bathroom mirror. Two hours of fitful sleep left him looking like he'd been on a three-day drunk.

It was seven in the morning and the man he was supposed to pick up in an hour lay dead in the Arlington morgue. Mullins' day wouldn't be much better. The overnight interrogation by Detective Sullivan was only the beginning.

Prime Protection would put him through an extensive debriefing and then draw up an official report. At least that should insulate him from any direct contacts with the media or the security department at the Federal Reserve. If Luguire's death drew the interest of a congressional committee, then that was a different matter. He'd be called to testify and there would be no hiding behind a company document.

Whether Prime Protection or anyone other than Detective Sullivan cared about Mullins' assertion that Luguire had been murdered would soon become apparent. And without compelling physical evidence, even Sullivan would move on to other cases.

Mullins' cellphone scooted along the vanity toward the basin. He snatched it up before the vibrate mode dumped it in the water. "Kayli" flashed on the caller ID.

His heart rate jumped. "Everything all right?"

"Yes, Dad. But are you okay?"

"You heard about Luguire?" He grabbed a towel from the rack and dabbed his cheeks and eyes.

"Sandy called a few minutes ago."

"Who?"

"Sandy Beecham. You met her. Her boy Luke is Josh's age."

"Right. Your neighbor." He folded the towel and set it on the vanity. "She called this early?"

"Her husband works for the Fed. She knows you're with Mr. Luguire."

"Not any more."

His daughter said nothing. Mullins knew his bitter tone put her off.

"Sorry. I got called by the police last night and went to the scene."

"I figured as much, but I wanted to make sure you knew."

"Thank you, sweetheart."

"So, you want breakfast?"

"Where?"

"Here. Josh is still sleeping. But seeing Paw Paw when he wakes up will make his day."

Mullins glanced at his watch. Five after seven. "I'll be there in thirty. Have a fresh pot ready."

He clicked off and then speed dialed the number to his supervisor's direct line. As he expected, voicemail answered the call. "Ted. I spent most of the night with the Arlington police. I'll be in at ten. Obviously, we need to talk."

Mullins pulled a clean blue suit and white shirt out of the closet. His face might look like hell but his wardrobe would be fresh.

He checked the safety on his Glock and dropped an extra ammo clip in his pocket. His request for a leave of absence would be a courtesy. He wouldn't take no for an answer. He knew what he had to do. He just didn't know where to start.

Chapter Seven

"Start at the beginning." Ted Lewison slid Mullins a mug of fresh coffee.

The two men were alone at the conference table. Lewison, the younger by a few years, could see his employee was upset. That was a first. The veteran Secret Service agent never got rattled, never displayed emotion. In a company with low-maintenance professionals, Mullins was no-maintenance.

Lewison respected Mullins. He learned things from the man, things the U.S. Army hadn't taught him. The military had been the quickest way for Lewison to get out of his poor African-American neighborhood in Baltimore. He'd spent twelve years in the service, gaining experience as an MP and warrant officer. He commanded protection details for politicians and high-profile civilians visiting war-torn regions all over the globe.

Twice he'd lost so-called dignitaries, and both times the men had deviated from security protocol, claiming they knew how to take care of themselves. Their deaths had been blemishes on his record even though they'd clearly gone against Lewison's orders. He resented being held accountable for someone else's arrogance and stupidity.

He took an honorable discharge, applied for a minority business loan from a Washington community development organization, and spent ten years building Prime Protection into one of the premier personal security firms in D.C. His company couldn't be held responsible for Luguire's suicide and therefore he placed no blame on Mullins for the desperate action of a troubled client.

Lewison knew Mullins had developed a good relationship with Luguire and suspected the man was grieving for the loss of a friend. Understandable. Once they got this debriefing behind them, Lewison would find Mullins a new assignment. The best therapy would be to get him back in the field as soon as possible.

Mullins took a sip of coffee, his fourth cup of the morning. "When's the beginning?"

"Yesterday morning will do. I'm not interested in trying to reconstruct some psychological profile. I'm confident if something seemed wrong before then, you would have reported it."

"Yesterday was no different. I picked him up at eight."

"Where?"

"The garage under his apartment building. I always phone him after I enter and check the location. Luguire steps straight from the elevator into the car. No more than six feet."

"How did he seem?"

"A little preoccupied, but that's not unusual. We exchanged pleasantries. He opened his briefcase and started reading documents. He had meetings at his office, and then I took him to an economic symposium at Georgetown. One of those lunch and panel deals. That went till two. I drove him back to the Fed. He had a late afternoon security meeting."

Lewison cocked his head with heightened interest. "Security? Did that involve you?"

"No. Transaction security." Mullins smiled. "Luguire said he wished we could create a virtual me who could stand guard at the window."

"What window?"

"He was referring to when the Regional Federal Reserve Banks made funds available to banks through a discount window, not so dissimilar to you or me going up to a teller. Now it's all done electronically."

Lewison relaxed. "Nobody carries cash anymore."

"Including Luguire." Mullins detailed the drive to Clarendon and the swing by the ATM. "And that's one of the reasons I know Luguire didn't commit suicide."

"He didn't?" Lewison asked the question with genuine surprise. "An accident? Was he cleaning a gun?"

Mullins leaned across the table. "Luguire was murdered. I don't know how or why, but there's not a doubt in my mind."

"Do the police think that?"

"The homicide detective is considering the possibility." He repeated his conversation with Sullivan, including the "tough-ass" phrase in the note.

"That's not much to go on."

"I know. And I'm not suggesting we put it in the report. I'm well aware that would be dragging the company name through the mud, even though we had no responsibility once he entered his apartment building."

"You saw him get in the elevator?"

"Yes. He used his pass card for entrance. He was alone."

Lewison clasped his large hands together on the table. "Then we're in the clear."

Mullins nodded. "The company, yes. But I'm not."

"You did your job, and you've made your views known to the Arlington police."

"Ted, I can't walk away from this. Luguire sent me a cry for help."

Ted Lewison understood Mullins had crossed the line between professional and personal. "We don't do investigative work."

"I know." Mullins stood from the table. "I've got vacation time. It started last night."

Lewison kept his seat. "You can't represent yourself as Prime Protection."

"I know."

"And when you run through vacation time, we'll talk about a leave of absence."

"Okay."

Lewison stood and offered his hand. "And when you need something unofficially, you call me."

"Thanks, Ted." Mullins shook hands and walked out.

He stopped by his small office to pick up extra clips and ammo for his Glock. The blinking red message light on his desk phone caught his eye. He rarely got a call on his direct line. Most friends used his cell, and since he'd been assigned to Luguire for nearly a year, few new business calls came to him. The phone was more of a glorified intercom.

He figured some enterprising reporter must be seeking information about Luguire. If so, the guy was out of luck. Mullins had no intention of talking to the press.

He decided to check the message anyway. He didn't know when he'd be back in the office.

"Mr. Mullins. I'm calling from Barnes and Noble at Clarendon." A woman made the statement in a pleasant tone. "The book you ordered has come in and you can pick it up at the register. Remember, after five, your receipt entitles you to enjoy a free cup of coffee in our cafe. Thank you." The call ended.

Mullins punched one to repeat the message. The woman's voice was familiar, but she spoke in such a sing-song, customer-service script that he couldn't place her.

He knew for sure he hadn't ordered a book from Barnes and Noble.

He also knew a rendezvous had been proposed at the bookstore only a few blocks from Luguire's apartment building. Someone was being very cautious. Someone was afraid.

Chapter Eight

Zaina Khoury brushed her daughter's silky black hair, a mindless activity that served to break the boredom of being confined to the apartment. She hoped today would be the day Fares returned. The guard had hinted that the work would soon be over and everything would go back to the way it had been—Fares' job, her home, and Jamila's preschool.

Jamila squirmed in her lap. Sesame Street ended and so did the distraction that kept the four-year-old still beneath the hair brush.

"Let me finish," Zaina said. "You want to look pretty for Daddy."

Jamila craned her neck toward the front door. "Daddy?"

"No, sweetheart. Not now. But soon."

As if to belie the words, the knob rattled and the retracting deadbolt clicked sharply.

"Daddy!" Jamila jumped from her mother and ran to the door. She froze as a stranger entered, carrying three bags from Burger King.

"Get away." The man waved the bags at the child.

Zaina stood from the sofa and Jamila ran to hide behind her.

"Take the burgers to the kitchen." He kicked the door closed behind him.

Zaina didn't move. She'd never seen him before. He looked at them with flat dark eyes that showed no more emotion than if he were watching two stray dogs in the street.

"Where's Chuchi?" she asked. Although she didn't like being cooped up in the apartment for two weeks, the Hispanic guard she knew only as Chuchi had been respectful, saying Fares was on an important mission to Washington, D.C., working to get their home back.

"Chuchi's done here. I'll be staying until this is finished. Now take these and put the food on plates. I'm not eating from a sack like a horse."

Zaina hesitated only long enough to see the man shove the bags at her. He wore a collared, peach-colored shirt and cream-colored slacks. The shirt opened two buttons down his hairy chest, revealing a delicate gold chain. A sheen of sweat clung to his swarthy face. She wasn't sure of his ethnicity. Somewhere in the Middle East, but not Lebanon. Zaina understood he wasn't someone you challenged.

She stepped toward him. "Okay. Come, Jamila."

"Your daughter stays," the man ordered.

"Why?"

"Because I say so. Because you'll work faster. And set proper places at the kitchen table."

Zaina turned around and knelt. "Jamila, Mommy needs you to wait here and talk to our guest. Sit on the sofa and tell him what happened on your TV show. Be a nice hostess. Can you do that?"

Jamila looked at the man.

"Listen to your mother. Then we'll have a nice supper. Maybe we can make something for your daddy and I'll see that he gets it."

Jamila scooted onto the sofa, pushing her tiny body into the far corner.

"I'll only be a few minutes," Zaina said, as much to the stranger as her daughter. She grabbed the bags.

He called after her, "Warm them in the microwave, thirty seconds." Then he turned to Jamila and smiled. "What did you see on TV?"

Zaina pulled plates from the cabinets and spaced them around the small Formica table. She put the settings for her daughter and her at one end so the whole length separated them from Chuchi's replacement. He made her nervous. If he was getting a message to Fares, maybe she could find a way to tell her husband how she felt. She would need to be subtle, but Fares knew her well enough to read between the lines.

Even though the bags contained only burgers and fries, she set out a full complement of flatware—knives, forks, spoons. She would re-heat his plate first, both being polite and getting him in the kitchen away from Jamila.

She punched start and the plate of food began rotating in the microwave. She didn't hear the finishing beep. It was drowned out by Jamila's scream.

Zaina ran to the living room. Her daughter lay face down on the sofa cushions, her hands clutching the back of her head.

The man stood over her. He held a knife in one hand; in the other was a clump of Jamila's hair.

"Something to send your husband." He jammed the severed tresses into his pocket. "Is my dinner ready?"

Chapter Nine

At four-thirty, Rusty Mullins pulled into the parking deck half a block from the Barnes and Noble in the Clarendon section of Arlington. Paul Luguire's apartment building was only a few blocks farther on North Garfield Street. He considered walking over there later on the off chance he might see Luguire's daughter.

Mullins took his time getting to the bookstore. What appeared to others as an amble stroll allowed him to scan the vicinity. A double-parked car or van would draw his attention. So would window shoppers who kept glancing over their shoulders. But nothing triggered the internal alarm bells he'd developed from over twenty years in the Secret Service.

Satisfied nothing was amiss, he checked his watch. Twenty to five. He entered the store and went straight to the second floor. He stood in the game section near the railing where he could view the entrance below. For the next twenty minutes, he browsed the merchandise, moving from games to children's literature to the adult genres, but always keeping one eye on the lower level. Shoppers came and went, most browsing like him, absorbed in the myriad of displays.

At five, he dropped his pretense and focused his attention on patrons and staff near the checkout line. Two cashiers worked the counter, keeping the customers moving so that the wait was never more than a few minutes. No one else seemed to be watching.

Mullins picked up a children's picture book from the bargain table and headed for the registers. His grandson, Josh, would like the story, and the purchase might deceive someone who had been told to be on the lookout for a man standing in line without any merchandise.

"Did you find everything you wanted?" the woman behind the counter asked.

"Yes. And you should have a book here for me." He handed her his credit card. "Under this name."

She examined the Visa card. "We do. I found it on the counter about an hour ago marked prepaid. Did you give one of our associates your card number over the phone?"

"No."

She nodded. "Good, because we're not supposed to ask for that information. Those sales are handled over the Internet."

"That's what I did," he lied.

The cashier frowned. "Well, someone didn't use the proper paperwork for the in-store pickup of an Internet order."

"Is that a problem?"

The woman retrieved a thin paperback from the shelf behind her. "No, but there should be a receipt. Did you happen to print one from your computer?"

"Sorry. I didn't think to."

She scanned the barcode and studied the register's screen. "The book's not listed in our inventory. It must have been the only copy and was deleted when you paid for your order." She handed him the book. "Are you okay with just your Internet receipt?"

Mullins didn't answer. He stared at the book cover. *Betrayal at Jekyll.* The author's name was Walter V. Simmons. Neither meant anything to him. Then he saw one of the quotes under the title.

Louis T. McFadden: "We have in this country one of the most corrupt institutions the world has ever known. I refer to the Federal Reserve Board and the Federal Reserve Banks."

"Sir? The receipt?"

He looked back at the woman. "No need. I've got the one on my computer at home. And I'll pay cash for the child's book. It's not worth putting on the card."

He gave her a twenty, collected his change, and let her put both books in a bag.

"Here's the receipt for the children's book," she said. "It'll get you a free cup of coffee."

"Thanks. I'll take you up on it." He left the register and headed for the cafe.

He got a cup of black coffee and sat at a table for two in the corner farthest from the traffic flow. The bag lay by his feet next to the wall. He wasn't going to display a book about the Federal Reserve like some hack spy in a hack-written spy novel. Then he saw her and he knew the book wasn't an identifier.

Amanda Church ordered a cup of green tea, and then turned to look for a place to sit. Her eyes lit up when she saw Mullins. Anyone observing would have thought she'd been pleasantly surprised to see a friend.

"Hi. May I join you?"

"Certainly." He stood and welcomed her with an outstretched hand. He didn't call her by name because she hadn't used his.

She set her cup on the table, clasped his right hand with her left, and gently pulled him into a hug. "No one here knows me," she whispered.

"Me either."

"You look good, Sam."

He indicated for her to take a seat. "You too." He decided against inventing a name for her. It was clear to anyone they knew each other and an overuse of names would sound contrived. "My coffee was free."

"You must have bought something. They didn't have the book I wanted." She pulled her cellphone from her purse, checked the screen, and set it down, rotating it in the process.

Mullins glanced at the face. In the split-second before it went dark, he read, "End if anything wrong."

Amanda was taking no chances. Her tight security measures meant she suspected either or both of them might be under surveillance.

"I saw Peter last night," he said casually. "He's hoping to get back with Mary."

She nodded. "Maybe. I think she dumped the other guy."

"That's what I heard too." Mullins understood they were in sync. The other guy between Peter and Mary was Paul, the folksingers from the 1960s, except this Paul was Paul Luguire. "I don't know any of the details."

Amanda laughed. "I do. But I'm not one to gossip."

"Since when?"

"Since I've got to get home and make supper for Herb and the kids."

Mullins bent down and picked up his books. "All right, I'll walk you to your car and you can fill me in."

They left, two friends who happened to run into each other and were catching up on mutual acquaintances. Mullins followed Amanda's lead, trusting her actions to be appropriate for her assessment of the situation.

Like Mullins, Amanda came out of the Secret Service. She was an agent experienced in the Treasury Department's efforts to thwart cyber-crime. In her early days, she and Mullins worked cases together. He respected her abilities. Their first case involved a Nigerian ring of credit card fraud. Even before the onslaught of their Internet scams, Nigerian con artists placed Nigerian immigrant workers in custodial jobs in medical offices. Cleaning at night, they would break into billing records and steal patient credit card numbers. Then they would mail-order merchandise until maxing out the card's limit.

Amanda came up with the idea to intercept the package deliveries. More than once, Mullins dressed up as a Federal Express employee, drove a real Fed Ex truck, and delivered the merchandise. As soon as the recipient signed for the delivery, Mullins placed him under arrest while a backup team raided the premises.

The operation was a big success, so much so that Amanda was assigned to more and more sophisticated electronic crimes. She crossed over from the government to the Federal Reserve when security concerns multiplied in proportion to the skills of hackers and the discontent of the populace that saw the Federal Reserve as the cause, not the solution, of the country's financial woes.

"Where's your car?" he asked.

"Right beside yours." She grabbed his arm. "Lead on."

They took the stairs to the second level and Mullins stopped behind his Prius. A Lexus sedan was on one side and an Infiniti SUV on the other.

"Which one of these limos is yours?" he asked.

"Neither. Let's sit in your car."

Mullins laughed softly and scanned the parking deck. The only people in sight were a mom and a toddler getting into a minivan six spaces away. He unlocked the Prius with his keyless remote.

Amanda slid into the passenger's seat and set her purse on the floor. "I don't think I was followed, but they could have put a bug and tracker in my car. I parked in Alexandria and took the Metro to Clarendon."

Mullins studied her for a moment. She was an attractive woman in her early forties, five or six years younger than he. He knew she was married to the novelist Curtis Jordan. Mullins had read some of his international thrillers, entertaining if a bit far-fetched. Either Jordan was a pseudonym or Amanda had kept her maiden name. Mullins suspected she provided Jordan with procedural and protocol information for his complex plots.

Today her confidence seemed shaken. He'd never seen her unnerved before, and the fact that they were sitting in his car told him she had no confidence in the normal channels of communication.

He decided to meet her head on. "Paul Luguire was murdered. I know it and I'm going to prove it."

She jerked her head around, eyes wide. Then she laughed. "You're amazing. Here I thought I was going to have to convince you. How do you know?"

Mullins reviewed everything he told Detective Sullivan: Luguire's mood, the plans for the Saturday ballgame, the withdrawal of one hundred dollars from the ATM, and the "tough-ass" insertion in the suicide note. "But you have something more concrete," he said. "At least that's what your precautions indicate."

She nodded. "Three days ago, a flag went up."

"A what?"

"An alert. I'm developing a security system that reviews transactions that are perfectly normal in every way except for frequency. Proper pass codes, account numbers, protocols, and hierarchy of approval. The theory is if someone hacked into the payment system somehow an increased frequency might be the first indicator of the breach."

"Makes sense," Mullins agreed.

"I'm in beta testing to set the parameters so that we're not swamped and paralyzed checking out false alarms. We're limiting the scope to Richmond before expanding. Three days ago a transfer of funds from the Federal Reserve in Richmond to a member bank in southwest Virginia popped up as an anomaly."

"Just one?"

"Yes. Everything was proper except in this case even one transaction tripped the alert. The order for the transfer came from Luguire. Such a matter wouldn't originate with him. It would be handled strictly out of Richmond.

"The bank, Laurel, is a small Virginia concern with interstate operations in western North Carolina and east Tennessee. It's had its share of problems, mainly due to loans for mountain land development that crashed in 2008 and 2009, but they've weathered the worst of it. I hesitated to bother Luguire with it because he might have initiated the loan somehow, but it just didn't feel right."

"He was high enough up someone probably thought the transaction wouldn't be questioned."

Amanda turned in the passenger seat and leaned against the door. "Exactly. And that's what the security software was designed to flag. I brought it to Luguire's attention on Tuesday. He claimed to know nothing about it, but said he'd check into

it. I never heard another word. Two days later he killed himself."
She shook her head. "I hate to admit it but I thought maybe
he'd transferred that money for his own gain and I'd uncovered
the beginning of a trail that threatened to expose him. So, this
morning after I heard about his death, I went back to the data
records and discovered the transaction was gone, completely
removed from the records."

"Couldn't it have been an error that Luguire caught and
simply reversed?"

"If that were the case, a reversal would have shown up.
Money might be created by the Federal Reserve but it doesn't
just disappear."

Mullins' mind went into high gear. Amanda's story offered
the first indication that Luguire's death might be linked to a
specific event. "What did you do?"

"I called the president of Laurel Bank, a man named Craig
Archer who would have known about the requested funds. He
denied any knowledge." Amanda reached into her purse on the
floor and retrieved a notepad. "Fortunately, I'd written down the
account number when I first discovered the transaction. I gave
it to Archer. He found no sign of the money coming from the
Fed window. Archer checked deposit records and discovered the
exact amount had been transferred into a new account opened
at a Laurel branch in Staunton, Virginia. He agreed to call me
back after he spoke to the branch manager."

She flipped through her notes. "Fifteen minutes later he
phoned with information that the account was in the name of
American Restitution and had been opened by the company's
president, Fred Mack. The initial deposit was nine-thousand
dollars and Mr. Mack claimed to be seeking 501c(3) status as a
non-profit organization raising money to assist victims of crimes
by either paying for plaintiff legal expenses, providing loans,
or in some cases outright grants to lessen financial hardships
because the prosecution of perpetrators seldom provided proper
restitution for the victims."

"How do you know these were the Fed funds? Was the number huge?"

"No. But an odd amount. Two-hundred-twenty-one thousand. Then the money moved on. Two-hundred-twenty thousand was wired out Wednesday, the day after the deposit. Yesterday, the president of American Restitution, Fred Mack, returned to the branch and said his request for classification as a 501c(3) organization had been denied. He withdrew the balance in cash—ten thousand—and closed the account."

Mullins thought through the implications of Amanda's story. "Well, if the Federal Reserve trail no longer existed, the money had to come from somewhere. It didn't just appear out of thin air."

"It didn't. Laurel Bank showed the originating account number. It was no longer from Luguire's Federal Reserve authorization but from a private account. An offshore account in the name of Russell Mullins."

Chapter Ten

For the third time, Sidney Levine cruised Q Street in search of a parking space. After six in the evening, something should have opened. Nearby Georgetown University was on summer schedule, the employees of those retail shops on Wisconsin Avenue that closed at six on Fridays should be leaving, and the social elite who lived in the more expensive townhouses should either be heading out of the city for the weekend or have their Beamers and Benzs in garages.

Sidney's basement apartment didn't come with a garage or even a designated parking spot. He had to fend for himself to find curb room for his 1999 Ford Escort. Finally, four blocks from his address, he snaked into a space vacated by a limo. Not so bad, except the hike to his building was all uphill.

He'd spent the day outside of Manassas, Virginia, on a farm, one of the new breed that eschewed chemical fertilizers and growth hormones for open pasture grazing and crop rotation. He hoped his freelance assignment would expand beyond one article to a series on the explosion of local farmers' markets. He knew people in the District who drove forty-five miles for home-cured hams and grass-fed beef. The craze to buy local wasn't just reserved for vegans and health-food nuts.

Sidney stopped halfway to his apartment and caught his breath. Thirty-eight, paunchy, and out of shape, he winded easily. He carried a backpack slung over one shoulder. It held his Nikon, digital voice recorder, and journals that he used for taking notes. The strap cut into him and he switched the load to his other side. He checked the bottom of his shoes for any trace of his barnyard excursion, something he should have done before getting in his car. As a guy who grew up Jewish in Greenwich Village, he knew his way around a farm like he knew his way around a nunnery.

He walked the rest of the distance slowly, wondering whether the Chinese take-out in his fridge would still be edible. He used the back entrance, a flight of outside stairs to the basement, because it was closer to his apartment. He'd check his mailbox in the lobby later.

Classical music sounded from the other side of his door. No one was home, no one meaning his sometimes girlfriend Colleen who had a key. The FM station provided his security alarm, an attempt to convince a would-be intruder that someone was inside. Colleen would have immediately switched the station to hard rock.

Sidney turned on his laptop before he turned on a light. He wanted to transfer the factual data from his interview notes along with the sensory impressions still fresh in his mind. If he finished in an hour, he'd ditch the Chinese leftovers and walk to Clyde's bar in Georgetown for a burger. Friday night, he might get lucky. Some women still found reporters exciting. Some desperate women.

He grabbed a beer and heard multiple pings as his email program loaded. That morning he'd forgotten his cellphone charging by the bed, and on the drive down and back, he opted for CDs rather than news radio. He'd been out of the loop all day. Something must have fired up his cadre of Internet followers.

Sidney sat at the keyboard and quickly scrolled through a list of new messages. All were from anti-Fed zealots and each subject line contained Paul Luguire's name. A sampling generated a range of words like death, suicide, murder, assassination, and liquidation—the more extreme ones coming from those elements Sidney considered nut jobs.

He jumped to the web site of *The Washington Post*. The story had been filed after press deadline and so was labeled Breaking News for the on-line edition. The quote "apparent suicide" from the Arlington Police Department muted Sidney's initial adrenaline rush. Even high-ranking Federal Reserve executives had personal problems. He didn't know much about Luguire other than the Fed Chairman had promoted him last year to a new position as the chief link between the Fed and Treasury Department. Luguire wasn't the public face to Congress or Wall Street like Chairman Radcliffe, but he would be privy to all the inner workings of the Board of Governors, a high enough player to set conspiracy-prone fanatics honking like startled geese.

Sidney moved from *The Washington Post* to the web site of *The Washington Times*. The woman who had replaced him on the economy beat had the same basic information with one additional detail. The "apparent suicide" quote was attributed to an Arlington homicide detective named Robert Sullivan.

He clicked back to his email. More than a hundred people wanted to know his take on Luguire's death. The irony struck him that the book that had cost him his job had created these Frankenstein monsters who now stalked him for his opinions on everything from President Kennedy's assassination to Queen Elizabeth's plan to rule the world. He glanced at the bookshelf above the laptop. Six of the volumes had the same title: *The Secret Revolution of 1913—How Bankers Stole America!* His layman's look at the Federal Reserve was meant to be provocative, but balanced. He'd had no clout over what the publisher chose to call it.

He got caught up in the conspiratorial currents of the anti-Fed and Occupy Wall Street movements, made the mistake of playing to them as book sales soared, and then found his credibility shredded by association. Like a politician receiving the endorsement of Castro or the Klan, the more he denied them, the stronger the perceived connection. And then the Establishment, the proponents of the status quo, and those legitimately attacked in his book hammered him down with accusations of bias and fringe journalism. His editor at the newspaper caved and Sidney found himself undone by his own success.

Still the book and these paranoid characters who embraced it paid his rent. He had to respond. But he would respond on his terms and with his standards. He was a journalist, albeit one in need of rehabilitation.

He started his blog. "No rumors. No speculation. No opinion. No coverup. Today I begin my personal investigation into the death of Paul Luguire."

Chapter Eleven

"Let's drive. We can't just sit here in the car." Without asking Amanda's permission, Mullins powered up his Prius and backed out of the parking space.

"Where to?" she asked.

"Anywhere till we've talked this through. I think better on the move. Then I'll bring you to your car in Alexandria."

He paid the parking attendant, exited, and maneuvered through the Clarendon side streets until he was on Washington Boulevard. When he realized he was unconsciously following the route to Luguire's office, he swung up the ramp to I-395 South.

"I want to head away from the city where there's less chance someone will see us together," he said.

"Good idea," Amanda agreed. "I keep thinking if that transaction hadn't been flagged, there's no way this would have come to light."

Mullins glanced at his passenger. She laid her head against the side window, eyes staring intently at something seen only in her mind.

"Do you think I'm involved?" he asked.

"Do you think I'd be alone with you in this car if I did?"

"Yes. If you had backup and wore a wire."

She turned and smiled. "Why, Mr. Mullins, are you trying to pat me down?"

"No. I'm trying to figure out why I'm not your main suspect."

"Because you're not smart enough."

"Ouch."

"And you're not stupid enough."

"Thanks for the vote of confidence. Explain please."

"My work at Treasury centered on ECSAP."

"I'm not that familiar with it. I was still on presidential detail when that stuff came down."

"The Electronic Crimes Special Agent Program grew out of ECTF, the Electronic Crimes Task Force created by the Patriot Act."

Mullins nodded. "I remember. One of those 'we're all in this together' initiatives."

"Don't be so cynical. It did unite federal, state, and local law enforcement in investigating cyber attacks on our financial institutions. We felt it was better housed in the Secret Service than in some closet within the FBI."

"I'll buy that. So, because I wasn't part of ECSAP I'm not smart enough?"

"No. It's because I was part of ECSAP. And I know I'm not smart enough. You might be smarter than me, but not by that much. I was in case management and the geeks I supervised may as well have been Martians for all we had in common. I mean they were into this stuff, not just computers, but cellphones, PDAs, anything that could create a potential attack, gain illicit access, or game the financial system in some way."

"You're saying this was an inside job?" Mullins put on his blinker for the Shirlington exit.

"At first I thought it was an inside Laurel job. That the bank president, Craig Archer, or someone close to him had obtained the two-hundred-twenty-one-thousand dollars through fraudulent means. Somehow gotten classified codes for the Fed's end of the transaction. Then when Luguire died, I thought blackmail was involved. That's the kind of thing that can drive a man to take his own life."

"I could have been partnered with Archer."

"Yeah, and pilfered Luguire's briefcase or some other source for his codes. But you and Archer fell off my suspect list when the record of the transaction was expunged. That was a sophisticated hack going beyond a bogus transfer. And then when Archer said the money had come from the offshore account of Russell Mullins—"

"You knew I wasn't that stupid," Mullins interjected.

"Correct. And it meant someone was not only smart, he was super smart with international access. Tracks were covered in an area of the Fed supposedly impenetrable and then the link is diverted to a fictitious account in the Caymans. I think your name was used just in case this came to light. Sends the investigators off on the wrong trail."

Mullins grunted, but said nothing for a few minutes. He slowed as he drove by the tall apartment building called Shirlington House. His one-bedroom unit was on the fourth floor. He scanned the parking lot for any sign of surveillance. Everything seemed normal.

He continued up the hill and into the cluster of brick buildings that formed Fairlington Villages, a housing neighborhood built in World War Two that had now gone condo. Kayli lived in one at the corner of South Columbus. Mullins liked living close to his daughter, and as he felt his stress level rise at Amanda's news, he wanted the assurance that everything was normal in her life as well.

He saw her VW Jetta parked near the entrance to her building. She and Josh would have finished dinner and were probably talking with Allen before Josh went to bed. For his son-in-law, the time would be three or four in the morning, but Kayli said he never missed a scheduled call. Mullins knew Allen was a keeper.

He relaxed and sped up. "Who else have you told?"

"No one. I wanted to check with you first."

"And now?"

She shrugged. "I don't know what to do. The scale of what happened is mind boggling. In addition to cold-blooded murder, we've got evidence of an operation that must have inside and outside participants. Luguire must have talked to the wrong person. Who can we trust?"

"Tell Radcliffe what you know."

"What proof do I have? All the evidence has been deleted. The only existing lead is the bank record of the wire transfer from the offshore account in your name. They'll be all over you in a heartbeat. If they silenced Luguire, you think they won't get to you or me?"

"And the only connection is the dollar amount?"

"Yeah. Two-hundred-twenty-one thousand. And that's a sticking point."

"How so?" Mullins asked.

"Why so little? With the addition of a single zero, the amount could have been ten times greater."

"Could be the size of the receiving bank. A larger amount would have drawn their attention. A small regional bank may not have as many systems in place. Who knows? End of day balance may not have been checked till the following morning. It happens."

"So, maybe they plan to repeat this operation through a network of small banks, hacking in a way so sophisticated that the whole U.S. money supply is at risk."

"We'd better hope that's all it is," Mullins said. "This could have been just a test. A demonstration of capability."

"That's why we need evidence. Something that can't be denied or covered up. Like it or not, Rusty, you've got a stake in this. Help me build a case so strong that no one can bury it. Then we'll take it to our old colleagues at the Treasury and Chairman Radcliffe. I'll keep monitoring the system inside while you work outside."

"You want me on the murder?"

"No. We need to follow the money trail. Let the police deal with Luguire. I'm going to talk to Craig Archer at Laurel Bank and tell him an investigator for the Federal Reserve will be calling on him Monday. Have you still got your photo ID clearance badge for access to our building?"

"Yes."

"Show him that. It should be enough."

Mullins thought a moment. "Okay. I'm on board."

"Good." Amanda reached over and grabbed his forearm. "Glad to have you back in the game."

Mullins nodded. He was in all right. But for more than Amanda bargained. He still wanted Luguire's killer more than anything.

Chapter Twelve

Craig Archer poured his third bourbon over ice. Friday evening, he sat in the easy chair in his spacious den and pressed the cold glass against his temple. The prominent vein on his forehead throbbed with each beat of his heart. He didn't want to guess his blood pressure.

He'd begged off the community theater charity dinner, the annual fundraiser chaired by his wife, claiming a splitting headache. She'd been pissed at him, but he'd been telling the truth. The pain began as soon as he got the call from the woman at the Federal Reserve.

Her accusation that he'd received a deposit from Laurel Bank's Fed account was ludicrous. Somehow they'd screwed up and now tried to put the blame on him. But then the exact amount showed up in another questionable transaction from an off-shore transfer into an account at the Laurel branch in Staunton, Virginia. That account had closed yesterday after being open less than a week.

And the transferring off-shore account no longer existed. Craig Archer found the transaction had been posted right before the close of business on Monday, and unnoticed because the branch employee who checked the daily balances left early that afternoon for one of the bank's mandatory training sessions. Another consequence of the FDIC sticking its nose into every aspect of his business.

Archer talked to his branch manager in Staunton, and they agreed the incident would go no further than the two of them.

At this point, the FDIC knew nothing, the Federal Reserve seemed unsure that what occurred wasn't an internal problem on their end, and the wire transfer from the Caymans in no way affected the asset base or loan portfolio of the bank. The two hundred twenty-one thousand hadn't been there long enough to be a loanable deposit.

Archer would comply with any requests for information, but he wouldn't bring the matter up to his board of directors. The loan debacles of the previous few years and the demands and increased scrutiny of regulators had nearly caused the bank to fail. He'd lost his title of chairman of the board and something like this could be the straw that broke the camel's back as far as the board's confidence in his leadership as president and CEO. Archer was sixty-three, his stock options were worthless, and his retirement funds tied up in real estate ventures that once looked solid but now would take years to recover their value.

He took a deep pull of the Wild Turkey. The liquor deadened the pain better than aspirin. Things would look better by Monday morning. The Fed would have discovered its error, and the transfer, well, coincidences do happen. Two-hundred-twenty-one thousand is a round enough number, and it went through a customer's account that had been properly set up. Thank God for that.

His cellphone vibrated on the end table by his chair. His wife's name flashed in the ID screen. Eight-thirty. She should be making her after-dinner speech. Maybe things wrapped early and she was going for drinks with some of her cronies.

"What's up, dear?" He spoke in a whisper so she'd have no doubt he was still suffering.

"Are you alone, Mr. Archer?"

The glass slipped from Archer's hand and shattered on the hardwood floor. One word flashed through his mind. Kidnapping.

"Mr. Archer?" The man's voice was calm, cultured, soothing.

"Yes."

"Sorry to alarm you. Your wife is fine. I just wanted to make sure you'd take my call."

"You stole her phone?"

"No. Temporarily borrowed her number."

"What do you want?" Archer's fear turned to anger.

"Nothing other than to give you a heads-up. I know you spoke with Amanda Church of the Federal Reserve this morning. And you'll probably be getting a follow-up visit from someone saying he works with Church. Technically, that's true, but he's really a third-party contractor."

"And who are you?"

"Agent Nathaniel Brown with the Secret Service. We're running a parallel investigation."

"Into what?"

"A possible cyber-crime. I'm with the Electronic Crimes Special Agent Program."

"You're investigating our bank?"

"No. We believe you're an innocent victim of an international money laundering operation. One that has assets in place within the Federal Reserve."

"Assets? What kind of assets?"

"Human assets. A person or persons in the pay of a criminal or terrorist organization. Someone who can make what happened happen."

"And this parallel investigation is separate from the Federal Reserve?"

"Entirely. And it's important it stays that way. Amanda Church and her colleague Russell Mullins are probably innocent, but they are in sensitive positions. I would be remiss if I didn't first clear them of any involvement."

"Mullins? That was the name on the Cayman account."

"Yes. Which makes it likely he was being framed."

"I see." Archer stood and paced unsteadily, trying to clear his head. "But why are you calling me?"

"I want you to cooperate with them. Tell them what they need to know. Technically, they don't have subpoena power or

the authority to make you divulge confidential information."
The man laughed. "They're not like us, the guys in the black
SUVs who can pretty much demand anything and everything."

Archer got the point. He needed to cooperate with this guy.

"We want to see how thorough they are in their investigation. So, assist them as much as you can without revealing your
bank's own confidential matters. Then I'd like you to write up
a report of that meeting and any subsequent conversations. By
hand is preferable, as it carries more weight in court."

"I'll be called to testify?"

"If we succeed in building a case. Your role in protecting the
integrity and security of our core financial institutions won't go
unnoticed."

That was the kind of publicity Craig Archer did want to
bring to his board of directors. And to have the FDIC and the
Fed in his debt would be huge.

"All right," Archer said. "If I can be of service, I'm happy to
help in anyway I can."

"Thank you. I'll be in touch early next week. In the meantime, tell no one. Not even your wife. And there's no need to
share your visitor is even from the Federal Reserve. It might
make your employees nervous."

"I understand."

The caller hung up. Archer took the phone from his ear and
stared at it as a reality check of what just occurred. For a split-
second he considered that Nathaniel Brown hadn't given him
any ID to show he was who he claimed to be.

But then the man had hijacked his wife's cellphone number.
In Archer's mind, that was far better proof that he was dealing
with the government than any wallet overflowing with credentials could provide.

Chapter Thirteen

At nine o'clock Friday night, Detective Robert Sullivan read through the autopsy report a final time. Paul Luguire died from a single gunshot to the right temple. Powder burns on his head and right hand were consistent with a self-inflicted wound. Luguire was right-handed. The only other notation made by the medical examiner was the presence of a small dab of aluminum sulfate on a nick under his jaw. The report stated it was most likely residue from a styptic pencil used to stop the bleeding from a shaving cut.

Sullivan jotted a note to remind himself to ask Rusty Mullins if he'd noticed it when he picked Luguire up for work. Then he locked the case file in his desk drawer and went to the office of the duty lieutenant Charlie Crouch.

"If you don't mind, I'd like to go home."

Crouch looked at the wall clock. "You sick?"

"No. I was up all night with the Luguire murder and worked through the day. I'm beat."

"Sure. Things are quiet. The captain will be happy to save the overtime."

"You know I work more hours than I put in for."

Crouch waved him away. "You don't have to sell me. Go home, Rob. If something comes up, I'll take it myself."

Sullivan started out the door.

"Hold up a second," Crouch said. "You might have a reporter waiting for you."

Sullivan turned. "At this hour? What's he want?"

Crouch shrugged. "He said he needed to talk to you about the Luguire case. I told him there was nothing new to report, and that you were tied up with other investigations."

"When was this?"

"About thirty minutes ago."

"You think he's gone?"

Crouch shook his head. "I don't know. He said he was here to give, not get information."

Sullivan stared at his supervisor.

"I know. I should have told you. But the guy's not with any real news organization. And I suspected you were trying to wrap up early. Frankly, I forgot about him."

"That's okay. If he's still here, I'll talk to him." Sullivan hesitated as a thought crossed his mind. "Charlie, do me a favor, will you?"

"What?"

"Put a call through to the M.E.'s office and ask that someone take a closer look at the shaving nick recorded on Luguire's autopsy report."

"What are they supposed to be looking for?"

"Damned if I know. But I saw an expensive Braun electric shaver charging in the bathroom."

As Sullivan entered the public waiting room, the duty officer at the desk gave a slight nod toward a white man sitting alone in a plastic chair by the wall. He wore black jeans and a blue dress shirt that was untucked, either through a style choice or sloppiness. The frumpy guy looked about forty, and if he was a reporter, he certainly wasn't television.

The man was writing in a journal, one of those blank page books that populated the swivel stands in stationery stores. He glanced up at the sound of Sullivan's footsteps.

"Are you waiting for me?" Sullivan asked.

The man snapped his journal closed. "Are you the detective on the Luguire case?"

"I am. You have information?"

"Maybe." The man stood. "My name's Sidney Levine. I used to be a reporter for *The Washington Times*."

"Used to be?"

"I wrote a book about the Federal Reserve. It did okay. But with a certain element it did really well. I was, shall we say, embraced by their extremist camp."

"Because of what you wrote?"

"Because of the way my book was interpreted."

"And how does this relate to Luguire's death?"

"I don't know. How did he die?"

Sullivan glanced over his shoulder at the desk officer. The man was watching to make sure Levine wasn't some loony about to go off the deep end. Sullivan mouthed, "It's okay," and turned to the reporter.

"Look, we issue our information through the press briefings. Nothing has changed since the last one. If you've got information regarding the death, I'll be glad to hear it. Otherwise, we're wasting each other's time."

"I have one question. Are you one hundred percent certain that Paul Luguire committed suicide? If you are, then I'm sorry I wasted your time. If you're not, then I might provide access to a suspect pool whose fervor against the Fed runs hot enough to include murder."

Sullivan studied the journalist. The man stood calmly waiting for his reply. Rusty Mullins' misgivings were contagious, but Sullivan needed hard evidence and a strong motive if suicide were to be ruled out.

"So what does that mean?" Sullivan asked. "You hand me a thousand emails?"

"No. I'd be your filter. Ninety-nine out of a hundred posts are pure junk and speculation. But kernels of truth are scattered here and there. These people aren't stupid. Luguire might have been a symbol of the Fed and bad money policies, or someone might have had a very specific grudge against him. Odds are whoever's behind his killing will want to get the motive out, even if hidden between the lines. That's what I'll try to elicit through my reports and my blog."

"And what's in it for you?" Sullivan asked.

"Your undying gratitude for starters."

The detective laughed. "Stand in line."

Sidney lowered his voice. "And some information that's more than spoon fed at the briefings. Things I can say are from a source close to the investigation."

Sullivan's eyes narrowed. "I don't know about that. I've been burned before."

"I'm not talking about something that would blow the case. Just enough to show a serious investigation is underway. I'll provide the speculation on theories to ignite the on-line response. Then, if something comes of it, I get the inside track on the story. You give me the game-winning interview."

"What do you really think?" Sullivan asked.

"About what?"

"About Luguire's death. Is this some desperate attempt to thumb your nose at your former bosses?"

"No. If it's murder, you have two of the strongest motives you could want. Money and power. The Fed embodies both, our country's money supply and an unequaled power to regulate it that many say is unconstitutional."

"Unconstitutional how?"

"Article 1, Section 8, 'The Congress shall have the power to coin money, regulate the value thereof, and of foreign coin.' There's a strong argument to be made that Congress has no constitutional authority to abdicate its responsibility to a central private bank that orders the Treasury to print money at its decree. Then that private bank holds the U.S. taxpayer responsible for the debt."

"So, why Luguire? Why now?"

"He could be a target caught in the middle. On the one hand, he's viewed as progressive and pushing for more transparency. There are powerful forces who want the Fed's actions to remain secret. Luguire agreed with the decision for the Chairman to hold a news briefing after their closed meetings. That happened for the first time in 2011, ninety-seven years after the Fed's founding. Such secrecy makes the CIA look like a town hall meeting in New Hampshire. The murder could be a message. 'Keep the doors closed.'"

"And on the other hand?"

Sidney pointed to the chairs behind him. "Mind if we sit?"

Sullivan debated taking the reporter back to an interview room, but decided to keep the discussion more informal. He wasn't sure where this was headed.

"Okay. I've got a few minutes."

They sat and Sidney leaned closer. "There are those who consider the Fed nothing less than the hand of Satan, not only running up debt that will destroy our country, but financing wars destroying other countries. I've heard a rumor that when Osama bin Laden was killed in Pakistan, they found evidence the target of the fourth plane on 9-11 wasn't the Capitol or the White House, it was the Federal Reserve headquarters on Constitution Avenue. Bin Laden saw the Fed as the primary financial resource funding our foreign policy."

"You're not serious," Sullivan said.

"I'm not. It's not my rumor. But there's truth that the Fed provides the deficit-spending mechanism that enables presidents to engage in military operations that couldn't be paid for otherwise."

"Luguire was killed by terrorists?" Sullivan didn't bother to hide his incredulity.

Sidney shrugged. "It's not out of the realm of possibility. At least foreign elements of some kind. There's also an international connection to the pro-Fed, pro-secrecy side."

"I'm listening," Sullivan said.

"In 2011, after an extended court battle, the Federal Reserve was forced to reveal it provided billions of dollars to foreign-owned financial institutions during the meltdown of 2008. In fact, nine of the twelve largest payments went to foreign interests."

"I didn't know that."

"Of course not. Makes for bad politics. You're out of work, you've lost your house, and the government bailout goes to foreigners."

"What was their justification?"

"These were financial firms doing business in the U.S. The impact of their failure would hurt Americans. I'm not saying that's not a valid reason, but the court battle broke ninety-seven years of secrecy that hid the identity of foreign banks using our money, money we're having to back with debt-generating U.S. securities."

"And you hate secrecy."

Sidney smiled. "I'm a journalist. I even carry a journal to prove it. Banks, Wall Street firms, and companies are owned by people. People who at the top make lots of money. That's the arena you're playing in, Detective Sullivan. That's also your suspect pool."

"If Luguire was murdered," Sullivan said.

"If Luguire was murdered," Sidney agreed. "And that's the whole point of my being here. Was he?"

Sullivan sighed. This reporter's claims, wild as they sounded, couldn't be rejected outright any more than Rusty Mullins' claim of Luguire's intention to be alive the next morning. But making a deal with Sidney Levine went against every instinct.

"Look, I'm not going to be able to do what you want, at least not yet. The investigation is still in its early stages."

"At least not yet?" Sidney repeated the phrase most important to him.

"I will say Paul Luguire exhibited certain behaviors last night that were not indicative of a man planning to take his own life."

"Such as?"

"That's for you to learn."

"Then who was with him last night?"

"He had a driver provided by Prime Protection. Russell Mullins. You didn't get his name from me." Sullivan reached in his coat pocket and gave Sidney his card. "Call me if you come across something."

"Prime Protection. Sounds like they were sub-prime."

"A word of advice. Don't start the interview that way. Mullins won't talk to you. Or if he does, you won't hear him because he'll have knocked you unconscious."

Sidney tucked the card between the pages of his journal. "Know where I can reach him?"

"Yeah, but only if you wait till tomorrow."

"Fair enough."

Sullivan gave him the address for Mullins' Shirlington apartment, and then escorted him to the door of the police station. He watched him walk away in the opposite direction from the nearest Metro stop. He either drove a car or lived nearby. Sullivan would check him out in the morning.

He returned to his desk and opened the case file for Rusty Mullins' phone number. Mullins wasn't the kind of guy to talk to the press, but Sidney Levine had said some very interesting things and he could be useful. Sullivan wanted a second opinion about that. Rusty Mullins was just the man to give it.

Chapter Fourteen

"Paw Paw!" Josh squealed the words as he leaned over the back of the sofa and peered out the front window.

As Mullins parked his Prius, he caught a glimpse of his excited grandson. The beaming face of the boy magically lightened the weight he'd carried since Detective Sullivan called him with the news of Luguire's death.

Mullins picked up the CVS bag from the passenger seat. After dropping Amanda Church at her car the night before, he'd gone to the store and purchased a Nerf baseball, something Josh could carry to the T-ball game. Luguire's twin grandsons wouldn't be there, but Mullins felt an obligation to carry through with the last plan he and Luguire had made.

Mullins pressed the buzzer by his daughter's condo number and the electric lock clicked. Before he could step inside, the door of his daughter's unit opened and Josh scrambled out. Mullins hustled up the short flight of stairs and caught the boy as he leaped from the top step into his grandfather's arms.

"Ball, Paw Paw. Ball."

"Ball," Mullins repeated, and rattled the bag he held against the boy's back. Evidently, Kayli had primed Josh for their outing. He shifted the child into the crook of his left arm and let him pull the Nerf ball free. "See. You say ball, and Paw Paw makes a ball appear."

"Good thing he doesn't know the word pony yet." A young man stepped out of the condo. A boy Josh's age walked shyly by his side.

Mullins recognized the child. Luke. Josh's playmate from a unit on the second floor.

"I'll have to get a bigger bag. I'm Rusty Mullins. A.k.a. Paw Paw."

"Don Beecham. Luke's dad. Kayli said you were coming by for Josh." He walked back in the condo. "The girls have gone to some sale at Pentagon City. I'm afraid my wife enticed your daughter to join her."

Mullins followed him, but left the door open. "I hope I haven't held you up. Kayli could have called me to come earlier."

"That's all right. It was a spur of the moment thing. Sandy saw the ad in the morning paper. Stores opened at eight for some Summer Madness promotion. Then they both have hair appointments."

Josh squirmed to get down.

"Hold still," Mullins said. "We're going in a minute."

"Kayli left diapers and a clean outfit by the door." Don pointed to a blue bag adjacent to the threshold. "She said she'd pick Josh up at one."

"Okay. I can lock up. Thanks for holding the fort till I got here."

Don reached down and lifted his son. "Kayli said she didn't think you'd mind if Luke and I tagged along. He's never seen a ballgame."

Mullins hesitated. Last night Detective Sullivan had convinced him to talk to some reporter named Sidney Levine, and the guy woke him up at seven-thirty. Mullins agreed to meet him, and the ballgame seemed a safe, public place.

Don picked up on Mullins' reluctance. "But if you'd rather have time alone with Josh, I understand."

"No, it's not that. I've got some errands to run afterwards and that might not be convenient for you."

"We'll take separate cars. Better anyway because I don't know how long the game will hold Luke's attention."

Mullins considered the point. Having Luke along might keep Josh occupied. He'd find a way to exchange a few words with the reporter and be done with it.

"Good. The boys can try out the new ball. The game's at the field near William Ramsay Elementary School off North Beauregard." He set Josh down and picked up the diaper bag. "I'll lock up."

"I'd better follow you," Don said. "I'm not sure where we're going."

"Okay." Mullins stepped back to let the father and son go first.

Don stood still. "Mr. Mullins, before we leave, I just want to say how sorry I am about what happened to Mr. Luguire. Kayli told us you were friends."

"Yeah, Paul was one of the good guys. You're with the Federal Reserve?"

Don nodded. "I'm on the congressional liaison side. I had the privilege of briefing Mr. Luguire a few times whenever he had business on the Hill." He stopped, and then pursed his lips, not sure what to say.

Mullins filled in the silence. "Although he understood politics, he wasn't one for bullshit. That's a rare combination."

"Yes, sir. Any idea why he killed himself?"

Mullins examined the younger man's face. Genuine concern was the only thing he saw. "If, and the police haven't said for sure, but if he did, then he must have lost hope. That's what suicide is, the ultimate loss of hope."

Chapter Fifteen

The T-ball game quickly became a Keystone Cops comedy. A kid would take a swing at the ball set on a waist-high tee, sometimes miss everything, sometimes hit the tee, sometimes actually connect with the ball. When that happened, everybody moved, no matter where the ball went, and it was a race to see whether any baseman could catch a throw before the batter ran past him. Both teams must have been nearing the total in *The Guinness Book of Records* for most in-field home runs.

Mullins sat with Josh on his knee, giving a dramatic play-by-play interspersed with tickles. Luke played with a toy truck in the dirt at the foot of the bleachers despite Don's encouragement for him to watch the game.

At the end of the third inning, Sidney Levine walked from his car where he'd been watching the stands. Rusty Mullins had told him he'd be there with his grandson, and he'd be wearing a Washington Nationals cap. He didn't tell him he'd be sitting with a friend. Sidney waited, expecting Mullins to take a walk or find some other way to distance himself from the other spectators. Finally, he figured Mullins wasn't planning on giving him enough time to warrant leaving his seat.

Don Beecham caught the man's movement out of the corner of his eye and reflexively grabbed Luke as he stepped near the boy.

"Mr. Mullins?" Sidney asked.

"Hi, Sidney," Mullins said warmly. "How have you been?"

For a second, Sidney was surprised by the greeting that made him and Mullins buddies. He quickly determined Mullins wanted this to play out as a chance meeting. "Good." He nodded to Josh. "Somebody got a big brother in the game?"

"Nah, we're just out on a lark. You got a boy playing?"

"My nephew," Sidney improvised. "I can't stay for the whole game, but I wanted to make sure he saw me."

"Good for you."

"Listen, I hate to bother you. I know it's been a tough week, but I've got a question about something that's come up with my job. That is, if you've got a moment."

Mullins lifted Josh and set him beside Don. "Do you mind watching him? I don't want to bore people with shop talk during such an exciting game." Then he gestured toward Sidney. "Excuse me. This is Sidney. Sidney, Don." Without giving them time to engage in more than a nod, he leaned over to Josh. "You stay with Mr. Beecham. Paw Paw's got to talk to the nice man." He stood and turned to Don. "We'll be in the parking lot if you need me."

Mullins took command, walking briskly toward his car.

Sidney hurried to catch him. "Why the charade?"

"Don works for the Federal Reserve."

"Oh." He took the fact as ample reason for Mullins' actions.

Mullins leaned against the door of his Prius. "So, why are we here? Why couldn't we do this over the phone?"

Sidney reached in his hip pocket and pulled out a paperback. "For one thing I wanted to give you this. More importantly, there's no substitute for sizing up each other face to face."

Mullins took the book and glanced at the title. *The Secret Revolution of 1913—How Bankers Stole America!* The author was Joseph Sidney Levine. Mullins thought of the book Amanda Church had purchased for him at Barnes and Noble. "Is this your version of *Betrayal at Jekyll*? Are you claiming the Federal Reserve is quote, 'one of the most corrupt institutions this world has ever known.'"

Sidney gave an appreciative nod. "You're already doing your homework."

"Not really. Somebody gave it to me yesterday. Is your book like it?"

"Tamer. Less on the conspiratorial approach and more on the economic consequences of a central bank basically running with little oversight. But I had *The Washington Times* byline to my credit which got me a mainstream publisher, not a POD."

"POD?"

"Print-on-demand. Those are books that are printed only when a copy is ordered. It's used by self-publishers or when the print run has gotten so small that printing one at a time is more practical."

"Detective Sullivan called me last night."

Sidney smiled. "I thought he might. Did he tell you I was trouble?"

"You could be. But he also considers you a potential resource. He told me about your disciples."

"I wouldn't go so far as to call them disciples. Most of them simply look for validation of their beliefs and don't want to hear anything to the contrary."

"Sullivan said one thing that caught my interest and frankly it's why I agreed to meet with you."

Mullins paused, but Sidney didn't jump in with the obvious question. Too many reporters, especially the fringe ones, wanted to pepper interviewees with what they thought were provocative questions with little interest in the answers.

Mullins continued, assured that Sidney was a good listener. "You spoke to Sullivan about international involvement, both anti-Fed and pro-Fed."

"Yes. The anti-Fed is obvious. Extremists and terrorists see capitalism and the banking system as a great evil. The pro-Fed is more subtle. There are companies and financial institutions who have benefited from the Fed's ability to infuse money into them under the protection of the Fed's secrecy and independent authority."

Mullins looked skeptical. "Are you talking about international financiers? The so-called Jewish banking cartel set on ruling the world?"

"Most definitely not. I'm Jewish, and yet I was branded antisemitic by the critics of my book who use that as a knee-jerk response. J. P. Morgan was Episcopalian. John D. Rockefeller, a Baptist. This is about money and power, not Zionism or some mythical cabal conspiracy."

Mullins took another look at Sidney's book. "Rockefeller and Morgan are the bankers?"

Sidney shook his head. "You haven't read as much history as I thought."

"I've been busy protecting presidents and arresting counterfeiters."

"Some claim that's all the Fed is—legalized counterfeiters." Sidney walked to the Prius and leaned beside Mullins. "Representatives of Rockefeller, Morgan, and the Rothschilds bankers of Europe held a secret meeting in 1910 at Jekyll Island off the coast of Georgia. This is fact. They traveled in secret, used alias names, and created a scheme for a privately held central bank. Then they got the right people elected, secured the votes, and persuaded Woodrow Wilson to sign the legislation in late December of 1913, a highly unusual time when no one was in Washington. Even the name Federal Reserve was calculated to obscure because the banks weren't federal entities and they had no reserves."

Sidney pointed to the book in Mullins' hands. "Read the preface. It's what Woodrow Wilson supposedly said three years later."

Mullins flipped through the first few pages till he found the quote.

"I am a most unhappy man. I have unwittingly ruined my country. A great industrial nation is controlled by its system of credit. Our system of credit is concentrated. The growth of the nation, therefore, and all our activities are in the hands of a few men. We have come to be one of the worst ruled, one of the most completely controlled and dominated Governments in the civilized world, no longer a Government by free opinion, no longer a Government by conviction and the vote of the majority, but a Government by the opinion and duress of a small group of dominant men."—Woodrow Wilson, 1916

"He doesn't call for them to be killed," Mullins said.

"And neither do I. Also, there's evidence the quote was cobbled out of two statements Wilson made before the Fed was even founded. I talk about the discrepancy in the book, but the publisher excerpted it for the front and the proper context doesn't appear till page eighty-nine. A hook, they called it."

"So, the anti-Feds ignore that possibility."

"The Internet's not known for fostering calm rhetoric, and Woodrow Wilson never saw national debt at nearly fifteen trillion dollars. I told Sullivan I have access to the fringes, and if Luguire was killed because of his work at the Fed, something will arise out of that fringe."

Mullins closed the book. "I'm not investigating Paul Luguire's death."

"Not officially."

"I'm not investigating Paul Luguire's death period."

Sidney held up his hands. "Okay. Then why are you interested in the possible international connection?"

"Curious. The possibility expands the scope of the case beyond our shores. As a former Secret Service agent, I find that interesting."

Sidney smiled. "And I find it interesting that you would have me believe you think his death is a suicide but focus on international possibilities. Level with me, Mr. Mullins. Paul Luguire didn't commit suicide because you were close enough to him to have spotted warning signs. Tell me what you think off the record, and I'll float it out there to see who bites."

Mullins felt the short burst of vibration from the cellphone in his pocket. A text message. He looked at the boys on the field. "Paul Luguire was supposed to be watching his twin grandsons play here today. We planned to see the game together. It was the last conversation we had, and five hours later he was dead."

"You don't make plans for after your suicide."

"And you don't get a hundred dollars from an ATM to cross the River Jordan."

Sidney whistled. "He did that?"

"I'm sure they have the bank security footage of me getting the money for him on his way home."

"And the international angle?"

Mullins thought for a second about his real international interest, the creation of a Grand Cayman account in his name. "I told you, it broadens the scope of the investigation. An investigation I'm watching only from the sidelines."

"Does that include anything I might uncover?"

"I'm not one to turn down good conversation."

"Conversation is a two-way dialogue."

Mullins stuck out his hand. "That's what I hear. Good luck, Mr. Levine. I'd better get back to my grandson."

Mullins headed to the small stand of bleachers. He could see Josh now playing in the dirt with Luke. Don Beecham wasn't watching the kids or the game. He was staring at him.

Mullins stopped and pulled the phone from his pocket. He expected to see a message from Kayli that she needed to change the pickup time for Josh. He used his hand to shield the screen from the glare of sunlight.

The text read, "Our person of interest expects you 9am Monday. Follow through."

The sending number was blocked, but Mullins knew the message had come from Amanda Church. She'd spoken with Craig Archer at Laurel Bank. She'd used the power of the Federal Reserve to make the appointment.

As an ex-Treasury agent, he would do what he did best. Follow the money.

Chapter Sixteen

Immediately after leaving the T-ball game, Sidney Levine sent a text message: Call me ASAP! Twenty minutes later, as he crossed over Key Bridge into Georgetown, his phone rang. Caller ID read Colleen's Cell.

He answered in a whisper, "Hey, babe, you at work?"

"Yeah. I was screening a rough cut of the Italian architecture doc for the powers that be."

"On Saturday?"

"National Geographic scheduled the damn thing for the week after next. They're already running on-air promos, and, of course, now they want changes."

"Guess you'll be camping out in the edit room."

"You got it. What's up?"

"I need your car."

She sighed. "Jeez, Sidney. Did the Escort die again?"

"It's running like a champ. I'm on a story. A big story. But a guy I need to follow has seen my car."

"For the day?"

"Maybe a couple days. A simple swap."

"Except my Audi doesn't break down."

Sidney laughed. "I thought you were stuck in edit hell."

"Okay. When do you want to get it?"

"How about now? I can be at the post house in ten minutes."

"I'm going into a meeting with the sound designer."

"Put the keys under the mat. I'll do the same."

"Sidney, you could leave your keys in the door and nobody would take your car."

Sidney knew he'd won. "I owe you, babe."

"Damn right. You make the national debt look like chump change."

◇◇◇

Sidney spent the afternoon in the parking lot of Shirlington House waiting for Rusty Mullins to return to his apartment. The temperature rose into the high eighties and Colleen's black Audi turned into an oven. He rolled down all the windows and moved the car to a space in the shade. He wondered if tailing Mullins wasn't a mistake. The guy might not know anything. He insisted he wasn't investigating, but his reason for seeing Sidney didn't ring true. The international aspect of the anti-Fed sentiment definitely meant something to him.

Even if the ex-Secret Service agent undertook a one-man crusade to find Luguire's killer, he might work only the phone and Internet. But Sidney's face to face with Mullins left him feeling the older man wasn't an armchair detective. If he had a lead or a line of inquiry, he'd go to the source in person. And he'd do it soon.

Sidney used the time in the car to write his news blog on his laptop, upload it via his 4G wireless card, and tweet the availability of the post to his Twitter followers. He kept one eye on the rearview mirror and the other on his computer screen as reactions multiplied to his report that Paul Luguire displayed behavior merely a few hours before his death that undercut any rationale he contemplated suicide. The theme most commonly woven through the thread of responses was that Luguire had been summoned by Congress to testify before the Banking committee.

Luguire was known as a straight-shooter who didn't dodge questions with evasive answers, and that made some powerful people very nervous. Most dangerous of all, Luguire wasn't a prodigy of Goldman Sachs, the firm whose executives hopped back and forth between Wall Street and the Fed so frequently they shouldn't have bothered changing offices. He was an outsider who had seen behind the curtain.

Sidney became so engrossed in the online gossip that he nearly missed Rusty Mullins pulling into the parking lot. The blue Prius flashed in his mirror as it crossed behind him, appearing so suddenly that Sidney didn't have a chance to duck down. Just as well because that reflex action might have attracted Mullins' attention. Instead, Sidney started the engine, figuring Mullins would expect a person sitting behind the wheel of a parked car to do one of two things: get out or drive off.

Sidney backed out of his space, angling so that the driver's side window stayed farthest from the Prius parked six cars away. He checked Mullins in the rearview mirror and saw him grab a suitcase and multiple hangers of clothing fresh from a dry cleaners. Had he been running normal Saturday afternoon errands, or was he preparing to leave town? The grandchild was no longer with him.

If Mullins planned a flight out of Reagan or Dulles, Sidney knew he was screwed. Tailing Mullins at an airport might not be impossible, but learning his travel plans and not being seen on the same plane would require a string of luck stretching the odds to lottery-winning proportions. Mullins could even be leaving the country, if his international interest represented a very specific target.

Sidney had to be prepared for what he could control. He left Shirlington House and fueled the Audi at a nearby Shell station. He used the bathroom, bought snacks, drinks, and sandwiches, and returned to the apartment parking lot. Mullins' car hadn't moved. Sidney found a spot far enough away and off the route Mullins would walk that he felt relatively secure he could avoid detection.

By ten o'clock, Mullins hadn't reappeared. Sidney decided Mullins was spending Saturday night in. He left for home. He packed an overnight bag, grabbed a few hours sleep, and was back at Shirlington House at four-thirty in the morning.

Five hours later, Rusty Mullins emerged from the high-rise apartment building carrying the suitcase and a hanging bag.

Sidney knew only one thing. Mullins wasn't headed for church.

Chapter Seventeen

Craig Archer clutched a cup of black coffee and wandered through the lobby of his own bank. At eight-forty on Monday morning, the arriving tellers and customer advisors were surprised to see their president. Normally, he stayed in his suite of executive offices on the third floor and came and went by the rear elevator.

Although he greeted employees with a smile and a cheery "Good Morning," his appearance wasn't reassuring. Small groups clustered in the break room and worried that an announcement was imminent. Further layoffs, or the FDIC had taken over the assets. He would utter the dreaded words, "Laurel Bank has failed."

Ironically, Craig Archer waited in the lobby to dispel the very gossip his presence created. He wanted to intercept his visitor from the Federal Reserve before the guy flashed his credentials. Better to greet him as if he were a personal friend and not an investigator. An on-site Fed would set the rumor mills working overtime.

Archer took U.S. Treasury Agent Nathaniel Brown's request for secrecy at more than face value, going so far as to enter into his electronic calendar a nine o'clock meeting with Walter Thomson, a name he made up for the benefit of his administrative assistant so she would have an explanation for the man in his office.

Archer caught the eye of his senior teller. "Lexie, can I borrow your key to the front doors?"

"Yes, sir. But it's only twenty till."

"That's okay. I'm expecting a friend and I forgot to tell him to come in the back. If he gets here before nine, I'll re-lock."

"All right." The woman took a key from the pocket of her blazer. "I'll be at my window."

Archer stood a few feet from the glass double doors. The drive from D.C. took around four-and-a-half hours depending upon which side of Washington you started from. He hoped this Russell Mullins wouldn't be late. Otherwise, Archer would turn into the equivalent of a Wal-Mart greeter once the bank opened.

A trim, middle-aged man wearing a crisply pressed, dark-blue suit walked up to the door. He eyed Archer and gave a nod. The man couldn't have looked more governmental than if he had the U.S. flag tattooed on his forehead.

"Mr. Mullins?" Archer mouthed from behind the glass.

The man nodded again.

Archer unlocked the bolt and pushed the door open.

Rusty Mullins gave a quick glance over his shoulder just long enough to make sure the black Audi had followed him from the motel.

Archer re-locked the door and then offered his hand. "Craig Archer. A pleasure to meet you. You made good time."

"I drove down yesterday," Mullins said. "Thank you for seeing me on such short notice."

Archer relaxed. He'd expected a confrontational attitude from some arrogant Washingtonian who viewed Roanoke as a hick mountain town. "We want to do what we can to clear up whatever happened, especially if illegalities occurred outside of our control." He gestured for Mullins to follow. "We can speak in my office."

Moving quickly through the lobby, Archer dropped the keys at Lexie's window and led Mullins to the back elevator. When they were safely ensconced in his office, Archer said, "Would you like some coffee? My assistant will be here shortly and can brew a fresh pot."

Mullins waved the offer aside. "Thanks, but I'd rather get right down to business. Time could be critical in learning what happened so we can prevent a reoccurrence."

"Certainly." Archer indicated for Mullins to take a seat at a small conference table in one corner of his spacious office. "What would you like to know?"

"Walk me through how the account in question was set up."

Archer picked up a file folder from his desk, and then joined Mullins at the table. "I had my manager at the Staunton branch scan and email me the account documents." He flipped open the file cover and slid the top document to Mullins. "This is a photocopy of his driver's license."

The double photo, one small, one larger, showed a dark-skinned man. His features weren't Hispanic, although that would be the common assumption in Florida. Mullins thought of his favorite detective novel, *The Maltese Falcon*, where Hammett described Joel Cairo as "The Levantine." The word sent him to the dictionary where he learned "Levant" meant the land around the eastern Mediterranean.

He studied Fred Mack's features carefully. His educated guess pegged the man as Syrian, but Mack could have been a third-generation American. Mullins wasn't one to jump to conclusions.

He read the address on the license aloud. "4908 Palm Crescent Drive, Sunrise, Florida. Did someone ask why he was opening a business account in Staunton, Virginia?"

"Mr. Mack said he was in the process of relocating. A major benefactor of his company lives in the area and wanted the organization to be in close proximity. Mr. Mack said he really couldn't say no."

Mullins looked across the table at the open file. "Who was the benefactor?"

"He said the benefactor insisted on remaining anonymous."

"And this organization supposedly helps crime victims gain restitution?"

Archer nodded. "That's what he said."

"And a local address?"

Archer grimaced. "No. That's where we're lacking critical information. Mr. Mack said they hadn't completed negotiations for office space yet. He had a P.O. box at the main post office in Staunton and used the Florida address as a physical location, something we're required to have on file along with a photo ID."

"Let me guess. There's no such address."

"No. There is. I used Google Earth and it's a residence. Sunrise is a town about forty-five minutes north of Miami. I could see the house and it looks like there's a For Sale sign in the front yard. At least it's the right size. The satellite view doesn't show what's written on it."

"Can I see the rest of the documentation?"

Archer pushed the thin file to him.

Mullins quickly skimmed the papers, most of which were bank forms and disclaimers including the record of the initial nine-thousand-dollar deposit and signature cards for the account. Fred Mack was the only person with signing privileges.

"Did you check the tax ID number for the company?" Mullins asked.

"No. We had no reason to think there was a problem. And he signed the form attesting that the information he provided was true and accurate."

Mullins laughed. "Yeah, that only works for people whose information is true and accurate."

Archer reddened. "He was a customer. Frankly, we need accounts and deposits, and we did everything the law required us to do."

Mullins turned up his palms. "Look, I'm not here to bust your chops. I'm just trying to find out what happened and how I might reach Mr. Mack. So, he opened the account on Monday a week ago and closed it on Wednesday two days later?"

"Yes. I knew none of this till your colleague Amanda Church called me."

"And by then it was too late."

"I know how it looks."

Mullins stared at the man. "Tell me how it looks."

Archer licked his lips nervously. "Mr. Mack opened the account for the sole purpose of passing a large amount of cash through it."

"And somehow broke the authorization codes for your Federal Reserve window and managed to reverse the entire transaction and create an offshore source in the process. Then the money transfers into eleven other accounts that turn out to be bogus. We have no idea where the funds really went, but they started with the Federal Reserve and somebody, somewhere, got real cash. I might be wrong, but that's not your normal Staunton, Virginia customer, is it, Mr. Archer?"

"No, it's not."

Mullins held up the copy of the driver's license and pointed to Mack's face. "And I find it hard to believe this man pulled the stunt off alone. He had help."

"Not from me or any one in Laurel Bank."

"That's your opinion."

Archer bristled. "Part of my opinion. I think you should look to your own house, Mr. Mullins. What are the odds that someone here came up with the name Russell Mullins for a Cayman account?"

Mullins nodded, conceding the point. "So, you understand why I have a personal interest in discovering who's behind this, as I expect you do as well."

"Most assuredly. And we're implementing a thorough review of every procedure involved in establishing and monitoring Mr. Mack's account."

"When he closed the account, did Mr. Mack say what his plans were?"

"No. He expressed disappointment that his 501c(3) application had been denied and he apologized for wasting our time."

Mullins sifted through the file documents again. "Who in the branch opens new accounts?"

"Normally customer advisors handle that, but if they're tied up, the manager helps out."

"And your manager dealt with Mr. Mack personally?"

"An associate opened the account. Carl Andrews, the manager, closed it. Because of the large, although brief deposit, Carl wanted to meet Mr. Mack next time he came in."

"Get him to park his money a little longer?"

Archer shrugged. "I prefer to call it building customer relations. When Mack told him he would be withdrawing the balance, Carl made an effort to keep the account open in case the 501c(3) problem was quickly resolved. He waived service fees in consideration for the amount of money that appeared to be moving through." Archer paused. "Carl said that was an odd moment."

"How so?"

"Mr. Mack seemed surprised at the additional funds. At least that was Carl's impression. Then Mack said he'd forgotten the transaction would be taking place."

"He forgot over two-hundred thousand was coming to an account he'd just opened?"

"Yeah. I guess that's another reason to think Mack wasn't in this alone."

Mullins gathered the papers together. "May I have copies of these?"

"They're for you."

"Did you tell your branch manager I was coming this morning?"

"No. I said only that I wanted to review the file because of the amount of money that moved through such a short-lived account."

"I understand the person who checks overall daily balances was out the afternoon the wire transfer occurred."

"Yes. FDIC compliance training. We're a small bank and don't have redundancy systems in place. When she ran the numbers the next day, the deposit had come and gone from our balance sheet."

Mullins thought a moment. "How long in advance had that training session been scheduled?"

"Six weeks. She had to drive to Richmond."

"And she had to confirm her attendance beforehand?"

"Yes. As soon as we got the notice."

"Thank you, Mr. Archer." Mullins closed the file and stood. He looked at the notepad by the phone on Archer's desk. "Can I have a sheet of that paper? I want to give you my personal cell-phone number in case you think of anything else, and especially if Mr. Mack returns."

Archer pulled the top sheet free. "Certainly. Is there anything else I can do?"

"Not at the moment. Let's keep this conversation between us. You can appreciate the sensitive nature of what's transpired."

Archer watched Mullins jot down the number. The bank president took it, folded the paper once, and then tucked it in his wallet. "I won't say a word, but if you learn something that could help us avoid a similar problem in the future, I'd appreciate anything you would share."

"Fair enough." Mullins shook Archer's hand. "Meanwhile, I was never here."

Archer smiled. "Russell Mullins never walked in this building."

"Thank you. I can find my way out." Mullins opened the door and left, heading straight for the elevator.

Archer watched him leave, and then closed his office door. He went to his desk, pulled out a fresh legal pad, and began to write everything that just occurred. When Agent Nathaniel Brown called, Archer would be ready.

Mullins stepped off the elevator on the ground floor. Instead of returning to the lobby, he exited through the employee entrance. He crossed the rear parking lot and walked two blocks in the opposite direction from where the black Audi had been facing. He'd made Sidney Levine when he left his apartment in Shirlington, but to try and evade the reporter would have made him suspicious. Mullins didn't have a problem being followed to a public bank, but the next leg of his investigation needed to be solo.

He walked to the corner of the cross street where he could see two blocks to the bank. The Audi was in the customer lot in a space farthest from his Prius. Sidney could watch both the lobby door and his car. Mullins looked around, not seeing what twenty years earlier would have been a common sight. A pay phone. He wondered if Roanoke had eliminated all of them. He turned and retraced his steps to where he'd seen a Fast Break Food Mart. Sure enough, on the outside wall near the corner of the building, was a public phone. It wouldn't work for Clark Kent to change into Superman, but it more than sufficed for Mullins.

He skirted the door so that a cashier couldn't see him, took a handkerchief from his pocket to avoid fingerprints, and dialed 911. He repeated the bomb threat twice to make sure the responder got the address.

The sirens wailed as he stepped back into the bank's employee parking lot. As people streamed out of the building, Mullins walked around the side and cautiously checked the customer lot. He saw a police officer telling Sidney Levine to move his vehicle. Then a firetruck screeched to a halt, blocking his view. Mullins hurried to his Prius, eased it forward on quiet battery power, and circled behind the bank.

He relaxed when he merged onto I-81 with no Audi behind him and nothing but interstate between Roanoke and Miami.

Chapter Eighteen

The rush of cop cars, their blue lights blazing and sirens wailing, caught Sidney Levine off-guard. As people poured out of the office building, Sidney scanned the faces for Mullins but couldn't see him.

"Are you waiting on someone?" The police officer shouted the question as he bent closer to Sidney's window.

Sidney rolled down the glass. "I was going into the bank. Has there been a robbery?"

"Possible gas leak. We need you to clear the area now."

Gas leak my ass, Sidney thought. He looked past the officer to the stream of people flowing out the doors and across the street beyond the perimeter rapidly being established by the police. If Sidney got out and joined them, he'd be away from the car if Mullins drove away.

The cop made the choice for him. "Move the vehicle, sir. We need the working space."

As an emphasis of his point, a firetruck jumped the curb and stopped facing the building. Mullins' Prius disappeared behind the wall of red and silver metal.

"Yes, sir," Sidney said. He backed the Audi up and drove out the entrance. Another police officer refused to let him turn left onto the street going in front of the bank. As Sidney drove through the intersection, he craned his neck out the window to see around the firetruck. Mullins' Prius was gone.

Sidney had no doubt that Mullins orchestrated the chaotic scene. Somehow he must have phoned in a bomb threat to mask his escape. Sidney assumed Mullins spotted him. Then another possibility crossed his mind. What if Mullins saw someone else following him? Someone whose presence posed a real threat.

Sidney looked in his rearview mirror. No cars trailed him. He took a deep breath, telling himself not to let his imagination overwhelm the rational side of his brain. He needed to focus on what he could learn. Mullins had spoken to someone in that building, and he'd gone into the lobby before the bank opened. A distinguished-looking man admitted him. As soon as the emergency vehicles left, Sidney would find out who Mullins saw and why.

Meanwhile, his best option was to return to the Hampton Inn on I-81 in case Mullins hadn't checked out. Maybe he was in Roanoke for more than one night.

Mullins' car wasn't in the hotel lot. Sidney parked on the side of the building where his own room had been. He'd received his receipt under the door at four-thirty that morning, left his keycard and five dollars for the maid on the nightstand, and staked out Mullins from the Audi.

Sidney checked the time before getting out of the car. Nine-fifty. There was a good chance the front desk thought he was still in his room. He walked to the entrance, grabbed a cup of coffee and blueberry muffin from the complimentary breakfast buffet, and nonchalantly approached the registration desk.

A cheerful blonde looked up from her computer and smiled. "Can I help you?"

"I'm checking out of 207 and left the key in the room."

"Was everything all right?"

"Yes. Except I forgot to set my alarm and overslept. I was supposed to have breakfast at nine with someone I met last night. Russell Mullins. Has he checked out?"

"Do you know his room number?"

"No." Sidney motioned toward the flat-screen TV mounted on the wall in the lounge. "We came in at the same time and baseball was on. We both paused to watch the end of the second inning and wound up staying for the whole game. More fun than watching it alone."

"Uh huh," the woman said, her fingers dashing over her keyboard like a concert pianist's. "Sorry. Mr. Mullins has checked out."

Sidney shrugged. "Thanks anyway. I'm leaving as well."

"We still provide wake-up calls."

"Good. Would you call me at home? I oversleep there too."

She laughed. "I'll put that in the customer suggestion box. It's about as likely to happen as any other request."

"I always suggest getting rid of the suggestion box."

Thirty minutes later, Sidney watched the last police car pull away. He entered the Laurel Bank lobby and surveyed the line of tellers returning to their windows. One woman gave the others instructions.

He approached her and read her gold name badge. "Excuse me, Lexie. I was supposed to meet a friend here, but in all the excitement we must have missed each other."

"Someone who works at the bank?"

"No. But he had an appointment. We were catching up afterwards. At ten."

"I'm sorry. It's been so confusing with the bomb scare that I don't know who's been here."

Sidney stepped closer and rested his arm on the marble ledge of her window. "He was coming before nine because he told me someone would have to let him in. Maybe his meeting was delayed, but I don't want to wait around if he's gone."

Lexie nodded. "I think I know who you mean. Was his appointment with Mr. Archer?"

Sidney took a chance. "Yes. That's the name. Rusty didn't tell me his title."

"Rusty?"

"My friend's nickname."

"Mr. Archer is president of our bank."

"Then I don't want to bother him. Would you check if my friend's still with him? Russell Mullins."

"My pleasure." Lexie picked up her phone, anxious to please someone associated with a guest in the president's office. "Linda, it's Lexie. Is Russell Mullins still with Mr. Archer? His friend's in the lobby."

Sidney saw confusion on the teller's face.

"But I saw Mr. Archer let him in this morning," she said. "Thin reddish hair, nice blue suit. Maybe fifty." She listened a moment. "And you're sure that's the name?" She listened again. "No, there's no problem. I'll let him know." She hung up.

"Something wrong?" Sidney asked.

"That was Mr. Archer's administrative assistant. The person I described was named Walter Thomson. She has no appointment listed for a Russell Mullins. Are you sure you were meeting today?"

Sidney laughed. "I thought so, but I could be wrong. This is embarrassing. I'm probably at the wrong bank."

Lexie smiled. "There are one or two others in town, but ours is the best."

"I'm sure it is. Sorry to trouble you." Sidney walked out the lobby, wondering why Russell Mullins used his real name at the Hampton Inn but set up his appointment under an alias. He could only conclude that the hotel required a photo ID and a bank interview didn't. Why would Mullins meet with a bank president using a phony name?

Sidney sat in the Audi, uncertain what to do. His first reaction was to return to the bank, identify himself as a reporter, and confront Archer. But he might be blowing a key strategy of Mullins' investigation, an investigation that could net Sidney an exclusive. He decided to confront Mullins instead, maybe force him to reveal his plan. If Mullins was headed back to D.C., then he had over an hour's lead. Sidney started the car. He'd take advantage of the Audi's superior horsepower and find Mullins as soon as possible.

Archer's handwritten report took five pages of his legal pad and he composed it carefully for accuracy in case he ever had to testify in court. The bomb scare had unnerved him. He suspected the incident was tied somehow to Mullins and the mysterious call from Agent Nathaniel Brown. He looked at his phone. The agent was due to call and give him his next set of instructions. Archer had cleared his schedule and he hoped once he'd completed his task, he'd never hear of Russell Mullins or Nathaniel Brown again.

The buzzer from his intercom startled him. "What is it, Linda?"

"Lexie called from downstairs. She said someone had come in saying he was supposed to meet your morning appointment."

Archer felt his stomach knot. Was Agent Brown in the bank?

"Did you tell him Mr. Thomson had gone."

"Yes, but that wasn't the name he gave. He was looking for Russell Mullins. I just wanted to see if the right name had been entered in your appointment calendar. I wasn't the one who put it in."

The knot tightened. Someone had been following Mullins. "I don't know that name," he stammered. "I met with Mr. Thomson."

"Thank you, sir. That's what I told her."

Archer grimaced. He hadn't wanted his lie to go beyond his assistant. "So, you were correct. Anything else?"

"Yes. A Mr. Brown is on line two. He says you're expecting his call."

Chapter Nineteen

The history of Roanoke, Virginia is forever linked with the railroad industry. The Norfolk and Western line not only made Roanoke a major transportation hub, but it also produced the finest steam locomotives in the world. Jobs and commerce roared through the city like a freight train thundering through the Shenandoah Valley. Soot and cinders weren't dirt, they were signatures of prosperity.

Until the coming of the diesels—cleaner, quieter, and made elsewhere. Over two thousand workers were laid off, and as the railroad industry abandoned the power of steam, it also abandoned Roanoke. When Norfolk and Western merged with Southern Railways to form Norfolk Southern, the headquarters of the new company was established in Norfolk, Virginia. Roanoke remained an important hub, but the clout of manufacturing and leadership had evaporated like steam from a leaky boiler.

Some remnants of the golden age survived as part of Virginia's Transportation Museum. But other warehouses and industrial buildings fell into disrepair.

Craig Archer was a little surprised that Treasury Agent Nathaniel Brown suggested they meet behind one of the railroad ruins. The old Virginia Railway passenger station near the South Jefferson Street Bridge had been abandoned for years. A fire had done extensive damage, and although it stood beside active rail lines, a chain-link fence had been erected around it while funds were sought for preservation and renovation.

Archer pulled his Cadillac Escalade to the back corner of the depot lot close to one of the bridge abutments. Overhead, headlights cut through the gathering dusk as cars moved in a steady stream. Archer killed the engine and rolled down the windows. Usually the mountain air cooled quickly after sunset, but the June day had been a scorcher and heat radiated from the ground.

He thought about getting out and stretching his legs. Surely a breeze blew across the rail yard.

A pair of headlights rounded the corner of the dilapidated depot. The vehicle pulled close behind, wedging Archer's Cadillac against the bridge's footing. High beams flicked on, lighting up the interior and bouncing off the rearview mirror into Archer's face. What a hotdog, Archer thought. Just like in the movies.

Archer opened his door.

"Stay in the car," a voice shouted. "Put your hands on the steering wheel."

Archer obeyed. He heard footsteps approach his window. He turned his head toward the sound. "Agent Brown?"

A man stepped alongside Archer's SUV. The high beams lit the right side of a swarthy face. The light glinted off coal black eyes. "Craig Archer?"

The words were tainted with a foreign accent. Maybe Middle Eastern, Archer thought. "Yes. Can I see some identification?"

The man reached his right hand inside his dark jacket and held it there. "Can I see the documents?"

"Okay." Archer turned to the manila envelope on the passenger seat where he'd stuffed his handwritten account of the meeting with Russell Mullins.

The suppressor muffled the pistol shot, reducing the sound to little more than a loud cough. The muzzle velocity of the bullet was also reduced, but still fast enough to smash through the skull behind Archer's ear and exit through his right temple.

The seatbelt and shoulder restraint kept his body dangling over the console. Blood and brains speckled the surface of the envelope on the passenger's seat.

The assassin walked around the front of the Cadillac and reached through the open window of the passenger's door. He grabbed the envelope by a clean corner and held it away from his expensive suit.

The open window had provided an escape route for the bullet and made its recovery unlikely. Too bad. But the blood on the envelope would be even better.

A freight train approached on an adjacent track. By the time it passed, the assassin and Craig Archer's handwritten report were gone.

◇◇◇

Sidney Levine waited for Rusty Mullins in the parking lot of Shirlington House till nine when he resigned himself to the fact that Mullins had given him the slip and gone elsewhere.

He kicked himself for not getting Mullins' cell number. The landline to the apartment was the only number listed and it was useless when Mullins was out of town. Detective Sullivan probably had Mullins' cell number, but Sidney knew he'd have to give Sullivan a reason for needing it. The cagey detective would want information in exchange.

Sidney decided to leave a message on Mullins' home voicemail. "I know about Walter Thomson. Call me." He closed with his cell number, feeling certain the name would force Mullins to get in touch.

When he got back to Georgetown, he logged onto his Internet account and Googled "Craig Archer Laurel Bank."

The first reference was less than an hour old and linked to *The Roanoke Times.* He clicked it, expecting a quote from Archer on the morning bomb scare.

The newspaper headline stunned him.

"Bank President Murdered!"

A chill swept through him. Russell Mullins had met Craig Archer using a phony name. Craig Archer was now dead. And Sidney had left Mullins a message proving he knew where Mullins had been and the name he used. If Mullins was a murderer, Sidney Levine had just made the biggest mistake of his life.

Chapter Twenty

Rusty Mullins felt his phone vibrate against his side. He looked at the clock on the dashboard. Nine-fifteen. Another forty-five minutes would get him to Daytona Beach. After twelve hours on the road, with only brief stops for lunch and dinner, he'd find a motel on I-95 and get a good night's sleep. Tomorrow he'd drive another four hours and face the task of tracking down Fred Mack.

The phone kept vibrating. Not an email or text message. Someone wanted him, and Mullins didn't want to be found. His daughter Kayli was the only call he'd accept, but he'd already spoken to her once that afternoon and let her, and only her, know where he was headed.

The ID showed an unfamiliar number with a 540 area code. Roanoke, if he remembered correctly. Craig Archer was the one person he knew there who had his cell number. Calling this late indicated he had important information.

"Hello." Mullins never answered with his name, an old habit from his undercover days.

"Is this Walter Thomson?" The man's voice was clipped and authoritative.

"Sorry. You have the wrong number."

Before he could snap the phone shut, the man said, "Russell Mullins?"

Without hesitating, Mullins broke the connection. The voice wasn't Archer's. A wrong number from Roanoke was odd enough. 540 and his Arlington area code of 703 would be hard to mix up, but using a wrong name followed by his name sent alarm bells ringing. When he reached a Daytona motel, he'd do a reverse look-up for the incoming number.

His phone vibrated again. A text message. "Call me. URGENT. AC."

Amanda Church. Mullins knew a trained agent who so carefully orchestrated their clandestine meeting at the bookstore wouldn't text his cell for a chat. He called the incoming number.

"What?" was all he said.

"I set up a Google alert on our friend. Ten minutes ago his name appeared in an online news update from Roanoke. He was found shot to death in his car by an abandoned railroad depot. No suspects."

"Suicide?"

"I've checked other wire services and that possibility's not mentioned. No weapon was found at the scene."

Mullins felt the ground shift under him. Archer murdered. A man who genuinely seemed in the dark regarding the dubious financial transactions that ran through his bank. Had Mullins failed to uncover key information during the interview, or was the Fred Mack file on the seat beside him worth a man's life?

And the reporter, Sidney Levine. He'd seen Mullins enter the bank. Could he have silenced Archer?

"Hey, are you there?" Amanda shouted through the phone.

"Yeah. Just surprised. Listen, I'm pulling into my parking lot. Let me check a few sources. Call you tomorrow."

"Right." She hung up.

They'd used no names. Mullins hoped the lie about his location would delay any eavesdropper from tracing the cell tower relays and pinpointing him fifty miles north of Daytona Beach.

He took the next exit, pulled into an Exxon station, and paid cash to fill the Prius. He had six hundred dollars left from the eight-hundred total he withdrew from two ATMs the previous day. He'd used no credit cards. The remaining wad of twenties would have to last till he returned to Arlington.

He extracted the battery from his BlackBerry, placed it in the glove box, and tucked the disabled phone under his seat. Not only was he losing communication, but also the BlackBerry's GPS service. He entered the Exxon mini-mart and bought a Snickers and a detailed map of South Florida.

An hour later, Mullins checked into a Holiday Inn Express at I-95 and Daytona's Speedway Blvd.

As the young man behind the registration desk programmed the keycard, Mullins asked, "Is there a business center where I can check my email?"

"Yes, sir." The uniformed night man slid the card into an envelope. "Your room is 211. The business center is on this floor beyond the elevators." He pointed down the adjacent hall. "It's open twenty-four-seven and we have three terminals and a shared printer. You should have no trouble getting an open computer at this hour."

Mullins thanked him, picked up his overnight bag, and headed for the business center.

He had the room to himself. He logged on as a guest and navigated to White Pages, Reverse Lookup. He typed in the Roanoke call from memory. After a few seconds search, "No number available" appeared on the screen. But there was a list of sponsors claiming to have the information for a fee. So much for the free lookup.

Maybe the number wasn't a private residence. He tried searching for a business. Same result. No free info, but a host of links promising to provide information for fees ranging from one dollar to ten dollars. Under the circumstances, Mullins wasn't about to use his credit card on an Internet site.

To hell with this, he thought. There was only one number he was worried about. He might as well check it directly. He typed in the information for a Google search.

The number appeared under the name Mullins had feared.

The Roanoke Police Department.

They had his cell number, they had his name, and they had a bomb threat and a murder occurring on the same day he came to town. They would find him a person of interest until he could be ruled out. And they would do their own reverse look up and confirm the number of the phone he answered belonged to a Russell Mullins.

But who was Walter Thomson and why did the caller think he was reaching him?

Mullins logged out and cleared the browser's history.

So much for a good night's sleep.

Sidney Levine cruised slowly through the parking lot of Shirlington House. Mullins hadn't returned and it was nearly one in the morning. If he'd killed Archer and driven back to Arlington, he'd be here by now.

Sidney returned to his apartment in Georgetown where he sat in an easy chair in the dark, avoiding the temptation to turn on his computer. The speculations of his Internet followers were noisy prattle, the musings of paranoid loners who found virtual companionship by inventing conspiracies for their own entertainment.

Sidney didn't need to invent anything. Something sinister had occurred right in front of him. He wondered why Mullins was interested in the president of a small bank, and why he would set up an appointment under a false name. Maybe he'd tried to protect the banker. Mullins was close to Luguire and his visit to Archer might have alarmed someone. If so, the plan failed. And Sidney recognized another possibility why Mullins wasn't home. He could also be dead.

If that were true, or if Mullins didn't surface soon, Sidney had no other recourse in his pursuit of the truth about Paul Luguire's death than to contact the one person officially assigned to the case—Detective Robert Sullivan. But telling Sullivan about Mullins' link to Archer might blow any game Mullins was playing. If Mullins was alive to play any game at all.

With that thought echoing in his mind, Sidney finally fell asleep.

Chapter Twenty-one

Kayli Woodson set the bowl of dry Cheerios on the floor in front of Josh and turned on The Cartoon Channel.

"The terrible twos," she said to herself. Truer words had never been spoken. Josh totally destroyed the banana she'd given him at the breakfast table, choosing to mash it between his fingers rather than eat it. Then he'd knocked over his cup of orange juice.

She was in no mood to battle her son. He could go hungry, eat the cereal, or pulverize it into dust. She didn't care. The vacuum cleaner could handle the mess better than she could handle his toddler attitude.

Kayli returned to the kitchen and checked her cellphone again. No missed calls, no text message. It was nearly nine and she hadn't heard from her father. Normally, when she first checked her phone there was "Good Morning Glory" on the screen or a short hello on voicemail for Josh.

She dialed Mullins' number. She heard no ring and her father's voice answered immediately. "Can't get your call. Leave a message." His phone wasn't silenced, it was off.

She cleared the dishes from the table, unable to relax. She understood her father well enough to know Luguire's death had set him off on a personal crusade. But she sensed there was more to it. Something else had gotten under his skin. The sudden trip to Florida and his vague explanation of falsified bank transactions indicated he pursued more than a simple investigation.

And he was out there on his own, without backup or Treasury Department resources.

Kayli wanted to share her concern with someone, even though her father had stressed keeping his movements a secret. She logged onto her Internet account and sent an email to her husband somewhere in the Indian Ocean. She didn't want to wait till the evening. "Call when you can. Need to talk."

She kept the phone close by as first she dressed and then changed Josh out of his pajamas. They were going to the park with Sandy and Luke. If Allen called, she could slip away while Sandy watched the two boys.

Sandy would understand.

◇◇◇

Mullins drove slowly past the house near the end of Palm Crescent Drive. The roof line matched what he'd observed on the Google Earth satellite photo, but the sign in the yard at 4908 didn't say For Sale or promote some political candidate's primary campaign. It read Foreclosure and gave the phone number of Goldlight Bank. Mullins wondered if there was a connection between Goldlight Bank and Laurel Bank.

The yard appeared well maintained but not overly landscaped. The pale yellow stucco exterior so common in Florida neighborhoods showed little wear. Mullins circled around the cul-de-sac and then pulled the Prius into the empty driveway. He parked in front of the double-wide garage door. The solid sheet of white metal closed off any view of vehicles inside.

He stepped out into the tropical heat and breathed cautiously. The humidity nearly choked him. He looked up and down the street. Everyone must either have been inside a protective cocoon of air conditioning or gone to work or to the nearby Sawgrass Mills Mall. He walked to the front door on a sun-bleached sidewalk bordered by white crushed stone. Drawn blinds covered the window for the living room or great room or whatever the hell real estate marketers now called the large front room of a home.

Mullins peered through the slats and made out the shapes of furniture in the shadowed interior. The house wasn't empty.

He rang the bell. A minute later he rang it again.

"No one's home." A woman stood in the yard on the other side of the driveway. She held a burning cigarette in one hand and a cane in the other. "You a bill collector?" Her voice had the tender tone of gravel sliding across a sheet of tin.

Mullins wasn't sure whether the old watchdog was a friend or foe to her neighbors. "Oh, no. I'm with an organization that tries to help people out of financial predicaments."

The woman took a drag on her cigarette and shook her head. "I'm afraid you're a little late for the Khoury family. I think they've skipped town."

Mullins pulled a folded photocopy of Fred Mack's driver's license from his pocket. He walked toward the woman. "Let me make sure I was sent to the right place. Is this Mr. Khoury?" He held the picture in front of her, keeping his thumb over the name Fred Mack.

"Yes, that's Fares. His wife is Zaina and they have a little girl named Jamila."

"The house still has furniture."

"I know. First week they were gone I went over every day and rang the bell. Since my Mort died, I spend most of my time playing red and black and staring out the front window. I never saw them leave."

"Red and black?"

"Solitaire. Mort and I played gin rummy at the table." She sighed. "Sometimes I look up from those cards and expect to see him sitting across from me. Keeps me from cheating."

Mullins stuck the photo back in his pocket. "How long have they been gone?"

"Three weeks. Maybe a little longer. They didn't even say goodbye."

"What was Mr. Khoury's job?"

She took another puff and a long chunk of ash dropped to the ground. She eyed him suspiciously. "You don't know?"

"That's why I'm here. To fill in the details and see if he's eligible for government aid."

"Fares worked as a landscape designer. He didn't have his own company or anything like that. I don't think he was a licensed landscape architect or whatever they call the top guy. He got laid off when the economy crashed and nobody was building new neighborhoods. That happened at the same time their mortgage payment ballooned."

"He told you this? You must have been pretty close."

"Zaina would invite me over for coffee, especially after I lost Mort. One afternoon she just started sobbing. Like to break my heart."

"They were losing the house?"

"She said they tried to work out something with the bank. Renegotiate. But nobody would help. That's the way it is, I guess. You're in the red or you're in the black. Money trumps everything."

"And they all left together?"

She shook her head. "Fares was gone first. Zaina said he was preparing an appeal that took him out of town. One last chance. Then a couple days later, she and the little girl were gone. I guess it didn't work. But they never said goodbye. Hell, I would have taken them in." She dropped the cigarette and snubbed it out with a fuzzy slipper. "An old Jewish widow taking in a Arab family. Well, they're people too. They have to have a place to live."

"Was Mr. Khoury angry about what had happened?"

"He never talked to me about it. But I would be, wouldn't you? Get into a house with a low interest loan and promises of roll-over financing only to have the rug pulled out from under you." She lifted the cane and swatted some invisible enemy. "I'd be mad as hell."

"Any idea where they've gone?"

"No. Just up and left."

"And they were Arabs?"

"Lebanese. Not the crazies. I thought they might be Christian since I know a lot of Lebanon is Christian, but they were

Muslim. And they were nice. Fares would pick up Mort's heart medicine when he went for his insulin."

Mullins' ears perked up. "Was Mr. Khoury diabetic?"

"Yeah. The bad kind. He had to take the shots. And he always carried orange juice or a candy bar with him." She looked at the Foreclosure sign. "I wonder how he's paying for his medicine. It's a shame, I tell you. Greedy bastards on Wall Street making millions while the family next door is destroyed."

Mullins nodded sympathetically. "I know. Makes you want to take things into your own hands."

"It does. Enough people lose their homes and this country will be in the middle of a revolution. Look at that Occupy Wall Street."

Mullins stuck out his hand. "I'm Harry Lockaby. Sorry to start talking without introducing myself."

The woman wrapped her nicotine-stained fingers lightly around his palm. "Judy Bernstein. If you talk to them, tell them I asked about them. And I'm watching the house."

"I will, Mrs. Bernstein. Can you tell me the name of the pharmacy where Mr. Khoury picked up your husband's medicine?"

Her eyes brightened. "That's smart. Fares may still come in for his insulin."

"Good thinking. I bet you're a hell of a card player."

The old woman beamed. "Got time for a hand of gin rummy? Penny a point."

"Maybe some other time when I've got more money. I have a feeling you'll clean me out."

"You do that. There's always an open chair at the table," she said wistfully. Then she added, "The CVS near Sawgrass Mills."

Mullins followed Judy Bernstein's directions to the pharmacy a few miles away. He stood in the pick-up line and waited his turn. Fortunately, the store marked a respectable distance between the customer being served and the next patron to insure some degree of medical privacy. A pharmacist wearing the name tag Harvey motioned him forward.

"Can I help you?"

"I'm getting the prescription for Fares Khoury."

Harvey looked surprised. "Mr. Khoury's back? No one phoned in an order."

"His insulin, right?"

"Yes. But we transferred the account to Staunton, Virginia."

Mullins scratched his head. "Gosh, I don't know what to say. I spoke to Fares last week and he expected to be home from his assignment tonight. I was going to drop it by the house."

"I'll check. Maybe we missed a fax." He entered data on a keyboard.

Mullins racked his brain for any knowledge about Staunton. "Was it the pharmacy near Mary Baldwin College?"

"I don't know Staunton that well, but this was the one on West Beverly." Harvey turned from the screen. "I don't have any record of a request."

"Well, I guess I misunderstood. I'll see if I can reach Fares and get it straightened out."

"That would be best," Harvey agreed. "Either Mr. Khoury or his doctor will need to authorize any change."

Mullins stood by his Prius in the parking lot. The sun beat down like a fiery torch. Eleven o'clock. He'd been in Sunrise less than an hour and faced another day in the car. Staunton was even farther than Roanoke. Well, he'd drive as far as he could, grab a few hours sleep at a motel, and be at the CVS on West Beverly when it opened.

Fares Khoury or Fred Mack or whatever name he now used had left a trail of insulin that Mullins wasn't about to lose.

Chapter Twenty-two

Amanda Church wanted to skip work. With Rusty Mullins in the field and out of communication, she needed to be able to react at a moment's notice to any new development.

But the security department at the Federal Reserve stood on high alert. The previous day Amanda sat through a review of all protection measures being taken to safeguard the governors of the Federal Reserve Board as well as key officers. Although no evidence surfaced suggesting Paul Luguire's death was anything but a suicide, the tragedy generated anxious assessments of the vulnerability of the central bank's leaders.

Now the Tuesday morning session bogged down into details of budget and the practicality of twenty-four-hour surveillance. No one mentioned a murder in Roanoke, Virginia. That wouldn't happen till someone connected a Russell Mullins who saw Craig Archer with the Russell Mullins who was the last person to see Paul Luguire alive.

Every time someone entered the conference room, Amanda expected the announcement that Russell Mullins was tied to the homicide of a bank president.

When they finally took a break at eleven, she called her husband Curtis Jordan in Paris. After Mullins went underground the night before, she'd told Curtis everything. Too much was at stake to keep developments just between Mullins and her. Curtis' skills as a thriller writer meant he had the knack for determining patterns of action and how they might play out. She needed reassurance as Mullins' silence heightened her anxiety.

"Amanda, Mullins' name may come out." The sound of traffic rumbled underneath his voice. "That's a distinct possibility."

"But we're not ready to have our suspicions out in public." She whispered her concern over the secure line at her desk. "Mullins is making progress."

"You've got a reasonable explanation and the evidence to back it up. You told Mullins his name had surfaced on an unusual transaction and he went to check it out. Keep it personal for him. He'll have to provide his own alibi, and I'm sure he'll have one—either gas or hotel receipts."

Her husband's comforting words eased her fear. "Okay. I'm good with that. But I don't like being out of touch with him."

"Mullins is a smart guy. He'll get to you sooner rather than later. Remember, you're the only link he has to the Federal Reserve. Remind him you need each other to connect the dots and form a more complete picture."

She took a deep breath. "All right, Curtis. I'm just edgy. I'll feel better when you're back."

"Me too. But I need to stay in Paris till I finish this story."

"I know. You can't disappoint your fans."

He laughed. "You mean I can't disappoint the people who'll give me the big advance. That's why they call it a deadline."

"I'll call tonight," she promised.

"Okay. But don't assume your cell and the home line are secure. Anything critical you have to share needs to be communicated another way."

"Curtis. Hello. You're talking to an ex-Secret Service agent."

"And you're doing a great job. The right people will know it even if the public never does. That, my dear, is the secret part of Secret Service." With another laugh, he hung up.

Amanda laid the receiver back on the cradle. She checked her watch. The security meeting would begin in ten minutes. Her conversation with her husband uncovered some pitfalls in her planning. She and Mullins should have anticipated that he might have to go off the grid and ditch his cellphone. There was a good chance she'd have to follow suit, especially if Mullins got tied into the murder of Craig Archer.

The phone on her desk rang. She snatched the receiver, thinking that her husband had forgotten to give her some instruction.

"Yeah."

"It's me."

She recognized Mullins' voice.

"I'm on a pre-paid. Can we talk?"

"Yes."

"I tried your line a few minutes ago and it was busy. I figured you were in your office."

"The place has been nuts since Luguire died. But I've got eight minutes before the next meeting."

"Good. Here's what's happened and here's what I need you to do."

◇◇◇

Sidney Levine slipped the keys to the Audi under the driver's floor mat and closed the door. He found his keys under the seat of his Escort where Colleen left them. She was still stuck in edit hell and claimed to have no time to exchange keys in person. Just as well, Sidney thought. Less chance for her to question where he'd been. He'd filled her gas tank and run the Audi through a car wash. That would be enough to keep him in her good graces.

Thirty minutes later, he drove his car past Mullins' apartment building. The Prius still wasn't in the lot and Sidney had no clue as to where Mullins could be. He knew only one man who might have the answer. Detective Robert Sullivan.

But contacting Sullivan posed a risk. Sidney didn't want to admit he trailed Mullins or suspected the ex-Secret Service agent used a false name while meeting a man who was murdered the same day.

He needed a plausible story. When in doubt, tell the truth—selectively. He whipped the Ford Escort in a U-turn and headed for the Arlington Police Department.

◇◇◇

The fax was on Sullivan's desk when he arrived Tuesday afternoon. Per his request, the M. E. took a second look at the shaving nick under Luguire's jaw. He noted that the aluminum sulfate consistent with the ingredients in a styptic pencil had closed the wound but not masked its depth. The new analysis revealed a shallow puncture from a pin or needle.

An odd place for an injection, Sullivan thought. He wondered if Luguire had worn a new shirt the day he died. Once, Sullivan had forgotten to remove all the pins from the packaging and jabbed himself in the neck.

In light of the discovery, the M. E. re-ran the blood work with more exhaustive tests. Nothing unusual appeared other than a slightly elevated reading for norketamine, a chemical not particularly dangerous in itself, except it's the breakdown product of ketamine, a pain killer that works by creating the sensation of separating the mind from the body—a kind of euphoria accompanied by physical numbness and loss of mobility.

An electric shaver in the bathroom, a shaving nick that wasn't a shaving nick, and trace levels of a chemical that could have been the byproduct of a potentially mood-altering and physically debilitating drug. Sullivan mulled the new facts and then phoned the M. E.

Five minutes later all he had were the words "inconclusive" and "suspicious" and an understanding that ketamine breaks down almost immediately, which makes it difficult to detect. He clipped the updated autopsy report together with the preliminary findings and closed the case file folder.

Another examination of Luguire's apartment would be needed. This time he'd look for anything that could explain the skin puncture, and he wanted to know if Luguire had the habit of keeping new shirts at his office. The cleaning crew had emptied the wastebaskets the night Luguire died. Now it would be like looking for a needle in a haystack after the haystack had been moved.

Sullivan hadn't asked Russell Mullins whether he noticed a dab of styptic on Luguire's face. Secret Service agents, especially those who served on presidential protection, were trained to study faces. Mullins should be an ideal observer.

The detective flipped open the case folder and found Mullins' cell number. Immediately the call went to voicemail. Sullivan left his name.

The intercom buzzed before he could take the receiver from his ear.

He punched the line. "What?"

"Your boyfriend's back." The desk officer laughed. "You got your own groupie now?"

"What are you talking about?" Sullivan snapped.

The officer dropped the comedy. "That reporter who came in a few days ago. He's here asking for you."

"Levine?"

"Yeah, that's the guy."

Sullivan dropped the case folder in his desk drawer. The M. E.'s update would stay confidential at this point. But if Mullins had helped Levine develop his own theory, then Sullivan wanted to hear it.

"Clear him through."

Sidney entered the interview room as Sullivan held open the door.

"You want some coffee?" Sullivan asked. "It tastes like crap but it's hot."

"No thanks." Sidney slipped into a chair and pulled out his notepad.

Sullivan sat across the table. "What's on your mind?"

"Just checking in. Any info that raises questions about the cause of death being suicide?"

"You could have asked me that over the phone."

Sidney shrugged. "But then I couldn't look you in the eye when you dodge my questions."

Sullivan leaned across the table, his eyes locked on the reporter's. "I have nothing to add other than I've asked for additional blood work."

"Why?"

"Did you talk to Mullins?"

"Yes. He told me about Luguire's cash withdrawal and plans to meet at the ballgame."

"Then you have your answer. Mr. Mullins is a credible witness with extensive law enforcement experience."

"And the new blood tests?"

"I expect to see them soon." Sullivan didn't consider his statement a lie. He would take a look at them again.

"Then they must be more complex. Any specific drug at the top of your list?"

"I'm not a damn pharmacologist. Maybe something that had an unexpected side effect. You hear them listed on TV commercials for miracle prescriptions that, by the way, might create severe depression and thoughts of suicide."

Sidney jotted down possible drug reaction. "Was he under medication?"

"Not that we know. Mr. Luguire was a private man and lived alone. We are making inquiries, but nothing has come to light, and it would be irresponsible for me or you to say otherwise."

Sidney nodded as if he shared Sullivan's ethical standards. "So you're considering he might have been drugged unknowingly."

"That's a bit of a stretch. We want to determine if some compound eluded the basic blood screen, and then we'll focus on the possible source."

"Would Russell Mullins be a suspect?"

Sullivan didn't hide his surprise. "Mullins is the one claiming Luguire didn't commit suicide. Why would he do that if he killed him?"

"You're the detective, but it strikes me as a damn good way to insure Mullins that he wouldn't be a suspect, especially if he knew a more comprehensive blood test would reveal a chemical agent."

Sullivan thought about the code words, "as tough ass nails," that Mullins interpreted as Luguire's attempt to alert him. That information would have to stay confidential. "Interesting theory, but Mullins' concerns are what prompted my request for more tests."

"Mullins isn't even a person of interest?"

"Not in any official sense."

Sidney leaned back in his chair. "Okay. Then you know he left town."

Sullivan's bushy eyebrows arched. "When?"

"Sunday."

"He tell you where?"

"Not directly. I overheard him on his phone. He went to Roanoke."

"Do you know why?"

"No. I didn't ask but I assume it has to do with his investigation of Luguire."

Sullivan eyed Sidney with skepticism. "You didn't ask him? Don't tell me you suddenly went respectful."

Sidney laughed. "Hardly. He got this phone call at the ballgame. The one he was supposed to watch with Luguire. That's where we met. He had his grandson with him and a friend from the Federal Reserve."

"Who?"

"I only got a first name. Don. Anyway, Mullins took a call and walked a little distance away for some privacy. The kids were noisy and with the parents shouting he had to raise his voice a few times. During one snatch of the conversation, he said he'd be in Roanoke the next day. I checked his apartment yesterday and today. He hasn't returned. I thought maybe you knew why Roanoke and where else he might be heading."

"No." Sullivan turned his palms face up on the table. "Look, I'd tell you if I knew. Mullins wasn't under any travel restrictions. Maybe it was something he'd planned for a while. Maybe he just wanted a break."

"Maybe." Sidney pushed back his chair. "That's all I've got. When do you think you'll have the blood report?"

"When I get it."

"And when will I get it?"

"If and when we decide to make it public."

Sidney didn't push him. He got up from the chair and smiled good-naturedly. "I'd appreciate a heads-up when that happens. I don't have an assignment editor scheduling me for press briefings."

"All right." Sullivan stood. "I've got your number." He shook Sidney's hand and held it an extra second. "Let me know if you hear from Mullins."

◇◇◇

Sidney whistled as he walked to his car. Something was brewing. Sullivan had signaled the case had moved beyond his simple due diligence to rule out unlikely alternative explanations. And Sidney managed to whet Sullivan's curiosity about the Roanoke trip. He felt confident the detective wouldn't give him up as the source if he spoke with Mullins.

Hell, Sidney could even tip Mullins that Sullivan asked him about Roanoke. Sidney would say he hadn't told Sullivan he followed Mullins. And he wouldn't say a word to either man about the murder of Craig Archer. Sidney had one goal: stir the pot and see what boiled to the surface.

◇◇◇

When Sullivan returned to his desk, he called Mullins' cell. Again, he went straight to voicemail. No ring meant Mullins' phone wasn't on. Was that because he was in a meeting, had a dead battery, or wanted to be off the grid—untraceable?

He logged onto the intrastate law enforcement database and targeted Roanoke. The major crime list prioritized a homicide from the previous night. Craig Archer, president of Laurel Bank, had been found shot to death in his car beside a Roanoke rail yard. No witnesses, no suspects, no motive, no leads. A dead banker in a town visited by a man seeking the killer of a Federal Reserve executive.

Coincidence? Vigilante justice? Or was there more going on?

Chapter Twenty-three

Wednesday morning, the sixth day after Paul Luguire's alleged suicide, Rusty Mullins stood behind a pine tree at the edge of a clearing and studied a small farmhouse for signs of life.

He was there because Amanda Church had delivered all he asked and more. With the connection to the CVS pharmacy in Staunton, she told him she used contacts within the FDA and DEA to circumvent prescription privacy and obtain specific information regarding Fares Khoury's insulin use.

The neighbor, Judy Bernstein, had been correct when she told Mullins that Khoury took shots, but he used an injection device called a pen that provided measured doses without the need for vials and a syringe. Khoury required twenty units a day: ten in the morning and ten in the evening. One pen held three hundred units and there were four pens to a prescription. The pens he picked up the previous Saturday would last approximately two months. If Mullins were to spot the man through a visit to the pharmacy, it wouldn't be for a while.

Amanda then said she ran a report on all the credit checks conducted by local real estate rental agencies in the previous month, and Khoury's name popped up as having rented an inexpensive farmhouse five miles to the west of Staunton. Property records and aerial photographs showed the place to be about five hundred yards off a secondary state road and approximately one mile from the nearest neighbor. Nice and isolated.

The rental record listed Khoury as the only resident.

Amanda had given Mullins the detailed information over her secure line to his pre-paid phone the night before, as he neared Christiansburg, a town about thirty miles southwest of Roanoke. He found a mom and pop motel that, unlike Hilton or Marriott, wouldn't enter his name in a national database. He paid cash, caught a few hours sleep, and left the motel before dawn. He traveled two hours to Staunton and parked the Prius beside a farm road a quarter mile beyond Khoury's drive. He walked across a fallow field and through a copse of pines to approach the house from the rear.

Gray clouds masked the rising sun. A light mist hovered over the needle-covered ground and clung to Mullins' skin and clothing.

A silver Ford pickup was parked between the back porch and a shed. Mullins spotted a shiny new padlock securing the latch on the shed's door. Cheap shades were drawn over the farmhouse windows. No lights shone behind them.

Time crept forward from seven-fifteen to seven-thirty without any sign of life. The morning chill worked its way into Mullins' bones. He zipped his windbreaker tighter even though it pressed the holstered Glock into his ribs. He considered the possibility that Khoury might not be home. Someone in another vehicle could have picked him up, or another occupant could share the house despite the information on the rental application.

Mullins decided to circle to the front and knock on the door. If no one answered, well, doors had a way of blowing open. As he stepped from the shelter of the pines, a man emerged from the back porch. Mullins retreated behind the nearest tree.

The man stopped at the rear of the truck. He raised his arms high over his head and took a deep breath. He wore only a sleeveless undershirt and a pair of blue warm-up pants loosely cinched at the waist. His frame displayed not an ounce of fat. Even from the distance at the edge of the trees, Mullins thought the man looked gaunt, the face more haggard than the one on the driver's license. But he had no doubt that the man by the truck was Fares Khoury.

For a few minutes, Khoury let the drizzle coat his body. Mullins wondered if the deep breathing and natural shower were some ritual, a cleansing coupled with morning prayers. But the sky brightened behind Khoury so he wasn't facing east. Maybe the act was nothing more than an invigorating jumpstart on the day.

Abruptly, Khoury returned to the house, pausing only to wipe his bare feet on a mat.

Mullins decided to confront the man before he had the chance to dress. He crossed the yard and circled to the front. As he neared the door, he spied Khoury through the dining room window. He sat bare-chested at the table with his damp undershirt draped across the back of another chair. Khoury's attention was focused on four items before him—a cellphone, a foil packet, a pen-shaped object, and a white conical cap about the size of the tip of a tube of glue.

Mullins froze. He watched Khoury pick up the pen and twist off one end. He opened the foil packet and pulled out a paper wipe. He rubbed it over the exposed end of the pen and then used it to clean a spot on his abdomen. Alcohol sterilization, Mullins assumed. The man was preparing an injection.

Khoury opened the base of the conical container and removed a disposable needle. He attached it to the pen, twisted the bottom end one click and then pushed the plunger, the priming step to get his insulin to the tip of the needle. Then he twisted the pen further. Mullins guessed he was dialing in the measured dose of ten units called for in his prescription. Khoury pinched the flesh he'd cleaned on his stomach and pushed the pen's needle straight in. He pressed the plunger and sat motionless as the insulin flowed into his body.

Mullins waited until Khoury withdrew the needle, and then he moved quickly. He unzipped his windbreaker, yanked the Glock from his holster, and kicked the door right beside the knob. Without a deadbolt, the latch splintered away from the jamb, and Mullins was inside the house before the door slammed into the wall.

Khoury leapt from his chair, holding the pen like a dagger. His eyes widened as Mullins pointed the Glock at his chest.

"Set the insulin down. I know you'll need another injection this evening. No sense damaging the pen."

A tremor ran through Khoury's body. Mullins didn't know if it was a reaction to the medication or a shiver of fear.

As the spasm eased, Khoury whispered, "Don't hurt my family, Mr. Mullins. Please don't hurt my family."

The mournful plea sent a shiver through Mullins. The man was terrified. And Khoury knew him by name.

"I won't. Not if you cooperate." Mullins had no idea what leverage he held over Khoury, but he meant to play the hand for all it was worth. He waved the gun in a tight circle. "Sit down and push those things away from you."

Khoury laid the pen on the table and then used his forearm to sweep it, the used needle, the cellphone, and the alcohol wipe away from him. He sat, rested his elbows on his bony knees, and buried his face in his hands.

"What kind of warrior are you?" Mullins asked.

Khoury balled both hands into fists and pressed one into each cheek. His eyes never rose from the floor in front of him. "I never claimed to be a warrior. Just an errand boy. A simple man trying to hold his family together."

"Come on. You knew what you were getting into. You knew people would be killed."

Khoury lifted his head. His eyes glistened with tears. "The bombs are for the night. One to four in the morning. No one will be hurt. You know that."

"And Craig Archer at Laurel Bank?"

Khoury looked confused. "I'm done with the bank. I closed the account like I was told. And I kept receipts for everything. And the journal. Everything was as you requested."

"Then I'll take them."

Khoury ran his tongue over his dry lips. "You don't have them? Yesterday, the same day I got the letter, I returned from the post office and grocery store to find everything gone. I thought you had come and taken them."

"Yesterday? Don't you mean Monday when you were in Roanoke? The day Archer was murdered?"

"Murder?" The blood drained from the Lebanese man's face. "Who?"

"Don't act so surprised." Mullins lowered the gun to the floor. "Craig Archer. The president of Laurel Bank. But it's okay. So far no one's connected you to him."

"I've never heard of him. Does he work at the branch where I had the account?" Then Khoury cocked his head and Mullins could almost see the wheels spinning frantically in his brain. "So, this Archer was the thirteenth target? Your target? That's why you're forcing me to do your job. To take the blame. You're on the run."

Mullins said nothing. The bits of information pouring from the frightened man were too disjointed to knit into a cohesive pattern. Someone had lured Khoury into a conspiracy and then upped the stakes by threatening his family. Someone had given Mullins' name to Khoury as a major player in that conspiracy. Why? Because of his connection to Luguire? Because of his name being tied to the offshore account? And if there was a thirteenth target, what were the other twelve? Had Luguire been the first?

Mullins took a calculated risk to gain the man's confidence. He holstered the Glock.

Khoury let out a deep breath and then looked Mullins squarely in the eyes. "What have you done with my wife and daughter?"

"I've done nothing with your family. Obviously, we've had some communication screw-up. I plan to get things straightened out." Mullins walked to the other side of the table and sat across from Khoury. "Who gave you the information about me?"

"The Syrian who first met me in Florida. He gave only a first name. Asu."

Mullins nodded as if the name meant something.

"He promised if I opened the account at Laurel Bank and purchased the supplies he would see that I was made whole. We could stay in our house and I would have money till I could find another job."

"And no one would be hurt?"

"No one would be hurt."

Mullins thought Khoury was telling the truth. A desperate man hearing what he wanted to hear even though part of him must have known he was making a pact with the devil. "And then things changed."

Khoury glanced at the phone on the table. "Messages began coming from a new voice. British maybe. He told me I would have to drive the van. That you had another assignment. The honor of the thirteenth target."

"And he told you Craig Archer was that target?"

"He didn't say and I knew not to ask. He told me I had the twelfth and you would give me instructions. To make sure I did as I was told he said you had Zaina and Jamila." A sob caught in his throat as he spoke the names. "Please. I'll do whatever you ask."

"And your target and the others. Have they changed?"

"Of course not." Khoury's face suddenly became wary. "You don't have them, do you? You don't know. You're not Mullins!"

With a power beyond his small stature, Khoury shoved the table away from him. The edge caught Mullins across the chest, toppling him over in the chair. His head cracked hard against the floor molding. White sparks flashed in his eyes. When his vision cleared, he saw the table above him and heard Khoury running from the house.

Mullins staggered to his feet and drew his pistol. Outside, the truck engine roared to life. Mullins ran through the kitchen and jumped from the back porch just as Khoury threw the pickup in gear. Tires bit into the loose gravel, pelting Mullins with stones as the truck sped down the driveway and disappeared through the pines.

Mullins shook his head in disgust. "Rookie mistake," he muttered. "Holster your gun to build his trust. I might as well have handed it to him."

He returned to the dining room. As he suspected, the cell-phone was gone. But the insulin pen had rolled off the table and lay on a heating grate in the floor. Mullins picked it up with a handkerchief and slipped it in his windbreaker. The fingerprints could prove valuable.

He made a quick search through the rest of the house. On a nightstand by the bed he found a soft flannel bag. Inside was a copy of the Koran. Beneath it was a single photograph of Khoury standing beside a pretty woman and holding a darling girl of three or four. They were in front of their house in Florida. Zaina and Jamila, Khoury had said. Here was his family. The family someone held hostage. Mullins put the Koran and picture back in the bag.

On the dresser, he discovered an envelope. Without touching it, he read Fred Mack and the P.O. box Khoury had given the bank in Staunton. The letter was postmarked Miami. Mullins pried open the torn end with the back of his fingernail. Black hair spilled out. Using the handkerchief, he pulled the tresses and a folded scrap of paper free. "REMEMBER" had been scrawled in red lipstick across the ripped page.

He moved to the bathroom. The medicine cabinet held three more insulin pens, a box of disposable needles, and the alcohol wipes. Khoury had bolted without his medicine. He would have to find insulin somewhere.

The refrigerator contained a few slices of pizza, orange juice, and sandwich meat. Three-fourths of a loaf of bread was on the counter by the sink. Mullins searched through the drawers. The only other item that caught his eye was a receipt for a delivery of heating oil dated three weeks earlier. Khoury said he kept a journal and receipts but that someone had taken them the day before. Either this one had been overlooked, or, more likely, the rental agency had supplied a full fuel tank for the new renter.

Mullins left the receipt, the insulin supplies, the envelope, and the bag protecting the Koran on the kitchen counter. He walked to the shed and examined the door. The premium Abus padlock appeared new with no signs of weathering or tarnish.

Mullins realized that his search through the house and Khoury's belongings hadn't turned up a key. Khoury must have kept this one on the ring with the truck and house keys.

But a new lock was only as good as the wood holding the screws of the latch. Three kicks and the door yielded. Inside, Mullins found a bare concrete floor with rakes and other garden tools hanging from hooks in the wall.

Part of the concrete had dark circular stains. Another area showed traces of gray dust. Mullins ran his finger across one of the stains. He sniffed the residue. Oil. Probably heating oil. Then he took a pinch of the dust. The texture was granular and the smell strong. Fertilizer. Oil and fertilizer. A bad combination if these were the supplies Khoury had been buying.

Mullins studied the circle stains again. The diameters were consistent with ten-gallon cans.

He left the shed and went to the heating fuel tank on the far side of the back porch. A rap on the metal generated a hollow boom. The tank was nearly empty, and yet the receipt for a recent delivery was in the kitchen. Mullins suspected Khoury had been buying up limited quantities of ammonia-based fertilizer so as not to raise any alarms. He probably traveled to local feed-and-seed stores scattered throughout the small mountain towns of southwest Virginia. Purchasing the oil wouldn't have been a problem since the rental company ordered the delivery, but Khoury could also buy empty fuel cans during his shopping spree and siphon the oil out of the tank with a garden hose.

And Khoury said that the previous day everything had been picked up. A final countdown was underway, and Khoury, Mullins' only connection to a van and a bomb, was on the run with a cellphone and a desperate need to protect his family.

Mullins knew he needed to contact Amanda as soon as possible. She was in a position to alert the government agencies that a terrorist attack appeared to be imminent. He dialed her office on his pre-paid phone. Voicemail. "We need to talk" was all he said. He didn't want to leave any information that could be overhead by anyone other than Amanda.

Meanwhile, his best course of action lay in staking out the CVS in Staunton. With his prescription on record, Khoury might say he lost his pens and get a refill. As far as Mullins knew, there was no limit on a diabetic's insulin supply. Khoury had no reason to suspect that Mullins knew which pharmacy would be filling his prescription.

Mullins collected the Koran and family photograph, the letter containing the note and hair, the insulin, and the receipt for the heating oil. He carried them across the field to his car. The drizzle had ended and the clouds looked like they would break up within the next half hour. He would try Amanda again when he was in position in the CVS parking lot.

He loaded his evidence in the rear of the Prius, removed his windbreaker, and took off his shoulder holster. He tucked the Glock under the seat.

As he neared the entrance to Khoury's farmhouse, he slowed. The truck was parked on the driveway about thirty yards back from the main road. Mullins turned in and stopped, angling his car as a makeshift blockade. Khoury wasn't visible in the cab.

Mullins grabbed the Glock, opened the door, and slowly approached the pickup. He raised the pistol when his eye caught sight of the shattered glass of the passenger's window. Shards lay on the ground showing they'd been blown outward.

Mullins heard the buzzing. Khoury had fled not more than twenty minutes earlier, but that was enough time for the flies to find his body.

He lay across the passenger's seat, amid blood and brains. The driver's window was open. Someone had neatly and efficiently tied up a loose end, and Mullins had no doubt that whoever had murdered Khoury had tied him in as well.

Chapter Twenty-four

At ten-thirty Wednesday morning, Amanda Church raced down the hall from the conference room to her office, anxious to check her phone for any message from Mullins.

The meeting had run an hour over. Normally, she could have excused herself after updating her colleagues on her cyber-security projects, but Neil Osmond, the Fed's security director, wanted her to remain for the discussion of the final arrangements for the upcoming Fourth of July Open House.

As part of the PR campaign to dispel its image of secrecy and closed-door dealmaking, the Federal Reserve was turning its exhibit hall and cafeteria into a celebration called "Our Glorious Fourth." Photographs spanning one hundred fifty years chronicled the nation's Independence Day festivities and made the not-so-subtle connection that nothing was more "American" than the Federal Reserve.

Next Saturday's public event stood in sharp contrast to normal procedures for exhibitions at the Fed's headquarters at 20th and Constitution Avenue NW. Groups wanting to tour had to call days in advance, give detailed personal information more in keeping with admittance to Fort Knox, and then wait for a security clearance. The one-time departure from the screening process meant extra personnel and scanning equipment needed to be in place. Amanda's Secret Service background tapped her as a valuable asset for reviewing all aspects of the operation.

Ted Lewison, president of Prime Protection, had also been in the meeting. One awkward moment arose when Amanda's boss asked whether Rusty Mullins would be part of Lewison's detail. Osmond said Mullins knew the layout of the building as well as anyone.

Saddling Mullins with the assignment would ruin Amanda's ability to work with him in pursuit of Luguire's killer. She was ready to publicly question Mullins' fitness for duty while Luguire's death was still under investigation. If her doubts got back to Mullins, he would understand why she'd trashed his name. He needed to be isolated and insulated.

But Lewison had replied that Mullins was on vacation the next two weeks and unavailable. Mullins wasn't mentioned again.

Amanda unlocked her office and went straight to her phone. The message light flashed.

"We need to talk." Mullins' voice sounded calm and restrained, but the words told her something had happened. She noted the message had been left at eight-ten. She dialed the pre-paid from memory.

"I'm on I-85 near Harrisonburg," Mullins said. "A couple hours out of D.C."

"I'm in the office."

Mullins proceeded cautiously, not trusting the security of either his cellphone or Amanda's line. "I found our person of interest."

"You've talked?"

"Yes. But he won't be saying anything further."

Amanda understood Fares Khoury was dead. "You?"

"No. He abruptly terminated our conversation. Someone else got the last word. I wasn't there. But now that we've got a pair, I think we'd better play our hand. The game's not going to last much longer."

Amanda realized Mullins wanted to bring in law enforcement. Things were too hot for him. He could now be linked to Craig Archer and Fares Khoury and the longer he stayed off the grid, the more suspicious his actions appeared. She would have to give him assurances. "Anyone else know?"

"I made a call."

"What?" Amanda sat down, unnerved that Mullins had jumped the gun.

"A courtesy call to the locals. I didn't take any credit."

"Okay." She breathed easier. Mullins had phoned in an anonymous tip, and she was confident he'd been discreet. The situation could still be controlled.

"Look," Mullins said. "Something's come up. Time is critical."

Mullins' normally calm voice bore an edge. Amanda could hear he was ready to go it alone. "I'll take it to key people," she said. "People we can trust. But first we need to talk."

"I agree. Back to the beginning. At two."

Amanda checked her calendar. "Fine." She dropped the receiver on the cradle. Back to the beginning. Their meeting at Barnes and Noble would be at two. She'd be ready.

Mullins laid the cellphone in the cup holder between the front seats of the Prius. The traffic light at the bottom of the Shirlington ramp off I-395 was still red. He'd lied to Amanda about his location because he knew she'd want to see him right away. He needed time to think.

He reached in the pocket of his windbreaker and removed the envelope he'd taken from Khoury's farmhouse. It held the scrawled word "REMEMBER" and the severed tresses of black hair. He remembered the pitiful wail in Khoury's voice—"Please don't hurt my family." Those words were honest and heartfelt. Mullins thought about the photograph of Khoury and his wife and daughter tucked in the bag protecting the Koran. The happy family standing in front of their house. Before the foreclosure sign marred the yard. Before Khoury descended into some desperate scheme to get his home and life back. A scheme that left him dead in a pickup truck near Staunton, Virginia.

Mullins knew the local police in Staunton would be baffled. Hell, he was baffled. Khoury had grabbed only his cellphone and Mullins couldn't find it in the pickup. Its log of Khoury's calls was gone and Mullins had no way of tracing the number. Khoury said someone had come to the farmhouse the day before and taken his journal and expense receipts. Khoury thought it was Mullins, which meant there was a good chance he'd mentioned Mullins' name in the journal as someone he was expecting. When and how that journal would appear worried Mullins. It linked him to a conspirator in a planned bombing of an unknown target. Mullins now sat on too much information and too much evidence. He and Amanda would have to trust someone.

"Laurie, I'm looking at this from the outside in and I don't like what I see." Mullins spoke to his wife as if she sat in the passenger's seat. The words came so natural that at first he didn't realize he was talking to a dead woman.

And then for the first time since he buried her, Mullins heard her voice ring clearly in his head. "Not outside in, but upside down."

A horn blared behind him. He snapped back into the moment, drove through the green light, and headed home.

His landline had recorded one call. Probably a telemarketer, since most of the people Mullins wanted to hear from knew his mobile. But he'd had the cell turned off for more than a day.

Mullins hit the replay button and Sidney Levine said, "I know about Walter Thomson. Call me."

Mullins felt the hairs on his neck prickle. How the hell did Sidney Levine get the same name that the Roanoke police used when they called his cellphone? Mullins guessed the police found the slip of paper on which he'd written the number, made a routine check, and decided he wasn't important. He had no clue why they thought the number belonged to Walter Thomson. Sidney Levine knew something. Or had done something. Mullins used the landline's log memory to find the call. Monday night. 9:08. After Craig Archer had been murdered.

"Call me." Mullins could do better than that. By the end of the day, Sidney Levine would see him face to face.

Chapter Twenty-five

Curtis Jordan sat on a park bench and reviewed what he'd written. The story stood at a crucial point where he'd created the character motivations and relationships and only needed the trigger event to set the action in motion for his pre-ordained outcome. Most readers didn't appreciate the skill needed to construct the set-up so that the climax was both surprising and inevitable. But their appreciation of story structure wasn't his goal. The story either worked or it didn't. He achieved the desired impact or he failed. No author could write an apology to the reader as the epilogue.

Jordan closed his journal and capped his fountain pen. He tucked both in his briefcase and tilted his head back to let the rays of the late afternoon sun warm his face. Unlike many writers, Curtis Jordan could work anywhere. The park bench in Luxembourg Gardens was a favorite nook. The sounds around him, the splash of the fountain, children laughing as they sailed boats in the decorative pool, the hum of voices in a multitude of languages, all these merged into white noise, wrapping him in a creative cocoon while simultaneously stimulating his imagination.

His phone rang, breaking through the self-induced reverie. Amanda. She'd be at work. It was a little before eleven in the states.

"Hi, dear." Jordan shifted on the bench, angling away from the fountain.

"Mullins called."

"I told you he'd check in. Mullins isn't one to go rogue when he knows he can trust you."

"He's making progress. He found Fares Khoury."

"Good. Mullins is a smart guy."

"He told me Khoury was killed as he tried to leave the farmhouse."

"Did he see who did it?"

"No. He found Khoury's body in his pickup truck at the edge of the property."

Jordan picked up his briefcase and walked toward a more secluded section of the gardens. "What'd he do then?"

"He called the police."

"What? I thought he agreed to work outside the authorities?"

"He called anonymously. But with three people dead, Luguire, Archer, and now Khoury, Mullins feels the pressure to bring in real law enforcement."

Jordan stopped and looked at the flowers around him. "Doesn't he know that would be turning loose a herd of elephants in a garden? Surely he's worried about tipping off whoever killed Luguire, especially if he's getting close."

"I think Mullins wants to make sure the police have access to all the evidence without sharing how to interpret that evidence. He's in a ticklish position."

"So are you," Jordan cautioned. "You've got your own career and credibility to think of. You want me to come home?"

"No, definitely not." She laughed. "You're like Mycroft Holmes, Sherlock's older, smarter brother who could solve cases without leaving his armchair."

"I prefer a park bench."

"Then sit on it and think. I'm meeting Mullins at two and we'll assess what to do from this point. I told him I'd be the one to take it up the ladder."

"Good. See if Mullins is tied to Khoury in any way. I imagine he's already a person of interest with the Roanoke and Arlington police departments."

"All right. But he got the Khoury farmhouse lead from me, and Roanoke is looking for a Walter Thomson and a Mr. Brown, two people Archer spoke with the day he was killed. Mullins is off their radar. I think he still has room to maneuver."

"He won't if he talks to the feds, but he'll understand that. What about the Arlington police?"

"They're anxious to write Luguire off as a suicide. When we prove he was murdered, they'll have enough egg on their face to feed an army."

Jordan didn't laugh. "Watch them. They're the unpredictable element in your backyard. You deserve the recognition for breaking the case, but timing's going to be critical. The Arlington investigation can unravel everything you've accomplished."

"You're giving them too much credit. I know these locals. They'll take the easiest way."

"Don't underestimate anyone, dear, especially Mullins. He's in this to find who killed his friend. He'll take risks where someone else would be more worried about covering his own ass."

"Are you saying you're worried about my ass?"

"Constantly, my love."

"I wish I was in Paris with you."

"Me too. But there can be only one Mycroft. Someone's got to do the leg work, and you've got great legs and a great ass."

"Save those lines for your book. Any real advice you'd care to share?"

Jordan sat on another bench secluded from the central garden. His mind raced through the information Amanda had given him. "Stay with the plan, but be ready to have Mullins and you come forward if connections are made from the outside. You're meeting him at two?"

"Correct."

"Then check the status of the investigations in Arlington, Roanoke, and Staunton right before you see him. Mullins will want an update, and the status of those cases will determine his willingness to continue working with you. If you're going to be a team, then both of you have to be comfortable working the leads unrestricted by a chain of command."

"And I'll be the link to that chain."

"Yes. Mullins will see the wisdom in that, especially since Luguire's death casts a shadow over him, no matter how undeserved that shadow might be."

"All right. Will you be working late?"

"Yes. So call anytime, Sherlock."

Chapter Twenty-six

Detective Robert Sullivan logged onto the Roanoke Police Department's secure site as directed by the lead homicide investigator in the Archer murder case. Sullivan's counterpart had agreed to upload the video files from the Laurel Bank security cameras in the lobby and drive-through ATM.

Sullivan was forced to be more specific than he wanted in order to gain access to the footage. He said a key person in an Arlington investigation had claimed to be at the bank the previous Monday. If he showed up on-camera, then Sullivan could cross him off the list. When the Roanoke detective asked the suspect's name, Sullivan gave him the first one he thought of that wasn't Mullins. Sidney Levine.

Sullivan didn't like playing games with a fellow officer, but he also didn't want to get Mullins embroiled in a Roanoke fishing expedition. Reading between the lines, he could tell the Archer case was going nowhere. If he saw Mullins at the bank, then he'd alert the local police.

He typed his temporary password and found the folder labeled "Laurel Bank—Monday, June 29th." The files inside were organized into two subfolders: lobby cameras and external cameras. Sullivan started with the lobby cameras. There were three, one angle above the front door facing the tellers and two behind the teller line, splitting the counter in two sections to allow closer framing of the customers.

The three cameras were designated A B C and their video files were broken into hour segments starting when the bank opened at nine.

The Roanoke Police Department internal website had a built-in playback window and all Sullivan had to do was drag the chosen camera hour into the viewer. He shuttled through the wide angle of the lobby, figuring if he saw someone resembling Mullins, he'd cut to the reverse angle for a positive ID.

He ran through the morning up to the bomb scare and evacuation. No one of Mullins' build or age appeared. But after the bomb scare, the first customer walking into the bank caught Sullivan's attention. He loaded the matching file from the teller's viewpoint.

Sullivan froze the frame. Son of a bitch, he thought. I told the Roanoke police the truth.

Sidney Levine leaned close to the teller in earnest conversation.

"The little prick said he didn't follow Mullins," Sullivan muttered. He found Sidney's cell number in the case folder and called.

As soon as the voicemail beep ended, Sullivan said, "Mr. Levine. Drop by the station as soon as you can. There's been a break in the case and I want to show it to you in person."

Sullivan reclined in his chair. He looked forward to making the reporter squirm, but the bigger questions still came back to Mullins. Had he or hadn't he gone to Roanoke? Where was he now? And why had he disappeared?

Chapter Twenty-seven

Amanda Church dispensed with the elaborate maneuvers of leaving her BMW elsewhere and riding the Metro to her rendezvous with Mullins. Instead, she found a spot in the Clarendon public garage where he'd parked the previous Friday. She felt confident no one was following her, and since Mullins had ditched his personal cellphone, she knew he was traveling undetected.

She left the convertible unlocked. Better to have a looter simply open the door rather than slash through the roof. She walked to the nearest stairwell and descended to the ground level. Rusty Mullins stood leaning against the wall of the bottom landing.

"Change of plan," he said. "Let's take a walk."

"Where to?"

"Whole Foods. Lots of noise, lots of people. And I'm hungry."

He waited till she stepped beside him and then they strolled toward the grocery store across Clarendon Boulevard a block away.

"How have you been?" Amanda asked.

"Compared to what?"

"Compared to working with the full backing of the Secret Service."

He laughed. "The paperwork's a breeze but the pay leaves a lot to be desired."

"When this is over, you should come inside the Fed. Your stock will never be higher."

They stopped at the crosswalk to wait for the light. Mullins edged closer and lowered his voice. "If there is a Fed. This is much bigger than a trumped-up suicide."

"I know. We're talking about three murders."

"We're talking about a terrorist attack."

Amanda snapped her head around. "What?"

Mullins stepped off the curb. The "Walk" light shone and to stand still would have drawn attention. "You think it's too hot for soup?"

"I think it's too hot period."

"Then let's get a salad. It's the kind of meal you can draw out while we talk."

Whole Foods bustled with activity. Amanda and Mullins found the section with hot entrees, sandwiches, and salads to the left of the grocery aisles. Even though the prime time for lunch had passed, traffic still moved through the food lines at a steady pace. They went down the salad bar across from each other.

Mullins loaded his plate in an intricate pattern that looked more like a construction project than a meal. "Go through the register ahead of me and tell the cashier I'm paying for both of us."

"Wow, you are in disguise. Pretending to be a gentleman."

"You do what you have to."

They climbed a short flight of stairs to a mezzanine area where tables accommodated no more than four people each. Turnover was constant, and Mullins took the lead, heading to an open table in a back corner. He wanted to see if anyone else prolonged eating in the munch-and-move-on environment.

"So, can you talk now?" Amanda asked the question as she slid into the chair opposite him.

"Yes. Just ignore the lettuce between my teeth." Mullins gave a brief summary of what they'd already discussed in detail over the phone: the meeting with Archer, the foreclosed home in Florida, and the conversation with the neighbor Mrs. Bernstein. When he got to the encounter with Fares Khoury earlier that morning, Mullins took Amanda through the events beginning with his hike across the field. He concluded with the phone call he made to the police from a pay phone at a BP station on I-81 twenty miles north of Staunton.

"And they found nothing," Amanda said.

"What?" Mullins dropped his fork by his plate. "No body?"

"No body, no truck, no sign that Khoury had been in the house."

"Well, I wiped down everything I touched and I took a few things I thought would be useful. This was before Khoury was killed."

"Like what?"

"He had a copy of the Koran, a picture of his family, and his insulin pens. But his clothes should have been there."

"I monitored the report the investigating deputies filed. They chalked it up to a prank call. What about the journal and expense ledger he mentioned?"

Mullins shrugged. "Nothing. He said he thought I'd picked them up the day before while he was away from the farmhouse, along with the fuel and fertilizer."

"Twelve targets?"

Mullins nodded. "That's what he claimed. I was to take the thirteenth, and he was upset that he was assigned the twelfth. He said it wasn't part of the deal, and that no one was to be hurt. Oh, and there was an envelope with locks of black hair and a note with the single word 'Remember.'"

"You're saying he wasn't a willing participant?"

"He might have started out that way. Lured into a plan with the hopes of keeping his home. But he was definitely a man under pressure and desperately fearful for the safety of his wife and little girl."

Amanda stared at her plate of untouched salad and thought a moment. "Why bring him into it? Surely there are enough fanatics around who would line up to volunteer."

"Two reasons. First, an Islamic extremist has a greater chance of being on the government's radar. Second, Fares Khoury had the social and business experience that fit his assignment."

"I understand the first point but why the second?"

Mullins leaned over his lunch and lowered his voice. "Someone had to pull off setting up the bank account. That person's not a brainwashed zealot in a suicide vest. Then Khoury assembled quantities of the fertilizer through multiple small quantity purchases. He was a landscape designer. He would know what to buy and how to ask for it."

"But he turned into a bomber, not in a vest but a van."

Mullins shook his head. "I don't know about that. He might have been just delivering it. Designing a detonator wasn't within his skill set. Whoever was controlling him was worried whether Khoury would go to the next level. The threat to his family provided the leverage."

"What was the target?"

"He didn't say." Mullins thought back to his final words with Khoury. "I asked him, but that was the question that spooked him."

"Because you didn't know?"

"I didn't ask what they were. I asked if the targets had changed. The idea seemed so preposterous that he suspected I wasn't Russell Mullins."

Amanda gave up any pretense of eating and slid her plate to the side. "So your name is embedded in the conspiracy from financing to execution."

"Yes. I think that must be because of my connection to Luguire. I'm somebody's fall guy."

"But why? You've got no ties to Islamic terrorists."

"You know that and I know that, but who knows what kind of links have been fabricated. If the investigation stops with me, then I'm the buffer, the insulation protecting the real brains behind the operation."

"Wouldn't an extremist group want the credit?"

"Yes. But a foreign government wouldn't."

Amanda's eyes narrowed. "You think this is state-sponsored?"

"I think it's multi-layered, and your initial fear that there's an inside element has to be taken seriously."

"I hoped I was wrong."

Mullins reached across the table and laid his hand on Amanda's. "If it is inside, then you'd better be damn careful."

"No one knows what we're doing."

"Which means we could both be set up."

"Me? I'm the one who told Luguire about the fund transfer."

"And who did he tell? And who can testify that your conversation with Luguire ever took place?"

Amanda took a deep breath. Mullins had zeroed in on the problem. "So we should go public?"

"And the rats will go back into the shadows."

"But there's a bomb out there." Her voice rose in excitement.

Mullins glanced at the tables around them, but no one seemed to have overheard. "There are twelve bombs," he whispered. "I believe Khoury's is targeted for Richmond."

"Richmond?" Her mouth dropped open. "It's the twelve."

Mullins saw that she understood. "Yes. The twelve branches of the Federal Reserve. A coordinated attack on the central banking system of America." He rattled off the cities from memory. "Boston, New York, Philadelphia, Richmond, Atlanta, Dallas, Cleveland, Chicago, St. Louis, Minneapolis, Kansas City, and San Francisco. No corner of the continental United States will be untouched."

"And the thirteenth target must be the Federal Reserve headquarters in Washington."

"Maybe not."

"But surely they'll want that prize."

Mullins nodded. "They want it, but you and I both know the security in D.C. is extremely tight. And the money doesn't add up."

"What do you mean?"

"A total of two hundred thirty thousand flowed through Laurel Bank, counting the Federal Reserve transfer and the initial deposit by Khoury, aka Fred Mack. That's ten thousand for Khoury and twenty thousand for each of the other eleven cities."

"Why only ten thousand for Khoury?" Amanda asked.

"I don't know. Rural Virginia, or he might have received money earlier to rent the house and start his purchases."

"So, D.C. is being funded some other way?"

"Maybe," Mullins agreed. "Or maybe the thirteenth target is something else. Something that might be easier to pull off without the same cost or risk."

"July Fourth. The day of the public exhibit."

"That photography thing?" Mullins remembered Luguire said he had to be at the office for the holiday.

"Yes. The new, cuddly Federal Reserve dispensing with the procedure of prior approval for visitors. I spent the morning going over security arrangements."

"So, it's tight."

"And it's different. Extra guards, scanner installations, the perfect time for infiltration. No need for a truck bomb. They'll smuggle it in somehow."

Mullins' throat went dry. "And somehow blame it on me."

"Your name came up in the meeting. Osmond wanted to know if you'd be working security."

"Did your boss want me banned from the premises?"

"On the contrary, he thought it would be a good idea for you to be part of the team."

"Really?"

"Yes, but Ted Lewison said you were on vacation."

"Lewison was there?"

"Yes. Prime Protection is providing additional security."

"Good. Sounds like they'll need it." Mullins looked across the mezzanine. All of the tables had turned over since he and Amanda sat down. If someone was watching them, he wasn't doing it nearby. Mullins decided they could sit a little longer.

"When I said the rats would run back into the shadows, I didn't mean you and I could keep this to ourselves. If there are twelve bombs out there, then certain people need to know."

"Certain people?" Amanda echoed.

Mullins weighed the options. The Fourth of July was less than three days away. Homeland Security and the FBI needed to be involved and their investigation had to proceed rapidly. But, uncovering the full extent of the conspiracy, especially if the government had been penetrated, required secrecy. Mullins believed the secrecy extended to the Federal Reserve itself. The fact that Neil Osmond, head of Federal Reserve security, asked for him to be assigned to Prime Protection's detail could be a compliment or could be the final piece of the frame Mullins felt enclosing him.

"What people?" Amanda prompted.

"Outside the Federal Reserve. Take someone with you from the Secret Service whom you trust completely. Maybe Hauser." Rudy Hauser was the deputy director, second in command, and Mullins had known and respected him for years. "Tell him you want access to meet with the highest levels of the Bureau and Homeland Security. Hauser's got the clout to pull it off."

"Are you coming with me?"

"No. You don't need me. If I'm under surveillance, I shouldn't be seen with any federal law enforcement."

"Makes sense," Amanda agreed. "So, what will you do in the meantime?"

"Concentrate on staying alive."

"Good plan. You'll want to be in on the takedown, won't you? I'll get the clearance."

"Let's see what kind of response you get from Hauser and the Bureau." He pushed back from the table. "We'll go to my car and I'll give you the Koran, Khoury's family photo, his insulin pens, and the hair with the warning. Maybe that will bolster your story."

Amanda stood and picked up her salad. "I don't think I'll be eating much of anything between now and Saturday."

"Make it business as usual and let the intelligence community take it from here."

As Mullins' carried his plate to the trash, Amanda caught his arm. "Thanks for all you've done."

"Thanks for telling me about Luguire."

They walked back to the garage without speaking. Mullins' car was on the level above Amanda's. He reached under the driver's seat and pulled out a brown paper bag.

"I've sealed everything in a Ziploc. You can probably get fingerprints off the Koran, the insulin pens, and photograph. Maybe the envelope. If Khoury wasn't in the system, then the prints won't be of much use unless his body's found. I doubt if whoever mailed the letter left prints, but you might get lucky. Be sure and have them check out the name Khoury mentioned. Asu."

"Yes, sir." Amanda took the bag and tucked it under her arm. "Are we safe to get together Friday night? Doesn't matter how late. I'd like to bring you up to speed."

"Where?"

"My place."

"Will your husband mind?"

"He's in Paris. But don't get any ideas. I know twenty-one ways to kill you with my bare hands."

"It only takes one."

She smiled. "Believe me. I'm not worth dying for." She spun on her heel and walked away.

Mullins admired the view. She'd spoken the truth. As alluring as her movements were, Amanda wasn't worth dying for. Too much was at stake. For now, she was on her own.

Mullins had his game to play without her.

An ocean away, an old man sat in a wheelchair, a landline phone pressed tightly to his ear. He stared through split drapes at the clearing skies of evening. Rain left the streets of London shiny, reflecting the glow of the cosmopolitan capital of the United Kingdom.

"Remember Occam's Razor," he said. "Just like the simplest explanation will be the most plausible, the simplest plan will be the most effective."

He listened in silence a few minutes, the wrinkles on his brow furrowed deeper with concentration.

"Italy and Greece are teetering," he said. "The stability of the United States has never been more crucial. Be damn sure the conclusion leaves no doubt as to responsibility. We'll take it from there."

He hung up and continued staring out the window.

Dusk dissolved into darkness.

Part Two
The Execution

Chapter Twenty-eight

Detective Robert Sullivan smiled as Sidney Levine took the chair opposite his desk. The smile put Sidney at ease, which was its purpose. Sullivan wanted to establish a baseline of comfort that he could suddenly disrupt. Sometimes only a few seconds were needed to expose the truth beneath a pretense of lies.

"So, there's been a break, huh?" Sidney scooted to the edge of his seat. He opened his journal on his lap and gripped his pencil as if preparing to chisel The Ten Commandments in stone.

"I prefer to call it a development."

"A significant development?" Sidney wrote the words, not bothering to wait for confirmation.

The two men sat at the detective's desk where Sullivan thought Sidney would feel he was getting the inside scoop rather than a standard briefing in an interview room. Sullivan's partner was still on sick leave, although Sullivan suspected the illness could be diagnosed as flu in a bottle. Just as well because Sullivan wanted to play Sidney alone.

He took a closer look at the reporter. The late afternoon sun threw shadowed bars from the window blinds across Sidney's face. The faded jeans were the same ones Sidney wore the previous time but the untucked dress shirt had been replaced by an untucked, red and green Hawaiian shirt. Sullivan looked over the edge of his desk to Sidney's feet, expecting flip-flops. Black Nikes and white socks. Comfort and practicality.

Sullivan loosened his tie. The room grew warmer.

"Well?" Sidney squinted against the sun. "Significant how?"

"Significant in whether it ties into a crime committed last Monday in Roanoke."

"What kind of crime?"

"The murder of a bank president."

Sidney's eyes widened. "Murder?"

Sullivan interpreted the response for what it was, the forced reaction of a grade-B actor. "Yes. I checked the police reports after you said Mullins went to Roanoke."

"You think Mullins killed this guy?"

This time Sullivan believed Sidney's surprise. "A very interesting connection came to light." Sullivan stood, walked to the window and closed the blinds. "I want you to see what I saw courtesy of the Roanoke Police Department." He bent over his desk and swiveled his computer monitor around. Then he tapped the keyboard's spacebar. The video from the teller camera filled the screen.

Sidney recognized the bank lobby and immediately thought Mullins was about to appear. Sullivan had connected him to Archer's workplace. One sickening split-second too late, Sidney understood the true reason he sat at Detective Sullivan's desk. Transfixed, he watched his own image step to the teller window and play the ingratiating role of confused friend with all the sincerity of a door-to-door salesman.

Sullivan tapped the keyboard and the video froze.

Sidney closed his journal. "I can explain."

Sullivan picked up his notepad, sat on the edge of his desk and waited.

"I followed Mullins to Roanoke. I borrowed a car so he wouldn't recognize me, but I guess he did."

"The man's a trained Secret Service agent."

"Yeah. I was stupid. And I was stupid not to tell you."

"That's the first honest thing you've said."

"I told you Mullins went to Roanoke. That was the truth."

"Then why wasn't he on the security cameras?"

Sidney's eyes widened again, this time in unmistakable astonishment. "But I saw him enter the front door of the bank."

"When?"

"Before it opened. I'm not sure of the exact time. Eight-forty. A quarter to nine. Someone had to unlock the door."

"Did you see who?"

"I was a block away, but I saw a man wearing a dark suit. He could have been Archer."

Sullivan hopped off the desk and took a step closer to the reporter. Even his short height was enough to force Sidney to look up. "Oh? How would you know what Archer looked like?"

Sidney wasn't so stupid that he didn't know when he'd been out-foxed. He threw up his hands. "Okay. I saw the story and his picture on the Internet. I knew Mullins had an appointment with him."

Sullivan shook his head. "Archer had an appointment with a Walter Thomson."

Sidney stood and leaned into Sullivan's face. "I saw him walk into the damn bank. Either Walter Thomson was another meeting or Mullins gave a fake name."

They stared at each other for a few seconds. Then Sullivan asked, "Why did you lie to me?"

Sidney stepped around Sullivan and walked to the window. He took a deep breath. "Mullins struck me as a man who looked for answers in the field, not from behind a desk. He was on to something, and I thought following him would be the best way to discover what it was."

"Then why even tell me he went to Roanoke?"

"Because I was at a dead-end. Mullins disappeared." Sidney pointed to the computer monitor with the freeze-frame of him and the teller. "She told me Walter Thomson had been with Craig Archer that morning. Yet Mullins used his own name when he registered at the Hampton Inn. That didn't make sense. When I learned Archer had been killed, I didn't want to believe Mullins did it. But I pointed you to Roanoke figuring you had the contacts, and if Mullins was guilty, then he needed to be caught."

"Why not go to the Roanoke police?"

"Because Mullins might be playing some angle as a tactic of his investigation. If he is, then the last thing I want to do is screw him up. I tried to have it both ways. Let you discover Mullins' Roanoke activities on your own while giving Mullins room to operate. I've been trying to reach him. I even left a voicemail on his home phone saying I knew about Walter Thomson."

Sullivan smiled. "You told a potential killer you knew he'd been with the victim?"

Sidney laughed. "I was on a roll of stupidity all right. At the time, I didn't know Archer had been killed. Since then, I've been looking over my shoulder."

Sullivan thought for a moment. The room was quiet with only the rush of the air conditioner filling the silence. Then the detective pointed to Sidney's empty chair. "Sit down. At this point, I've got no choice but to believe you. But if you jerk me around again, I'll arrest you for impeding an investigation."

"What about the video? Why doesn't Mullins show up at the bank?"

"The lobby cameras don't run twenty-four-seven. Only the one over the ATM outside. The head teller activates the internal cameras during working hours, and on Monday she was flustered because Archer was hanging around the lobby waiting for someone. She didn't turn them on till nine."

"After Mullins entered."

"Yes. Then if he exited through the back door at the base of the stairs from Archer's office, he could have avoided both internal and external cameras."

"Have you given Mullins' name to the Roanoke police?"

"No. I only had your word he'd gone there. That wasn't good enough to risk immersing Mullins in an interrogation. Like you, I don't want to blow whatever he's working on."

Sidney returned to the chair. "How about my name?"

Sullivan sat behind his desk. "Not yet. Have you got an alibi for the time of Archer's death?"

"No. I left the voicemail for Mullins, but it was from my mobile. The police will say I could have placed it from anywhere."

"Why leave it if you killed Archer?"

Sidney nodded appreciatively. "Thank you. Good point and I won't hesitate to raise it. And what would be my motive?"

"The motive for most murders. Cover up another crime. Some tie-in to Luguire and the Federal Reserve. Remember, you came to me. You could be working a story and sniffing out how much I'm uncovering."

"And the reason for my voicemail to Mullins?"

Sullivan leaned over his desk. "Simple. Give the impression that you thought Mullins was alive, when you'd already killed him."

Sidney paled. His mouth dropped open as the accusation left him speechless.

"It's a possibility I can't discount. Mullins disappeared from a town where only you knew he was present. From a hotel only you knew he booked."

Sidney's voice returned in staccato bursts of denial. "No. No way. I simply followed him. Then there was this bomb scare. He had to call it in to give me the slip. I swear."

Sullivan ignored his protests. "You also deal in information. Archer's executive assistant told the Roanoke police that Archer received a phone call from a Mr. Brown shortly after you left the bank. She saw her boss write several pages on a legal pad that she assumed she'd need to type in a word processor. When she asked Archer about them toward the end of the day, he said that wouldn't be necessary. A manila envelope lay on the corner of his desk. The woman was skilled at reading upside down. Archer had written the name Nathaniel Brown across it."

"I don't know a Nathaniel Brown."

"Neither does anyone else in Roanoke. But whatever was in that envelope could have been the motive for Archer's death. You see, the blood splatter from the head wound made quite a mess in Archer's car. Except for one spot on the passenger's seat where something had been on the upholstery. Something that had the dimensions of a nine-by-twelve manila envelope.

"I think Archer drove to that abandoned depot to meet someone. Someone he could have thought was going to pay him for information. Or he could have been a whistleblower thinking he was turning over evidence of some kind of banking irregularities. The kind of evidence that an enterprising reporter would like to get his hands on."

Sullivan pointed his finger at Sidney's chest. "An enterprising reporter like you."

Chapter Twenty-nine

Zaina Khoury understood there were degrees of misery. As distraught as she'd been with the forced move from her home and confinement to an apartment somewhere in Miami, the arrival of the man called Asu had created fear for her and Jamila's safety. The vision of him holding a clump of Jamila's hair still haunted her. He was a man incapable of compassion. Maybe incapable of passion period. He never eyed her lustfully but only as an object to be despised, like she and Jamila were unclean animals, better housed in cages than shared living quarters.

At times of daily prayer, Asu would send them to the back bedroom. He never prayed himself and their obedience to the Islamic observance drew no sign the man either respected or practiced the teachings of the Koran.

He ordered them about as if his own words came from Allah, to be obeyed without question or delay. Zaina wanted to stand up to him, and if she had only herself to care for, she would have challenged him. But Jamila undercut her courage. Any act of defiance would be taken out on her child. Zaina knew that as well as she knew Fares' plan to keep their home had been hijacked as coldly and deliberately as the airplanes on 9-11.

Then came a glimmer of light. Asu had to leave, and in his place, Chuchi returned. Chuchi, the Hispanic man, who showed them courtesy and respect. The guard who Asu claimed wouldn't be returning. Something had changed. Zaina saw that

Asu wasn't the infallible mastermind he pretended to be. One call to his cellphone Saturday night had altered things. Someone had ordered Asu elsewhere, and Zaina's degree of misery had lifted a notch.

She stood in the doorway to the bedroom, watching her daughter sleep. Jamila sprawled out diagonally across the mattress, the legs of her Little Mermaid pajamas bunched up to her knees. When Zaina joined her, she'd have to scoot Jamila to one side without waking her. To Fares' side of the bed. Her breath caught in her chest and she sobbed silently, not wanting Chuchi to hear her crying.

His cellphone rang. She heard him mute the television before answering with his name. A pause, and then he spoke softly.

"Yes. We are fine."

English, Zaina thought. On other calls, Chuchi talked in rapid-fire Spanish. Asu didn't speak Spanish. The first day, she'd asked him a question in Syrian Arabic, and he answered without thinking. At first, he'd been angry, like she'd tricked him. Then he gave a cold smile and told her his name was Asu and that he'd been born in Damascus.

"They will be ready," was Chuchi's second and final sentence. The sound of the television returned.

Zaina returned from the bedroom. "Was that Asu?"

Chuchi paled. "He told you his name?"

"Yes." Zaina picked up Chuchi's unease. "Just his first name."

Chuchi looked away. "He is coming to take you to your husband."

"Really?"

Chuchi only nodded, and still didn't look her in the eyes. He wasn't a good liar. He changed the channel till he found a soccer match.

"Would you like something else to eat?" Zaina asked. "There's some ice cream left."

"Will you have some?"

"Yes. There's enough for both of us."

Chuchi got up from the chair. "I'll fix it." He pulled the phone from his belt and stared at it, as if debating whether to turn it off for the evening now that he'd received his instructions. He went to the end of the sofa, retrieved his overnight bag, and found his charger. "Battery's low." He took it with him to the kitchen.

Zaina heard him open the freezer and then pull two bowls from the cabinet. Her glimmer of light grew a little brighter.

Chapter Thirty

Curtis Jordan found the toughest part of creating a story to be controlling the characters. Well-rounded, strong-willed people were a writer's greatest asset, but they could also be a royal pain. Too many times a character exerted his or her own personality with such force that it changed the course of the narrative.

This phenomenon wasn't unique to Jordan. He'd discussed it with other authors who experienced the same dilemma. Most commonly, a minor character took over. Created for some specific purpose, they refused to leave the stage. A quirk or trait designed to make them suitable for a single story task led to unexpected directions and consequences. A minor motive became a major obsession, rippling out into aspects of the narrative it was never intended to influence. The majority of Jordan's colleagues attributed a character's unpredictable behavior to the author's subconscious where possibilities and connections constantly churned.

Jordan agreed with that theory, although the very nature of the subconscious meant the process was out of conscious control. He was an author who meticulously plotted events. Errant characters shook up his plans, but many times their impact made the story stronger. Jordan stayed alert for the opportunities these rogues, as he thought of them, presented. A skillful writer turned them to his advantage, particularly in the thriller genre, where the unexpected propelled the story.

Like real life, most of these character-generated events could only be shaped after the fact. Jordan's ability to manipulate them to achieve his original goal marked the genius of his writing and the power of the collaborative fusion of the conscious and subconscious dimensions of his mind.

But this Wednesday night, as he sat at the writing desk in his Parisian hotel room, his characters lay lifeless on the page. He suspected his subconscious refused to let go of the complex situation facing his wife. When his cellphone rang, he wondered if a third dimension of the mind existed that controlled mental telepathy.

"Hello, dear. I was just thinking of you." He got up from the desk and lay back on the bed.

"You're such a liar," Amanda said.

"No. It's true. I can't get a word to stick to paper, worrying about you and Mullins."

"That's why I called."

Jordan glanced at his wristwatch. Ten past midnight. "Are you still at the office?"

"Yes. On my line. I wanted to tell you about my meeting with Mullins."

"Is he coming in?"

"No. He's staying clear. He agrees with me that there's got to be someone involved in the conspiracy from the inside."

"Did he say who?"

"No. He even said he's not so sure of me."

"That's being suspicious to a fault. If he doesn't trust you, how's he going to make any progress?"

"He was kidding. He knows I wouldn't have told him about Luguire if I were involved. Besides, he's figured out all twelve Federal Reserve Banks are being targeted by terrorists."

Jordan sat up and grabbed his pen and journal. "And he's telling you to sit on that information?"

"No. He told me to get a meeting with Rudy Hauser. Mullins trusts him and he knows I do as well."

Jordan jotted down Hauser's name. "Does Mullins want to be there?"

"No. He's concerned if he's under surveillance any approach he makes to a government agency could spook the conspirators. He understands we're walking a fine line to keep them unaware that we're on to their plot."

"Mullins knows there's not much time."

"Khoury told him there's a thirteenth target, and I told him it must be the Fourth of July event at Washington headquarters. I urged him to come with me because by then we'll have no more need for secrecy."

Jordan thought a few minutes, giving time for any workings of his creative subconscious to bubble up. "Okay. Is Mullins expecting you to report on your meeting with Hauser?"

"He wants to stay clear of me too."

"Then how are you arranging communication?"

Amanda hesitated, and Jordan sensed she was holding back. "Amanda, I don't want you out on your own with this."

"I know. It'll be Friday night. That's our plan. Everything should be set by then."

Jordan gripped his phone tighter. "Remember, you're the only one with official responsibility. If Mullins does an end-run around you, the questions will be, what did you know and when did you know it? Washington's favorite mantra for skewering a scapegoat. You need to keep Mullins close and you need to keep him accountable."

"I will. Don't worry."

"And give him a report on the meeting with Rudy Hauser. He'll want to know what steps are being taken. He'll expect the counter-terrorism measures to be completely imperceptible so he'll count on you as his source for the government's plan."

"I've got it. I understand how important Mullins is."

"All right." Jordan sighed. He had no more advice to give her. "Now that an investigation is moving into official channels, we'd better limit our calls. I don't want you accused of sharing confidential information with me. Maybe telephone me on your cellphone with some chitchat that can be tapped without raising suspicions."

"The good wife checking up on her husband?"

Jordan laughed. "On second thought, maybe I should be the one checking on you." He hung up before she had a chance for a comeback.

In Washington, D.C., Amanda dropped the receiver in the cradle and got up from her desk. Had her husband's last comment been a joke, or had he given her a warning? The man had uncanny insights. The traits that attracted her to him were also traits she saw in Rusty Mullins. For that reason alone, she wanted to stay close to Mullins. As close as necessary.

Curtis Jordan went back to his writing desk. He reviewed the paragraph he been re-working, but instead of continuing, he let his thoughts roam free. What he wrote next wasn't a sentence but a heading. "Rogue Characters." He underlined it, and then centered one name beneath it. "Russell Mullins."

Chapter Thirty-one

Sidney Levine realized he shouldn't have had the fourth beer. Or he should have had something to eat. When Sullivan cut him loose from the station, he'd been shaken. Shaken by the bank video, shaken by the detective's accusations, and shaken that he hadn't seen how events could be turned against him.

As a reporter, he took pride in not just uncovering a story but also analyzing its impact and implications. That's what had drawn him to the Federal Reserve, an institution cloaked in secrecy and wielding unparalleled power over the United States and the world as well. But the links Sidney tried to forge in his investigation of Luguire's death had ensnared him instead. And Mullins was either out there as a potential murderer or a potential victim whose body was yet to be discovered.

Sidney got up from the table and felt the room tilt slightly. He left a twenty under his last bottle of Heineken and negotiated his way through Clyde's bar scene without waiting for a bill. The staff all knew him. His waiter waved good night and then hurried to the table before the twenty disappeared.

Outside, the muggy air refused to cool. Despite the heat, streetlights illuminated throngs of young professionals and summer tourists on the Georgetown sidewalks. Sidney wanted to get lost in a crowd and so he went with the flow, aimlessly drifting up Wisconsin Avenue.

He'd left his car halfway between Clyde's and his Q Street apartment. When the physical exertion and heat had sweated out the beer and cleared his head, he realized he'd walked beyond both his car and his address. The car would be fine for the night. Sidney headed straight for his apartment, anxious to get on his computer and float Craig Archer's name as someone who had possible dealings with Paul Luguire and was now dead. Sidney knew no reason other than Mullins' visit to the banker as to why there should be a connection. But that was the beauty of the Internet, making anonymous speculation without a shred of evidence.

Sidney stopped in the hall outside his apartment and listened. No music. His heart rate surged. He'd left the FM station playing when he'd gone to meet Sullivan. Then a gentle swell of orchestral strings broke the silence. He put the key in the lock and opened the door.

Without turning on the light, he hurried to his desk and opened his laptop. The screensaver, a quill pen smashing a sword, came to life as the device woke from hibernation.

"Don't turn around." The gruff voice barked the words from behind.

Sidney's knees weakened. He gripped the back of his desk chair to keep from collapsing. "What do you want?" The question came as a strangled whisper.

"Who is Walter Thomson?"

"Mullins?" The name was both an answer and a question to the intruder.

"Sit down."

Sidney rolled the chair from the desk and nearly fell into the seat.

"Now, swivel around slowly."

Sidney twisted the chair to face the man. The glow of the computer screen revealed a murky figure standing against the far bookcase. He held something in his right hand. A dull black tube extended toward the floor. Sidney shivered at what he saw as a gun with a silencer.

The man raised his right arm and snapped on a small flashlight. The brilliant halogen beam struck Sidney squarely in the eyes.

"Who is Walter Thomson?"

This time Sidney clearly recognized Rusty Mullins' voice.

"You, I guess. The name you used when you met with Craig Archer."

"Who told you that?"

"The teller. I went in the bank after the bomb scare. Said I was supposed to meet you. The teller phoned up to Archer's office and was told the only appointment of the morning had been with Walter Thomson."

Mullins studied the reporter's eyes. No signs of shifting, just a frightened deer-in-the-headlights gaze devoid of cunning and calculation.

"You gave her my name?"

Sidney nodded. "I was hoping they could tell me where you'd gone. As soon as I understood you used a phony name, I left. I thought maybe you were working undercover."

"And why did you leave that message on my home phone?"

"I didn't have your cell, and I didn't know where you were. I was trying to force you to make contact so I could find out what was going on."

"Who else did you tell?"

Sidney glanced away for a split-second.

"Don't lie to me."

"I'm not. I'm thinking." Sidney was afraid to say Detective Sullivan, but maybe that was his only chance. If Mullins was a killer and he thought Sidney hadn't said anything, then he might silence him permanently. "Detective Sullivan."

"Anybody else?"

"Not from me. But Sullivan knows I'm trying to reach you. If something happens to me, he'll know you did it."

"You know what happened to Archer?"

Sidney's voice failed. He nodded.

"Is that why you told Sullivan?"

"I didn't tell him about Archer. I just said I'd overheard you say you were going to Roanoke. I didn't want to implicate you in anything you weren't involved with."

"And you didn't want me getting away with murder if I was guilty."

"I figured Sullivan would learn about Archer's death on his own."

"So, now he thinks I killed Archer?"

"No. I don't think he believes you saw Archer. He thinks I killed him and that I'm trying to frame you."

Mullins considered both the story and the man telling it. He laughed. The dumpy reporter was as likely to be an assassin as he was to score the winning touchdown in the next Super Bowl.

Anger replaced the fear in Sidney's eyes. "You find that funny?"

"I do." Mullins crossed the room to the light switch and turned on the overhead. "More importantly, I believe you. Now why doesn't Sullivan believe you?"

Sidney took a deep breath and tried to stop his hands from shaking. "He saw me on the bank's security cameras and he didn't see you. I lied to him while he thinks you've played straight. He's concerned you've disappeared. He didn't say it, but I'm afraid he thinks you're dead and that I might have killed both you and Archer."

Mullins sat down on a worn sofa next to the bookcase. "What were you planning to do next?"

Sidney nodded toward the computer. "Log on. Post a few inquiries about Archer and wonder about a connection to Luguire. See if the viral tide washes anything up."

"Has Sullivan told the Roanoke police about me?"

"He hadn't when I saw him. Like me, he didn't want to screw up something you had working."

Mullins glanced at his watch. Nine-thirty. "Was Sullivan pulling second shift?"

"I don't know."

"When did you see him?"

"Around four. He left me a voicemail earlier about a break in the case. That's what lured me into the station."

"Call him."

"Now?"

"No," Mullins snapped. "On Christmas."

Sidney brought up the list of recent calls, recognized the Arlington Police Department, and punched callback. "What if he's not there?"

"Then tell the duty officer to find him. You've got information you'll only give to him." Mullins got up and stood beside Sidney's chair. "When he comes on the line, give the phone to me."

Sidney expected Sullivan to be out, but the officer who answered put him on hold and in less than minute, Sidney heard the familiar voice.

"Sullivan."

"It's Sidney Levine. Hang on a second."

Mullins took the phone. "This is Mullins. Don't say my name out loud."

"Okay. Where are you?"

"Where are you?" Mullins demanded.

"At my desk. Alone."

"We need to talk face to face."

"All right. Come on in."

"No way," Mullins said. "We need to sort things out first."

"Have you got blood on your hands?"

"No, but three people were killed within hours of being with me."

Sidney moaned and rolled his chair away.

"Three?" Sullivan asked.

"Yeah. And I'm afraid there might be more."

"So people die who are with you and you want to see me face to face."

Mullins had to laugh. "Yeah. But you're a cop. You don't count."

"How about the reporter?"

"Sidney's fine. He's not a hostage, if that's what you're thinking. A hostage has to be of value to somebody."

"Thanks a lot," Sidney muttered.

"All right," Sullivan said. "It's your show. Where do you want to meet?"

"There's an apartment on Q Street. I'll give you the address."

Sidney jumped from the chair. "He's coming here?"

Mullins waved him to be quiet, and then gave Sullivan directions.

"I'll be there in less than thirty," the detective promised.

Mullins handed Sidney the phone. "You expecting company?"

"No. My girlfriend's working tonight."

"Okay." Mullins pointed to the computer. "Don't post anything till we talk to Sullivan."

"Sure." The shock at Mullins' break-in had transformed into excitement. Sidney didn't know Mullins' game, but right then he didn't care. He was a player.

As if reading the reporter's mind, Mullins said, "Sullivan might not want to talk in front of you."

"I'll keep this meeting off the record. I swear."

"But if he's adamant about it, you might have to take a hike."

"This is my place. I have a right to be here."

Mullins stepped closer. "You don't want me as your enemy."

Mullins may have been ten years older, but Sidney knew the man could take him without breaking a sweat.

"You've kept your head so far," Mullins said. "I appreciate that you didn't go for an easy headline tying me to Archer. You knew there was something bigger going on. Well, it might be so big that you won't just be writing a story, you'll be writing a book."

Sidney felt the adrenaline rush he thought was gone for good.

"That's if we play it right," Mullins added. "Play it wrong, and you'll be writing my obituary, assuming you're still among the living."

Chapter Thirty-two

Kayli Woodson thumbed through the current issue of *Entertainment Weekly*, but her mind wasn't on the "who's in/who's out" gossip of Hollywood. She had problems of her own. Ten o'clock and no word from her father. To make matters worse, her husband Allen missed their seven o'clock call, and Josh refused to go to bed because he hadn't said good night to either Daddy or Paw Paw.

She finally got Josh down an hour late and read his favorite stories till he fell asleep. She wanted to go to bed, but her mind kept racing. She hadn't seen her father so keyed-up since her mother's illness, and at least then, she'd been able to share part of the burden.

Her cellphone vibrated on the end table beside her chair. The caller ID read RESTRICTED.

She grabbed it. "Hello." She heard the sound she hoped for. Silence. The line was dead for a few seconds.

"Hi, babe. Sorry I missed the call." Lieutenant Commander Allen Woodson sounded exhausted.

"You okay, honey?" Silence again as the communication routing delayed both ends of the connection.

"Yes. We had an all-nighter."

Kayli knew her husband couldn't talk about his work, especially over a POTS line. As an O-4, he supervised a UAV squadron—unmanned aerial vehicles—and Kayli assumed most of his operations occurred during daylight. But with high-tech, infra-red, and only God and the Pentagon knew what else, Allen had a twenty-four-hour job.

"You're good to call. If it hadn't taken forever to get Josh to sleep, I'd wake him."

"What was wrong with him?"

"He misses you. So do I."

"I miss you both. Maybe we'll have a better connection Saturday. If you can work me in around the Washington Nationals."

Kayli laughed with delight. "It's a deal. I'll let you know the TV time." Her spirits rose at the prospect of seeing her husband face to face. In that brief exchange, she learned Allen would be docking at Bahrain on Saturday—the matching port to the Washington Nationals. Before he deployed, they had assigned Major League teams to all the possible ports of call. TV meant Skype, the video connection he wasn't allowed to use at sea.

"Sounds good," Allen said. "Sorry the time is so short."

"That's all right. I know you have a lot to do." Kayli understood he was telling her the port destination had come up suddenly. Usually orders were posted several weeks out and their coded exchange might allow the chance for her to meet him.

"Anything new with your dad?"

Kayli's brief respite of joy ended. "I haven't heard from him in two days. Not since he called on his way to Florida. That's not like him."

The silence on the phone was longer than the transmission delay.

Finally, Allen asked, "Is he working with anyone?"

"Not that I know. I called Prime Protection this afternoon and they said he was on vacation."

"Anyone at Federal Reserve?"

"He has a former colleague from Secret Service, Amanda Church, but he hasn't mentioned her. I'm not sure what department she's in."

"Don Beecham might know."

Kayli thought a second. "Dad and Don took the boys to a T-ball game Saturday. Dad could have said something."

"Maybe. But your father's tight-lipped about his work."

Kayli laughed. "Just like his son-in-law."

"Well, check with Don. It couldn't hurt. And when you do hear from your Dad, drop me an email."

When the conversation was over, Kayli looked at her watch. Ten after ten. Too late to phone Don Beecham. She'd try in the morning before he left for work.

And maybe her dad would call before then or send his text saying, "Good Morning Glory."

The comfort she gained from talking to Allen faded. Something was wrong. She felt it in the pit of her stomach. Her dad had been evasive about where he was going and what he was doing. Like the old days with the Secret Service. But this was different if he was on his own. She didn't doubt her father's abilities, but she also didn't doubt he could be too hard-headed and too independent for his own good.

Chapter Thirty-three

Rusty Mullins sat down on the sofa and balanced his coffee on his knee. "There are things I can tell you and things you're going to have to trust me on."

"No. I'm going to have to trust you on everything, especially the things you tell me." Detective Sullivan took a cup from Sidney Levine and hoisted it toward Mullins. "You'd do the same in my position."

Sidney returned to the kitchen to get the third mismatched cup for himself.

Sullivan's gaze followed him. "And I'm also not comfortable discussing the Luguire case or anything else in front of a reporter."

"Except I'm a writer. Not a reporter." Sidney pulled a folding chair from the corner of the room and sat opposite Mullins.

Sullivan took the easy chair and completed an equilateral triangle. "What the hell's the difference?"

"Like I told you. I don't have an assignment editor, which means I don't have a deadline. I can sit on this until we know what we're dealing with."

Sullivan shook his head. "Evidently Mullins already knows what we're dealing with. And the way I see it, I'm the only one here whose ass can wind up in a sling."

"There's plenty of trouble to go around," Mullins said. "And the stakes are too high for any of us to worry about our own asses. Now we're either working together or I'm walking out the door."

The ultimatum surprised Sidney and Sullivan. Mullins had called the meeting, and more importantly, he'd been off the grid for over two days. He bet their curiosity would win out. If not, then he was ready to make good on his threat.

"All right," Sullivan said. "My pension's not worth a crap anyway. But I'm not closing my eyes to a crime."

"No one's asking you to," Mullins said. "We're trying to prevent one. That's the new priority."

Sullivan leaned forward in his chair. "You mean there's more to this than solving the deaths of Luguire and Archer?"

"Yes. And the problem is that there's so much more some innocent people are going to get hurt or even killed because saving their lives could jeopardize a larger operation."

"What larger operation?" Sidney asked.

"That's the part where you're going to have to trust me. I'll paint the picture in broad strokes, but Federal agencies are dealing with it." Mullins looked at Sullivan. "They're not directly involved in your investigation, so I doubt you'll cross paths. It's also better if you have limited knowledge in case they blow it. There's no reason for any of this to come back on you."

"My pension insurance," Sullivan said.

"You can think of it that way."

"So what are we working on?" Sidney asked.

"This." Mullins took an envelope out of his jacket pocket. "I made a copy before I turned the original over to the feds. One side is a photograph and the other is the backside where someone wrote information about the picture." He passed the two copies to Sullivan.

"Looks like Florida," Sullivan said.

"Sunrise, Florida."

Sullivan read the handwritten note on the second copy. "'Fares, Zaina, and Jamila, age 3. November 2011.' Who are these people?"

"They lived in the house. That is until the bank foreclosed on them."

"Archer's bank?" Sullivan passed the photocopies to Sidney.

"No. The mortgage was held by a Florida bank with no connection to Archer that I could find."

"Then what do they have to do with Archer and Luguire?" Sullivan asked.

"The family's last name is Khoury. They're Lebanese. Fares Khoury used an alias to open a bank account at a branch of Archer's bank in Staunton, Virginia. I went to see Archer in Roanoke on Monday to ask him about Khoury. More accurately, Fred Mack, the false name used on the account."

"Freddie Mac," Sidney said. "The Federal Home Loan Mortgage Corporation, the public government-sponsored agency that buys and sells secondary mortgages. They got stuck with so much toxic shit that last year they sued seventeen banks for misrepresenting their bundled mortgage funds."

Both Sullivan and Mullins looked at Sidney with new appreciation.

"Jesus," Mullins said. "Freddie Mac. I should have seen the connection."

"Was Archer's bank one of the seventeen?" Sullivan asked.

Sidney shook his head. "Just the big boys. Maybe this Khoury saw himself as being screwed like Freddie Mac, or if his scheme was to defraud the bank, then maybe he was making a statement that Freddie Mac was just as culpable."

"You lost me," Sullivan said.

"The banks and related financial institutions were under pressure from the politicians to make homeownership more affordable. Banks are by nature adverse to risk, but they like making money. Politicians can tie them up in reviews, committee hearings, and banking regulations. Politicians want homeowners voting for them, and bank executives want shareholders approving bonuses that are larger than the GNP of most countries. Throw in the wink factor, plus a Federal Reserve and Treasury Department ready, willing, and able to infuse debt-generated capital into the system, and you have an unholy alliance."

Sullivan scratched his head. "What do you mean wink factor?"

"You get the banks, the feds, and the politicians in a room together. The politicians push the banks for looser mortgage underwriting and give them a wink. Freddie Mac and Fannie Mae wink to the banks they'll agree to buy their mortgages on the secondary market, the politicians wink at these government-sponsored agencies that they'll cover their risks, and everybody winks at the Federal Reserve and U.S. Treasury to provide the bailout money in case some of those mortgages go south."

"What about Wall Street?" Sullivan asked.

"Wall Street saw a gold mine in bundling all these new mortgages into investment vehicles and making an obscene amount of money while adding nothing of value. The brakes were off, loan screening and lending practices became a joke, and everybody was grabbing every dollar possible. Housing prices skyrocketed, but that didn't stop sales. Bigger mortgages made up the difference, and commissions at every step of the process turned mortgage lending and mortgage-backed securities into a feeding frenzy."

"And then it blew up," Mullins said.

Sidney waved his hands in a wide circle. "A goddamned mushroom cloud. The 2008 financial collapse left people unable to pay mortgages that were ballooning. Not just homeowners who lost their jobs, but people who'd been told they would simply roll-over escalating mortgages into new loans. But when real estate values plummeted, people who tried to refinance found they not only had no equity, they had a value deficit between the appraised worth of their home and the balance of their existing mortgage. Sometimes the appraisal was only half the mortgage balance. I interviewed one family whose payment went from a thousand dollars a month to seven thousand a month. They needed seventy-two thousand of new income just to stay even."

Sidney looked at the photograph of the Khourys. "If that happened to this family, they would have felt like victims. And who could argue? It was all a damn shell game, stacked in favor of everyone but those who could least afford to bear the loss. The poor and the taxpayer." Sidney handed the photo back to Mullins. "You think Fares Khoury, a.k.a. Fred Mack, killed Archer?"

"No."

"Why not?" Sullivan asked.

"Because I talked to him this morning. He didn't know who Craig Archer was."

"You believed him? I think the Roanoke police would like to decide whether he's telling the truth."

"I'd love for the Roanoke police to talk to him. But twenty minutes after he swore his innocence, I found him dead in his pickup with one gunshot to the head. Sounds familiar, doesn't it?"

Sullivan whistled under his breath. "Somebody shut him up."

"That's the way I see it. And somebody shut up Craig Archer. I don't know what Archer's game was, but I didn't tell him I was Walter Thomson. Either he or someone else wanted my identity a secret, or wanted to make it look like I'd given him a false name."

"Was Khoury killed in Staunton?" Sullivan asked.

"Yes. I found him at a farmhouse he'd rented."

"What do the Staunton police think?"

"They don't think anything."

Sullivan's round Irish face bloomed red. "I can't condone keeping the murder of that man from the authorities."

"I haven't kept it from the authorities. I placed an anonymous tip. I've learned when the deputies got there, the truck and the body were gone. They think my call was a prank."

Sidney pointed to the photo in Mullins' hand. "Somebody murdered that man and then cleaned up the scene after you left?"

"Yes. And pretty damn quick. I phoned in less than fifteen minutes. The deputies would probably have been there in under ten."

"Where were you when Khoury was killed?" Sullivan asked.

"Still in his farmhouse. That's where I found this picture."

"You let him go?"

Mullins reddened. "He sort of got the jump on me. My car was too far away to give chase. I found him as I was leaving."

"Do you think whoever killed him knew you were there?"

"Possibly."

"That makes no sense," Sullivan said.

"I know," Mullins agreed.

"What?" Sidney asked. "I don't understand."

"Why didn't they kill me?"

"They thought you were armed."

"Then why leave the body in the truck where I could find it and then remove it before the police arrived?"

"Did you touch anything?" Sidney asked. "Maybe they were hoping you'd incriminate yourself. You know, tie you to that death and then Archer and even Luguire sound plausible."

"He's got a point," Sullivan said.

"Maybe. If I'd called the police from the scene, they might have killed me and either left or removed both of us. But when I drove off, they could have thought I was on the run, and that suited them fine."

"Why?" Sullivan asked.

"Because Fares Khoury thought I was part of a conspiracy. He'd been told to expect me and that I was supposed to deliver the bomb to its destination."

"Bomb?" Sullivan and Sidney said in unison.

"Yes. Fares Khoury had assembled fertilizer and fuel oil. Yesterday, someone removed them and a journal he'd been keeping. Khoury thought that I was taking the bomb to Richmond to blow up the Federal Reserve Bank."

"My God," Sidney exclaimed. "That's the big picture?"

"No. There are the other eleven regional Federal Reserve banks as well."

Sullivan got to his feet and paced. "You're not keeping that to yourself, are you?"

"No. The information's being relayed to someone I trust. The relevant agencies are making a coordinated investigation. But we're not to breathe a word. They'll want to wrap this network up with one swoop. They've got the twelve locations, and they've got a target date."

"When?"

"July Fourth. This Saturday. But there's another complication. Khoury told me a thirteenth target has been added. The one I'm supposed to take out."

"Washington headquarters?" Sidney asked.

"That's what we think."

"That's quite a story," Sullivan said. "So, why are we sitting here?"

"Because too many things indicate internal complicity. And I think after the planned attack, the investigation will look for someone on the inside. My name has popped up too many places for me not to be the possible fall guy. In some ways, I'm made to order, a former insider who's now an outsider."

"Don't they know you're on to them?" Sullivan asked.

"Maybe not. Or maybe it's too late to change plans. Either way, I don't think they know the extent of my knowledge. That's why I'm staying clear of everything."

Sullivan returned to the chair. "I don't understand how you got on to this. Sounds like they were planting evidence you were never intended to see."

"Someone inside the Federal Reserve discovered a breach in cyber-security. An unauthorized transfer of funds had been made, supposedly by Paul Luguire. This person came to me the morning after Luguire died, convinced that the breach had been made by someone on the inside."

"Before Luguire's death?" Sidney asked.

"Just days before. The person had told only Luguire because of the implications such a security breach carried."

Sidney shook his head. "Not only a security breach but an operational anomaly. Luguire didn't deal with member banks. He worked with Treasury."

"Whatever. I don't claim to understand how the Fed works. But we think Luguire went investigating. To make a long story short, Luguire was killed, my name was linked to the account, and that's when we realized my connection to Luguire was being exploited. I was being set up."

"Why are you trusting us?" Sullivan asked.

"Both of you are too far down the food chain. But you have resources and access I can use."

"This plot smacks of terrorism," Sullivan said.

"I know. But I don't think Fares Khoury is a terrorist. I think he's the real fall guy. He pleaded with me to save his family. He thought I had control of them."

"He sounds like a willing participant to me," Sullivan argued. "He loses his home, he assembles the materials for a bomb, but then you catch him. How many suspects have you heard sing the tune 'Somebody Made Me Do It' when they thought the game was up? And I hate to say it, but the guy fits the profile."

"I found an envelope containing severed hair and a note with one word, 'Remember.' The hair is the same color as the hair of the wife and little girl."

Sullivan took a sip of coffee and thought about the meaning of Mullins' discovery. "He could have been forcibly recruited?"

"I saw his face. I know how to read a face. He was terrified for his family."

"Have you got this envelope?"

"No. I turned it over. Any fingerprints or DNA might be the only lead to who's behind the attacks. But I did hold back a few strands of hair." He pulled a small Ziploc bag from his pocket.

"What else have you got in your pockets?" Sullivan asked.

Mullins smiled, as he withdrew a larger Ziploc. "Khoury was a diabetic. I traced him through his insulin prescription. Here's a pen he used for his injections. I thought you could run a trace on the prints, just in case he turns up in the system somewhere."

"Won't the feds be doing the same thing?"

"Yes, they have the other pens. But they'll be concentrating on fertilizer purchases, fuel oil, van rentals, the litany of items in the vicinity of Federal Reserve property. They'll be all over the network chatter trying to intercept the bombs. Khoury's role is over for them, and unless there's some hit to a terrorist cell or handler, they'll focus on other areas. Not on rescuing his family."

"This doesn't seem like much to go on," Sidney said. "You know where the guy lived, but you don't know where they've taken his body."

"I'm looking for a link to the wife and child. Where'd they live before? Who else knew them?"

Sullivan reached out his hand. "Let me see that."

Mullins gave him the bag containing the insulin pen.

"What are these little white cones?"

"Packaging for the needles. You dial up the dose and use the pen till it's empty. You cap it with a sterile needle for each injection."

Sullivan held the clear bag up to the light and looked at the needles' silhouettes in their protective plastic. "I wonder if the pen is tamper-proof."

"Nothing's tamper-proof," Mullins said. "What are you thinking?"

"The M. E. reported a shaving nick under Luguire's jaw. A styptic pencil had been used to stem the bleeding. But I noticed an electric shaver in his bathroom. Further examination revealed the wound to be a needle puncture. I'd like to make a comparison."

Sidney rubbed his palms back and forth on his thighs in excitement. "Luguire was murdered by insulin? That's impossible to trace, isn't it?"

"No," Sullivan said. "Now we have tests for blood and urine, even from a corpse. Mystery writers love it, but it's not a very efficient method. Too unpredictable."

"Does everybody know that?" Sidney asked.

"No. I'm sure most of the general public still thinks it's an untraceable murder weapon. And that might be the point of using one of these." He tapped the pen with his forefinger. "Use it as the delivery device. If there was no insulin found, then its absence proved it had to be the murder weapon."

"And by focusing on insulin, you'd miss something else," Mullins said.

"Yes," Sullivan said. "But we've already found it. Norketamine, the chemical left from the breakdown of ketamine. Ketamine's a pain killer that creates a state of euphoria. Makes you feel like your mind's detached from your body. It also generates numbness and a loss of mobility. The substance is difficult to trace. Because I wasn't smart enough to have suspected the puncture wound to be from an insulin pen, I ordered broader and more extensive tests."

"Then ketamine would make Luguire controllable," Mullins said. "He wrote what he was told, but had the presence of mind to slip in 'as tough ass nails.'"

"And the use of a pen would be one more link to Fares Khoury," Sidney said.

Mullins nodded. "Or me, if I'm supposed to be in the conspiracy with him."

Sullivan let out a deep breath and set the Ziploc bag on the sofa beside Mullins. "So, while Homeland Security and the FBI are saving the country, we're supposed to save Khoury's wife and daughter using a photograph, a lock of hair, and an insulin pen? That's all you've got?"

"I've got you and Sidney. And I've got a name. Asu."

"Asu. Is that a first or last?" Sullivan asked.

"First. He's Syrian, and Khoury told me he's the man that initially approached him. Khoury thought I was holding his family hostage. That information came from Asu. If Asu doesn't have them, he knows who does."

"Do the feds have Asu's name?"

"Yes. So monitor the law enforcement channels for any requests for information on him. I also think we should start our own search in Miami."

"Why?"

"It's close to the town of Sunrise and big enough for Asu to have resources and space to hide. There's also Miami International Airport, a quick exit out of the country."

"You want me to float that name out as well?" Sidney asked.

"No, someone could be monitoring for hits on the name. Let Sullivan concentrate on Asu. I think your first inclination to inquire about a link between Luguire and Archer is good. Something to get your conspiracy theorists chattering."

"Okay. I'll work tonight. The Internet never sleeps."

Mullins turned to Sullivan. "You okay with this?"

"I get the picture. Right now the number of people we can trust are the three of us and your contact to the federal agencies."

"That's the size of it."

Sullivan pursed his lips, and then looked at Sidney. "You're the Federal Reserve expert. Mullins alluded to this cyber-security breach as a possible reason for Luguire's murder. Is there any other motive?"

"Not as compelling as someone circumventing the process of transferring money. The other hot issue is the Federal Reserve itself. With an election year and tough economy, the Fed's a lightning rod. Luguire was set to testify before Congress this week. President Brighton supports the Fed but if he loses re-election, it could be curtailed, subjugated to greater oversight, or dismantled entirely. And I'm not saying that would be a bad thing."

"But the more likely scenario is a terrorist attack with internal tentacles?" Sullivan asked.

"Definitely," Sidney said. "The Fed is seen as the funding source of every deficit-financed war or invasion, which is basically all of them for the last one hundred years. By lashing out at the Fed, they're lashing out at the heart of our capitalistic system."

"All right." Sullivan looked back at Mullins. "Then I'm satisfied we let the FBI, Secret Service, and Homeland Security work on the big picture."

"When do you have to issue another report on Luguire's death?" Mullins asked.

"I can say I need through the weekend. A few more interviews. Other than Sidney, everyone else has written it off as a suicide. I'll keep the M. E. quiet about his findings."

"Then let's get started. We have two days. That's not much time." Mullins held up the picture of the Khoury family. "Especially for this little girl and her mother."

Chapter Thirty-four

Zaina lay on the bed beside her daughter. The room was dark with only a trickle of light from the outside street lamps leaking around the window shade. The audio from the television in the living room floated as a constant murmur, unintelligible because Chuchi had thoughtfully lowered the volume when Zaina told him she was going to sleep.

But she hadn't slept. She forced herself to stay awake, mentally clicking off the hours and listening for her chance. The signal finally came in short, raspy bursts. Chuchi's snoring as he dozed in the chair. Zaina waited until she heard the sounds settle into the rhythm of surf breaking on a beach.

She slid off the bed, careful not to wake Jamila. If the child found she was gone, she'd cry out. Zaina tip-toed to the door and turned the knob. The hinges squealed as she opened it just enough to slide through.

The glow from the television illuminated Chuchi asleep in the chair with his head lolled to one side and his mouth open. Zaina stared at his belt. The phone holster was empty. She glanced at the apartment's front door. The deadbolt was surely locked and the key tucked in Chuchi's front pocket. She could never hope to retrieve it without waking him.

She glided past him, thankful that the apartment's cheap carpeting muffled her footsteps. The kitchen flooring posed the greater problem. Worn linoleum did little to keep the subfloor from creaking, and the first groan sounded like a tree snapping in half. Zaina froze. She heard Chuchi shift in the chair. But he would have to get up and turn around before he could see her.

In the gloom, she made out the shape of his phone still charging on the counter. Chuchi had left an empty glass between it and the sink.

The snoring resumed. Zaina slid her feet across the floor as if skating. She snatched up the phone, leaving it attached to the power cord. She knew some models chirped when disconnected. She couldn't remember if Chuchi's phone beeped when a number on the keypad was pressed, but she only needed three. 911.

She pressed the power button and the screen flared to life. In the dark kitchen, it shone like a searchlight. Zaina pressed the face of the phone against her abdomen. Then she tilted it enough to place her thumbs on the keypad.

The lock rattled in the front door.

Zaina dropped the phone back on the counter and grabbed the empty glass. She held it under the faucet and ran the water just long enough to fill it a few inches.

The door opened. Zaina couldn't suppress a sob as she recognized the slim silhouette entering the apartment.

Asu flipped on the overhead light and Chuchi snorted as he awoke.

"What the hell are you doing?"

Chuchi mumbled something, but Asu looked past him to where Zaina stood trembling in the kitchen.

"You bitch!" He charged forward, sweeping her aside with such force that she crashed into the refrigerator. The glass of water shattered on the floor.

Asu snatched up the phone. The screen was still lit. "Who did you call?"

"No one. I came for water." She pointed to the damp floor and broken shards.

"You take me for a fool? It's turned on."

"It must be fully charged," Chuchi said. "It always lights up when it's finished charging."

Chuchi looked to Zaina and the fear in his eyes terrified her. "I came for water," she sobbed. "I wouldn't risk Fares not getting our house."

Chuchi edged closer to Asu. "See. It says fully charged."

"We'll see." Asu opened the folder marked "Recent Calls." He scrolled to "View All Calls" and checked the list.

"That number," Chuchi said. "That's yours. The last call came from you. Nothing has gone out."

Asu shoved the phone into Chuchi's stomach. "That was stupid. Don't let it happen again." He turned to Zaina. "As for you, I'm glad to see you understand that betraying me would be betraying your husband." He smiled, but his eyes stayed lifeless. "I have good news. You will see him soon. We are going to meet him in Washington. We will leave before dawn, as soon as I have a few hours sleep."

"Thank you," Zaina murmured.

"Go back to your daughter. Chuchi will clean this up. It was his fault."

Zaina closed the bedroom door. She stood for a moment, unsure what to do. Her mind kept jumping between two images, both of Chuchi. One was the fear on his face as he watched Asu check the phone. The other was the fear on his face when he learned Asu had told her his name. It was the second image that scared her the most.

She crept to the far side of the room where Jamila's backpack sat in the corner. She unzipped the pocket containing a small box of crayons and Jamila's Little Mermaid coloring book. She visualized the landing on the ground floor. The row of mailboxes for her wing of the apartment complex. But she wasn't sure if what she needed was there.

She pulled a dark crayon from the box, unsure of the color in the low light. She flipped to the back of the book and tore out the last page as quietly as she could.

At four in the morning, Chuchi led the way down the stairs. Zaina held Jamila asleep in her arms. Asu brought up the rear, his right hand tucked under the left lapel of his sport coat.

A single fixture illuminated the ground floor landing and the exit to the street. Zaina saw the row of mailboxes on the right. She slowed her descent, scanning the wall with growing desperation.

"Hurry," Asu ordered.

There it was. Zaina lurched forward as if Asu's command physically propelled her. She stumbled on the bottom step, and as she fell against the wall, she pinched Jamila's leg.

The child woke with a cry.

"Shut her up." Asu jerked his head in the direction of the door.

Zaina steadied herself against the wall and regained her balance.

"Sshh," she whispered to her daughter. "Everything's okay. Mommy's here."

Asu ushered them out of the building.

He never noticed the folded paper barely visible in the slot of the box labeled outgoing mail.

Chapter Thirty-five

Mullins sat on the edge of his bed, staring at the pile of clothes on the floor. He'd dropped them when, at two in the morning, he'd been too exhausted to do anything but fall across the mattress.

Four hours of dreamless sleep did little to physically recharge him. His knees and shoulders felt stiff from the long days of driving. But his mind fired on all cylinders. The previous week's events played back and forth like scenes in a movie yet to be edited. Yet to be sequenced.

Cause and effect. What triggered what? Luguire's death. Archer's death. Khoury's death.

He looked at the nightstand where he kept the oak-framed picture of Laurie and Kayli. His daughter had just finished second grade. Laurie was no more than thirty, vibrant and healthy. Mullins loved the photograph for their smiles. The occasion had been Kayli's "fly-up" from Daisy to Brownie. For her, the simple ceremony had been no less dazzling than the Academy Awards.

Mullins' success with the Secret Service's presidential detail had depended upon reading faces and reacting with split-second timing to any cue of danger: a twitch, an eye shift, a clenched jaw. But these two faces that he loved shone with undiminished joy, connecting him to memories bittersweet to recall.

"Why, Laurie?" He picked up the photograph. "Why aren't you here when I need you the most?"

There was no answer. Just his wife's frozen smile.

He set the picture back and headed for the shower.

◇◇◇

Kayli brought her father a third mug of coffee. He sat at her kitchen table, a half-eaten slice of toast on the plate in front of him. She'd listened to his story without interrupting, even though the murders of Archer and Khoury generated fear for his safety.

Mullins took a sip of the refill. "So, my investigative team is now me, a washed-up journalist, and a local detective who seems to be hours away from retirement."

Kayli sat in the chair across from him. "And you don't think Amanda will prioritize the mother and child?"

"No. She can't. Once the facts are fed to the anti-terrorism network, the priority will be preventing the attacks. If leads to the bomb or this Asu character also uncover their whereabouts, then fine. But I'm not sure Amanda will elicit much sympathy for their plight. Khoury did collect materials for a bomb."

"Why just Amanda? Why weren't you debriefed?"

"For one thing, I'd still be trapped in an incessant process of interviews, especially since my name's linked to Khoury's bank account. When Amanda talks to Rudy Hauser, he might want to pull me in or he might agree with our recommendation to leave me loose so that no one's tipped off. But I wouldn't be surprised if I were under surveillance."

"That could be a good thing. You shouldn't be a lone wolf."

Mullins laughed. "Don't forget my two sidekicks."

"Yeah. The washed-up reporter and the cop on Social Security."

"They're sharper than I painted them. Detective Sullivan's experienced with good instincts and Sidney Levine's a persistent jackass, the kind of reporter I despise except when we're on the same side. They're each working all the angles they can access."

"What are you going to do?"

Mullins looked around the kitchen as if it harbored something crucial to his plan. "How much longer do you think Josh will sleep?"

Kayli glanced at the clock over the sink. "Seven-thirty now. He should stay down for another half hour."

"When does Don Beecham leave for work?"

"Most days he goes in early. He probably left around seven. Why?"

"I'd like to talk with him. Do you have his direct number?"

"No. Sandy would. And she has his cell."

Mullins hesitated, unsure how many people to involve.

Kayli read his mind. "Sandy won't ask any questions, if that's what you're worried about." Kayli rose from the table.

"Wait. I need you to help me with something else while Josh is asleep."

"Okay."

"Set up the video camera. I want to record my story here in the kitchen. Then I want you and Josh to check into a hotel at least through Saturday. You'll disable your phone and talk to no one."

"You're scaring me, Dad."

"I sure hope so."

◇◇◇

Mullins sat at his dining room table and carefully sealed the DVD in a bubble-wrap envelope. Then he wrote Kayli's return address in the upper-left-hand corner. Although the U.S. Postal Service should be as secure as any delivery system, Mullins decided to use a contact in the Pentagon to expedite the package directly into military jurisdiction without a mailbox drop. He could take care of that detail on his way to a noon meeting with Sullivan and Sidney at Sidney's apartment.

He pulled the pre-paid cellphone from his jacket and unfolded the slip of paper on which Kayli had written Don Beecham's numbers. Remembering that Amanda Church preferred to use the secure line at her desk, Mullins dialed Beecham's office.

"Beecham." The man sounded distracted.

"This is Rusty Mullins. Don't mention my name. Are you alone?"

"Yes. But I'm finishing an email for the Hill. Can I call you back?"

"How long do you need?"

"Five minutes."

"I'll call you." Mullins hung up.

Precisely five minutes later, Beecham answered on the first ring. "I'm alone with the door closed. What's this about?"

Mullins shifted the phone to his left hand and prepared to take notes on a yellow legal pad. "I'm not asking you to divulge confidential information, but I need you to keep this conversation confidential."

"Does this have anything to do with Paul Luguire?"

"Yes. You told me you were working with Luguire on his testimony for Congress. Can you tell me the nature of that testimony?"

Beecham hesitated. "Well, I shouldn't but if it can help." He laughed softly. "This is ironic as hell. It's secret testimony about transparency."

"Regarding the Federal Reserve?"

"Yes."

Mullins jotted "transparency" on his pad. "Why hide a hearing on transparency?"

"To keep the markets from reacting to rumors of possible changes and to keep the lobbyists and financial institutions from killing any ideas before they're fairly examined. The issue's extremely volatile. On the one hand, we've got a viable presidential candidate charging the Federal Reserve Chairman with treason, and on the other hand, Federal Reserve proponents exert tremendous pressure to keep things just the way they are."

Mullins thought about his conversation with Sidney Levine. "Hasn't it always been that way? The bankers claim they need secrecy to keep politics out of the money supply, and the populists claim we've sold our soul and our children's future to the greatest con game in history."

"You're right," Beecham agreed. "But the leverage has always sided with the Federal Reserve because most people and financial institutions want stability. Then the market and real estate crash of 2008 shifted the balance and the Tea Party launched a full-frontal assault. Facts got trampled in a rush to find a scapegoat."

Mullins felt he was getting the Fed's party line. "A scapegoat whose secrecy begs for scrutiny."

Beecham cleared his throat. "Look. I concede the point. That's why change is coming."

"Through these transparency hearings?"

"Luguire, Chairman Radcliffe, other executives and select board members are being questioned on their assessment of what more transparency would do to the financial markets."

"So, Congress is pressing the issue?" Mullins asked.

"Actually the courts set the stage. In 2011, they forced the Federal Reserve to reveal which banks were given bailout funds, and the number of foreign banks appearing on that list set off a tidal wave of outrage. For nearly a hundred years, the banking relationships, both domestic and foreign, were closely guarded to protect the identity of institutions needing emergency funds."

"Then who approves the loans?"

"All twelve regional banks are empowered to make loans to undisclosed recipients. It protects consumer confidence, and in some cases, prevents an unjustified run on a bank."

Mullins wrote "U.S. taxpayers subsidizing foreign banks" on his sheet of paper. "And the Federal Reserve provides funds to foreign banks by issuing U.S. debt and we don't even know which countries are benefiting?"

"Like I said, the Fed was authorized to operate with independence so its decisions were removed from politics, both domestic and foreign."

"And from basic oversight and audits. Could some central banks of other countries be embarrassed by their involvement with our central bank?"

"Yes. I guess. I'm not privy to that information. I'm focused strictly on relations with Congress."

Mullins wrote down Luguire's name. "And Paul Luguire, what did he think about the transparency issue?"

"Personally, he was for more open communication. So is Chairman Radcliffe."

"So, you were expecting the shit to hit the fan if the chairman reversed one hundred years of Federal Reserve practices. I suspect some foreign banks and their governments wouldn't want their financial dealings with the United States made public. Might not play well with the people back home."

"Banks and governments are also people. People with power. The question I try to remember isn't who stands to gain from any rule change but who stands to lose? And what will they do to protect their interests?"

Beecham's statement forced Mullins to examine Paul Luguire's death from two opposing viewpoints: persons, organizations, or governments unknown hell-bent on destroying the Federal Reserve and persons, organizations, or governments unknown hell-bent on keeping its operations in the shadows.

"What has Luguire's death done to the secret hearings?" Mullins asked.

"Delayed them a week. I was working on a confidential email regarding the schedule when you called."

"Does Luguire's death change the direction the hearings will take?"

"No. Paul Luguire had a reputation for analytical pragmatism. The chairman wanted Luguire's voice heard, but his testimony wouldn't make or break the outcome of the hearings." Beecham paused. "Are you thinking that Luguire was killed to stop him from testifying?"

"Not really. Especially given what you've told me. I appreciate your candor."

"I liked Luguire. I want to know the truth of what happened. But please keep our conversation between us. I shouldn't have told you what I did."

"I understand the hearings are secret."

Beecham lowered his voice. "Do you know Amanda Church?"

The question caught Mullins off-guard. "A long time ago. We worked together at Treasury."

"She came by my office earlier this morning. Said she knew I was friends with your daughter. She wanted to know if I'd seen you. If you seemed all right."

"Did she say why?"

"She said you were close to Luguire. She was worried about you, but that technically you were a person of interest in the investigation of his death. If she contacted you, it could be viewed as inappropriate."

"What did you tell her?"

Beecham laughed. "That you seemed fine to me. But then I don't know you as a trained Secret Service agent. I only know you as Josh's Paw Paw."

"Thanks. Paw Paw is a much more rewarding occupation. We'll have to take the boys to another ballgame soon."

"I'd like that. Good luck, Rusty."

Mullins laid the phone on the table. Interesting that Amanda Church had come to Don Beecham. She was covering all the bases, making sure people within the Federal Reserve believed they weren't working together. Their plan depended upon preserving the illusion that the plot hadn't been uncovered. That Khoury hadn't talked, and the investigation had stalled.

Mullins studied his legal pad. The sparse notes from his conversation with Beecham had been unconsciously written in two columns. He labeled one as Pro-Fed and the other, Anti-Fed. Pro-Fed included people and even countries adverse to Luguire's planned testimony. To what lengths would they go in order to protect their interests? According to Beecham, killing Luguire wasn't one of them. His role wasn't that crucial. Others might think differently.

On the Anti-Fed side, Mullins circled "Transparency" and "Outrage." The words fueled a domestic opposition that may or may not be violent. And there was a line of foreign terrorists who would love to launch an assault on the bastion of American capitalism.

Foreign or domestic, Pro-Fed or Anti-Fed, the only thing Mullins knew for certain was that three men were dead, a woman and child were held hostage, and the makings of a bomb powerful enough to rival the Oklahoma City disaster had been assembled and transported from Staunton, Virginia.

If Fares Khoury was telling the truth, eleven duplicates were heading toward their destinations, and a thirteenth target, unknown and possibly unprotected, was out there with Mullins' name assigned as its executioner.

Chapter Thirty-six

Sidney Levine rarely found himself in the role of host. On the odd occasion when his basement apartment became party central, it was because Colleen invited mutual friends over and took care of setting out food and drinks.

The Thursday lunch meeting with Mullins and Sullivan had been scheduled at a time before Sullivan officially went on duty and when Mullins would normally be running errands. Both men could drop off the radar screen to collaborate with Sidney in their efforts to rescue Khoury's wife and daughter. With unusual forethought, Sidney went shopping for a deli platter. He also picked up beer and soft drinks.

So, he became annoyed when neither Sullivan nor Mullins showed at noon. The three men had agreed there would be no phone contact, which meant Sidney could only wait. After twenty minutes, he suspected the other two had dumped him and were pooling their information without him. If so, they would regret it. He'd spent most of the night planting Internet seeds in an effort to link Luguire and Archer, and then he read posts as various blogs picked up the speculation and passed it along.

Most went off on wild tangents, spouting conspiracies against small banks who threatened to stand up to the bullying Fed and FDIC, those banks and bank leaders outside the cartel of the New Yorkers protecting their cronies with bailouts while smaller institutions were carved up. Or conspiracies that Archer had been silenced as revenge for the killing of Luguire. The theories grew more fantastic and ridiculous.

But two seemingly unrelated posts caught his eye. One tagged with the name Congressional Confessional claimed inside knowledge that Paul Luguire was set to give secret testimony on how the Federal Reserve used its anonymity to further the War on Terrorism. Luguire was going to reveal that freezing the assets of terror-sponsoring nations was only the tip of the iceberg. In order to secure the compliance of governments and international companies holding unpaid trade balances, the Federal Reserve made secret, low-interest loans with the receivable accounts as collateral. In other words, the American taxpayer could be holding a debt payable from Iran. A subprime mortgage to the unemployed looked like solid gold by comparison.

The other post appeared from Roanoke by someone named Mountain View and stated a person close to Craig Archer thought the murdered bank president had been involved in a sting operation that went bad. That morning Archer had a closed-door meeting with a man named Walter Thomson, and afterwards wrote a lengthy memo on a legal pad he refused to let his executive assistant type up. Then he received a suspicious phone call from someone named Nathaniel Brown, suspicious in that Brown refused to specify the nature of his business, only saying that Archer expected his call. No one at the bank had heard Archer speak of either Thomson or Brown before.

Sidney knew Walter Thomson was the name Archer fabricated to hide Rusty Mullins' identity. But why? And the phone call from Nathaniel Brown couldn't be verified, but sounded like it had been actually taken by Archer's executive assistant. Sidney knew she'd seen a manila envelope with Brown's name sitting on Archer's desk. It made sense that she would connect a mysterious caller with a lengthy memo Archer kept from her. The executive assistant had to be the blogger's source.

And a missing legal pad fit the shape of the object Detective Sullivan said had been removed from the interior of Archer's blood-spattered car.

Sidney believed the two posts had the smell of a government coverup. But was the information so sensitive that some dark op would murder two American citizens? If Sullivan and Mullins shut him out, he'd put his theories and their underlying evidence up on the web. To hell with them.

Two sharp raps sounded on the door.

Sidney's speculations made him so paranoid he stepped to the side as he called out, "Who is it?"

"Mullins. Sorry I'm late."

"Is Sullivan with you?" Sidney reached over and unlatched the door.

"No." Mullins entered and scanned the room. "You mean he's not here?"

"No. And I haven't heard from him."

Mullins didn't stop moving. He paced back and forth across the small living room. "I don't like that he's late."

Sidney closed the door and went to the counter that separated the kitchen from the rest of the apartment. "You were late." He pointed to the deli platter. "You want a sandwich? There's beer and sodas in the fridge."

The question brought Mullins to a halt. "What I want is Sullivan here. He doesn't strike me as a guy who misses an appointment."

"He probably says the same thing about you."

"I had to shake a tail."

Sidney's eyes widened. "Someone's following you?"

"I have to assume so. And I have to assume they're good and I might not spot them. I doubled back over Memorial Bridge twice before finally coming into Georgetown over the Key. The second loop on Memorial Bridge was spur of the moment."

"Maybe Sullivan was called in early. Another case."

"Maybe."

Sidney leaned over the counter, his pudgy belly brushing the cheese portion of the platter. "I found some interesting speculation on Luguire and Archer."

"Save it. Let's give Sullivan till twelve-thirty. Then we'll share information." He eyed the food. "But I'm not waiting on him for lunch."

Mullins constructed a triple-decker ham and cheese, liberally smothered with mustard, and carried his sandwich and a bottle of Heineken to the sofa. Sidney had cleared the coffee table and both men used it to hold their plates.

Sidney took a large bite of pastrami and rye. A heavy knock came from the door. He tried to say, "Just a minute," but the wad of food in his mouth muffled the words into a strangled cough.

"Just a minute," Mullins shouted. He waved for Sidney to stay seated and went to the door.

Sullivan entered. He wore a blue blazer, slightly frayed at the cuffs, and a white button-down shirt whose collar remained unbutton. In his left hand, he clutched a curled sheath of white papers.

"Nice of you to join us," Mullins said.

"Did you save me anything to eat?" He marched straight to the kitchen.

Sidney turned in his chair. "Help yourself to whatever you like. Beer's in the fridge."

"And it will stay in the fridge. I'm on duty at two."

"We thought maybe you got called in early," Sidney said.

Sullivan laid his papers on the counter, bypassed the bread, and started piling meat and cheese on a plate. "I was at my desk. Unofficially. Two things happened just as I was leaving. I received an email from the M. E. that the depth of the puncture wound under Luguire's jaw matches the length of the needle on the insulin pen. And the name Asu generated a hit."

"What do you make of the needle match?" Mullins asked.

"That an injection was made with an insulin pen, but the dose was ketamine, not insulin."

"Does ketamine come packaged in those pens?"

"No. Since ketamine is primarily used in veterinary medicine, that won't happen until dogs learn to inject themselves."

Sidney gulped down a mouthful of food and wiped his lips on his sleeve. "You're saying Khoury killed Luguire?"

"No way," Mullins said.

"I agree," Sullivan said, "but I took the pen to the M. E. first thing this morning. He said an injection by a regular syringe wouldn't have matched Luguire's wound so precisely."

"I don't get it," Sidney said.

"A diversionary tactic," Mullins explained. "Confuse things with too much coincidental information. If the suicide falls apart and the investigation persists, the clues will lead back to Khoury. But this would be after the shit hit the fan and everyone is looking for the bomb maker and his conspirators. Khoury and his insulin pens would close the loop."

"Couldn't that really be the case?" Sidney asked.

Mullins returned to the sofa. "Khoury was nothing but an errand boy collecting fertilizer and opening bank accounts. Luguire was killed by a professional just like Archer was killed by a professional. If Khoury was a trained assassin, he would never have let himself be ambushed up close in that pickup truck."

Sullivan carried his plate of meat and cheese to the chair he occupied the day before. "And you don't motivate a trained assassin by holding his family hostage."

"This Asu character?" Sidney asked.

Sullivan slid the papers across the coffee table to the reporter. "A postman found a note jammed in an outgoing mailbox in an apartment building in Little Havana. Fortunately, it was on his first round of the morning."

"This morning?" Mullins asked.

Sullivan nodded to the papers in Sidney's hand. "The note was written on a page torn out of a coloring book, neatly printed in red crayon. Read it," he told Sidney. "It's on the top fax sheet."

Sidney found the paragraph. "'Help. My daughter Jamila and I have been kidnapped by men named Asu and Chuchi. They say they are taking us to Washington, D.C. But I don't believe them. My husband Fares Khoury is in trouble. Please help us.' Signed Zaina Khoury."

"Did you get this from the feds?" Mullins asked Sullivan.

"No. I've got a friend on the Miami force. I floated the name Asu by him last night. He promised to check it out. When the mailman's discovery flashed across the department, he called immediately."

"What had you told him?" Mullins asked.

"I said I was investigating a homicide with drug connections to Miami and the link at the other end of I-95 might be a dealer known only as Asu."

Mullins nodded. "Plausible cover story. Your friend have a last name for Asu?"

"No."

Sidney passed the Miami report to Mullins. "So, the mother and daughter could have been removed any time from after the mail delivery yesterday up to just before the postman came this morning."

"Probably during the night," Mullins said. "Khoury was shot early before yesterday's mail delivery in Miami. If the wife and daughter were leverage, then Khoury's death meant they were no longer valuable. They'd either be let go or disposed of. They weren't released and we know they were alive to leave the building. Why risk that during the day? Now whether they're headed to D.C. or not is another matter. The captors might have created that story to buy cooperation."

"I agree," Sullivan said, "but only because the tenant across the hall from the mailboxes is a light sleeper. She heard a child crying and looked out her window. Two men were helping a woman and child into the backseat of a van."

"Helping?" Mullins asked.

"That's what she thought, but she said the taller of the two men had a tight grip on the woman's arm."

"What time was this?"

"Close to four o'clock. She'd also seen the van park on the street around midnight."

"Could she give a description?" Sidney asked.

Sullivan shrugged. "The van was just a minivan. She's pretty sure it was silver, although it was lit only in the front by a streetlamp. Not a cargo van, but she had no clue whether it was foreign or domestic. The Miami police checked some surveillance cameras in the area. They got a plate off a silver van. A rental leaving Little Havana about that time."

"Still not much to go on," Mullins said.

Sullivan smiled. "Except she recognized one of the men."

"Asu?" Mullins and Sidney asked together.

"No. The witness is an elderly Cuban-American widow who's seen most of the kids grow up in the neighborhood. The streetlamp illuminated the shorter man as he got in the driver's side. She identified him as Jesús Colina. He goes by Chuchi. A local punk who's been busted a few times for car theft and petty larceny. Definitely doesn't have the brains or the resources to orchestrate what's transpired."

"Could she be mistaken?" Mullins asked.

"I doubt it. Chuchi's uncle owns the building and keeps an apartment. Sometimes Chuchi housesits."

"Like the last three weeks?"

"You got it. The old lady says the uncle got a visa to visit family in Havana."

"So, Asu is the taller guy," Sidney said. "Did you tell your friend that Asu is Syrian?"

"Yes. And they're checking their local contacts in the Arab community."

"What about the FBI?" Sidney asked. "If there's suspected flight across state lines, they should be involved."

"They've been notified," Sullivan said, "along with highway patrol divisions in states from Florida to Virginia. The van's a Ford Windstar, but they haven't put out a public alarm."

"Because of the terrorist investigation?"

"I assume it's for the safety of the hostages," Mullins interjected.

"Right," Sullivan said. "I stressed that we have reason to believe Asu's been involved in two homicides. I let the Miami police assume they were drug-related. We're concerned that if

Asu learns we've got his name and the van description, he'll ditch the woman and girl."

"You mean kill them?" Sidney asked.

Sullivan looked at Mullins. The two lawmen understood the realities they faced.

"Asu's got nothing to lose," Mullins said. "Right now he must have some reason for keeping them alive. We don't want to force him to change his plans."

"Why's he coming to Washington?" Sidney asked.

"Because this is where it started and this is where it will end." Mullins' voice rang with determination.

Sullivan and Sidney were quiet for a moment.

Then Sullivan said, "I agree. We have to assume Asu is coming here. We now know Chuchi Colina was in Miami with the mother and daughter. Asu could have been in Staunton, which is why he didn't get back till midnight. Someone else must have helped him eradicate any trace of Khoury. Removing the body and truck was a two-person job. And he probably had help with Luguire."

"Why do you say that?" Sidney asked.

"Because I examined the flat tire that kept Luguire's daughter and grandsons from meeting him the night he died. The puncture was on the side. Someone used an ice pick."

Sidney set down his half-eaten sandwich. "At least two people in two locations. At the ball field and at Luguire's apartment."

"Probably," Sullivan said. "But Asu could have punctured the tire at the start of practice and still had time to get to Luguire."

"No," Sidney said. "We have to consider another possibility. Asu used Fares Khoury's family as leverage, right?"

"Yes," Mullins said. "Although it didn't start out that way."

Sidney stood. "Well, why not the same thing with Luguire? Only Asu does it by phone."

"What do you mean by phone?" Sullivan asked.

"Phone, iPad, there's a host of devices that let you send real time video. Someone's in the parking lot with an ice pick and God knows what other weapons. Someone's with Luguire and shows him his daughter and twin grandsons are in imminent danger unless he does what he's told." Sidney paused. "Did someone help them with the tire?"

"Shit," Sullivan muttered. "His daughter said a guy offered to help put on the spare. She didn't know his name. She'd already called her husband."

"Damn it," Mullins said. "I should have seen that. I couldn't understand how if Luguire had the presence of mind to write tough-ass in the note, he wouldn't simply have refused to write the note at all. Did this guy who volunteered have a kid with him?"

"She didn't say. I'll contact her right away." Sullivan looked up at Sidney. "You raised a good possibility, but we didn't find any video or record of an incoming email on Luguire's phone."

"It wouldn't have been his phone. Something as simple as FaceTime could have linked the phones of the two accomplices. Luguire's daughter would never have known they were being videoed."

Mullins shook his head. "That's true, but it's not getting us any closer. We know we're dealing with ruthless people. We don't know the fate of Khoury's wife and daughter."

"Well, what use are they now?" Sidney asked. "Khoury's dead. Is there some other family member under pressure? A brother? Father? Maybe they're going to be used as some kind of distraction."

"Or they are the bomb," Sullivan said. "It won't be the first time terrorists have used women and children."

Mullins stood and carried his plate to the kitchen. "They'll have a hell of a time getting through security at the Federal Reserve."

"Then maybe we're wrong about the thirteenth target," Sidney said.

Mullins grabbed a second beer from the fridge. "What'd you learn from your Internet sources?"

Sidney filled them in on the Congressional Confessional and Mountain View posts. "Amid all the hysteria, these two offered information that appears based on fact. Archer was writing a secret memo that might involve a man named Nathaniel Brown, and Luguire was set to give secret testimony how the Fed plays a role in the War on Terrorism that could sway the congressional committee to keep the Fed's activities secret."

"Lots of secrets," Sullivan said. "What do you think, Mullins?"

"I think the supposed testimony of Paul Luguire is a crock of shit. I know from someone close to the proceedings that Luguire was prepared to recommend the opposite."

"And why can't your source be lying?" Sidney asked.

"He doesn't have a reason to lie."

"Right. The best lies are told by those you think have no reason to lie."

Mullins didn't have a comeback. He knew the reporter was right.

"What it does show is Luguire's testimony was going to be controversial," Sidney said. "But how that fits in with a killer like Asu is beyond me. Al Qaida doesn't care about American politics, they just want to inflict damage and casualties."

"Well, I think we've speculated enough," Sullivan said. "I'll follow up with Luguire's daughter about the man at the ball field, and I'm going to circulate photos of Zaina and Jamila Khoury to the District police and the Maryland and Virginia departments surrounding D.C."

"Do you want me to keep monitoring the Internet?" Sidney asked.

"What do you think?" Sullivan asked Mullins.

"See if you can learn any more about the two bloggers, Congressional Confessional and Mountain View. Maybe draw them into a conversation. But be careful."

Sidney grinned. "I won't spook them."

"I'm not talking about them. I'm talking about you. Both of you." Mullins gave each of them a hard stare. "Watch your backs. And if you've got any family, you might want to get them out of town for a few days."

"My wife's leaving tomorrow to see her sister in Philadelphia," Sullivan said.

"My girlfriend's forgotten my name," Sidney said. "She's buried in an edit but I'll tell her to stay clear."

"How about your family?" Sullivan asked.

"They're covered," Mullins said. "They know to lie low till this is over."

"That's a laugh." Sullivan stood from the chair and straightened his blue blazer. "You and I've been in this business long enough to know it's never over."

Chapter Thirty-seven

Curtis Jordan closed his laptop and then pinched the bridge of his nose. He felt drained. For over twelve hours, he'd sat at the desk in his hotel room, following Internet postings and then writing as the ideas came to him.

He looked out the window. Dusk descended upon the streets of Paris, and the City of Lights began fulfilling its name. Jordan got up from the chair, stretched his arms over his head, and twisted from side to side. A brisk walk through Luxembourg Gardens and a light supper would take the kinks out of his muscles and the ache out of his stomach. He picked up his writing journal and fountain pen and headed for the door.

The phone rang. Not his cell but the one in the room. Jordan turned and stared at it. During the past year since he'd been coming to the Odéon Saint-Germain, he'd never received a call on the hotel phone. He returned to the desk and snatched up the receiver.

"Oui?"

"I'm at my office. I didn't want too many calls going to your cell."

Jordan heard the tension in his wife's voice. He sat at the desk.

"Amanda, what's wrong?"

"There's been a break. Asu's been traced to Miami."

"The feds?"

"No. The Miami police found a note from Fares Khoury's wife saying she and her daughter had been kidnapped. Asu was mentioned."

"So, you've got the feds looking for him?"

"Only the FBI."

"Does Mullins know?"

"He's the one who told me. I just got off the phone with him."

"I thought you were working separately till Saturday."

Amanda couldn't hide her irritation. "Mullins called me. He thought I should be in the loop and he's right. The lead was generated by police on the ground in Miami. I might not have learned about it otherwise."

"Okay. I'm sorry. Does Mullins have a contact in Miami?"

"I assume so. I asked, but he said it was better if I didn't know. Maybe he picked it up off the Internet."

Jordan rested his hand on his closed laptop. The computer still felt warm. "I doubt it. I was on the net all night. I tagged the word Asu for several sources and got no hits."

"Mullins said he's controlling the information so that the kidnapping case doesn't have a public tie-in to the terrorist alert. He's concerned Asu might kill the hostages if he thinks he's been made."

"He's right. We need to make sure that doesn't happen. Mullins is still good with you as the sole contact with Homeland Security?"

"Yes."

Jordan relaxed. "Then I suggest you proceed as planned." He paused a moment. "Does the name Sidney Levine mean anything to you?"

"No. Should it?"

"He's a reporter. Got canned from *The Washington Times* a year or two ago when he became overzealous in his criticism of the Federal Reserve. He wrote a book and spent time in the Occupy Wall Street and Occupy DC protests."

"Reporting or agitating," Amanda asked.

"Depends upon your point of view. I read a couple of blogs he posted last night. He was hinting at links between the deaths of Luguire and Archer."

Jordan heard his wife take a sharp breath.

"Jesus. How'd he put that together?"

"When you dwell in the world of conspiracy theorists, you see links everywhere. Sometimes you're bound to be right. The law of averages."

"And that's what this is? A reporter launching a hundred trial balloons?"

Jordan didn't answer his wife's question. Instead he asked, "Any way Sidney Levine could have gotten the Luguire-Archer connection from Mullins?"

"No. Mullins hates the press. And all inquiries going through Prime Protection are being told Mullins is on vacation and unavailable for comment."

"He might have approached Mullins directly."

"That would never happen. Mullins is solo on this, at least till I bring him in. What did Levine learn from the posts?"

"I saw that he got credible responses from two sources—a supposed Washington insider who stated Luguire was about to give testimony to underscore the need for the Federal Reserve to keep its autonomy and anonymity, and a post from a Roanoke source that Archer was involved in a secret operation for the Federal Reserve. If Sidney Levine follows through on either or both, he'll have the framework of a story that can help your investigation."

"Independent corroboration would be useful," Amanda agreed.

"If he is independent," Jordan mused. "I'd like to know more about Mr. Levine and I'm probably not the only one wondering where he sourced his information. Public speculation about Luguire and Archer could be dangerous."

"What are you saying?"

"I'm saying that what you don't know that you don't know will get you killed. Remember that and be careful."

Curtis Jordan gently set the receiver on the cradle. Thoughts of a walk and light supper evaporated from his mind. He sensed Amanda was in waters over her head, and though she would never admit it, she needed him. She needed his imagination.

He packed his bag and called for a car. The overnight flight would arrive at Dulles early Friday morning.

Chapter Thirty-eight

Thursday night Mullins drove by Prime Protection twice. The first time, at seven-thirty, he saw eight cars still in the lot. He moved on. He wanted to avoid crossing paths with any of his colleagues, not that he had to justify his presence. Staff often came and left at odd hours, depending upon the protection assignment. But all his fellow operatives knew he was on vacation.

When he cruised through at eight-thirty, he saw only one car, the vehicle driven by the night duty guard. He parked beside the rear entrance to the two-story, standalone building and grabbed his black leather briefcase from the backseat. Then he took his entry pass from the glove box and slipped the lanyard over his head.

He stepped out into the humid July air and stretched like he'd been riding in the car for three hours. High definition cameras recorded a wide angle of the parking lot with such fine resolution that digital magnification could make any subject identifiable. From his console at the front lobby, the night guard would recognize him. But Mullins knew the guard wasn't in the loop on the duty roster. Mullins was just another employee working late hours.

With the empty briefcase in his right hand and his shoulders slumped with feigned fatigue, Mullins walked from his car, held his ID against the door's security reader, and disappeared into the building.

He trusted his boss, Ted Lewison, had made good on his offer to provide unofficial assistance. He expected everything to be in his desk drawer just as he'd requested, no questions asked.

◇◇◇

Friday morning at six-thirty, Sidney Levine turned off his alarm and rolled out of bed. He made a quick check of blog alerts but found nothing new referencing Luguire or Archer. He was tempted to plug the name Asu into an alert program. Sullivan and Mullins had warned against any Internet search for Asu. Inquiries were to be restricted to the discreet channels authorized by the Miami police or FBI. But millions of searches happened every second. He wouldn't dig down into pages or multiple links. Just a quick Google on the chance he might get lucky.

He typed "Asu" with quotation marks to limit hits to one word. 44,300,000 results in .16 seconds. Sidney saw the problem immediately—Arizona State University, Appalachian State University, Arkansas State University, Augusta State University—every state university preceded by an "a" noun and all their subtopics. Asu was a hopeless inquiry. Narrowing the search by adding Syrian or Islam would cross the line. He cleared the search engine and headed for the shower.

Forty minutes later, he stuffed a legal pad and his journal in a backpack in preparation for a day of phone work. He and Mullins planned to meet Sullivan at the Arlington Police Department where the detective had a list of every medium to cheaply priced motel in the D.C. area. Sidney would handle the four metro counties in Maryland, Mullins would take D.C., and, as an Arlington police officer, Sullivan would check Northern Virginia. By working from the station, Sullivan would also be able to stay in contact with the Miami and FBI operations.

If Asu was bringing Zaina and Jamila to D.C., it had to be connected to Saturday's attacks. A motel for two days made more sense than renting an apartment. And it was the only search they could mount in the short period of time left.

Sidney turned on his FM tuner and made sure the frequency was set to 90.9 classical WETA. His girlfriend Colleen hadn't been by for a week. He might as well solder the dial in place. He paused, remembering Mullins' warning about family members. He couldn't be sure whether Colleen's edit was over today or tomorrow. He'd call her later.

He closed and locked the apartment door. He listened to a few measures of Handel's Water Suite, and then set out to save two people he didn't know.

At eight-thirty Friday morning, Asu sat in the van alone in the motel parking lot. He listened on his cellphone to his final instructions. Chuchi, the woman, and the girl were still in the room of the Comfort Inn in Lorton, Virginia, where they'd arrived at eleven-thirty the previous night after nearly twenty hours on the road.

Asu had booked two rooms ahead of time, smuggled in the captives, and then he and Chuchi had taken a shift of four hours each to stand guard during the night. The double doses of Benadryl that Asu had ground into their food kept the mother and daughter groggy for most of the trip. Now he just needed to follow the plan for this day and the next, and then he would collect his money and be on a flight out of Dulles to Frankfurt.

He ended the call with the two words, "I understand." What he clearly understood was the new element of risk that had been injected into the operation. He'd slipped up and been traced to Miami. Somehow the woman got a message past him. If it had been up to Asu, he would have made this a simple hit without all the complications, but he also understood the need for maximum impact. And he was being paid well. Very well.

So, the plan was being adjusted. He'd have to rent a new vehicle and ditch this one where it wouldn't be discovered for a few days. A Wal-Mart or parking lot for an Amtrak station. And they'd have to leave Lorton. The location was too close to D.C.

His instructions were to move to Harpers Ferry, West Virginia. The hour and a half drive from there to D.C. was manageable enough, but more importantly, West Virginia was one more state removed from the Capital. It might not receive the scrutiny of Northern Virginia or the adjacent counties in Maryland.

Asu would let the mother and daughter sleep for now. Then he would make sure they were settled at Harpers Ferry with an early check-in. He could leave Chuchi on watch while he took care of the final details.

The weather forecast for the Fourth was clear and sunny. The perfect day for a celebration. And no one would turn away a child, especially one bringing a gift.

Chapter Thirty-nine

Rusty Mullins, Sidney Levine, and Robert Sullivan sat crammed together in the Arlington police station. Mullins and the reporter shared the adjacent desk of Sullivan's absent partner. The detective connected an extra phone and the three men went to work like telemarketers in a boiler room.

Most of the motel desk clerks had been on duty only a few hours. Each was pressed to check the previous night for late registrations between 9 p.m. and 5 a.m., the potential arrival window matching Asu's likely departure from Miami. If the question generated a hit, they would ask for a description of the guests and their vehicle. They wouldn't request names. If a lead looked promising, Mullins or Sidney would check it out in person.

Four hours later, not a single inquiry netted a positive result.

Then, after calling out for a lunch pizza delivery, Sullivan tried the Comfort Inn in Lorton, Virginia, at the southern end of Fairfax County. A woman on the front desk said a man had checked in shortly after midnight. He'd pre-booked two rooms on a credit card. Two rooms for two nights.

Sullivan stood from his desk to catch the attention of Sidney and Mullins. Instinctively, they lowered their voices, continuing their conversations while trying to listen to Sullivan's side of his.

"Do you have a vehicle on the registration form?" Sullivan asked.

The other men turned in their chairs to face him.

"A silver Windstar," Sullivan repeated. "A family then?"

Sullivan listened for a moment. "Was that to avoid additional charges?"

He listened again. "Sure. That makes sense. But the vehicle's the wrong make so your guests aren't the ones we're looking for. Like I said, it's a parental custody issue, nothing dangerous. Certainly nothing to be mentioned beyond you and me. Thank you for your help."

Sullivan hung up. The other men had finished their calls and stared at him.

"So, what's the word?" Mullins asked.

"A match on the check-in time and the van. Two rooms had been booked by two men traveling together on business."

"Did she volunteer their names?" Mullins asked.

"No. But the rooms had to be guaranteed by credit card. There will be a name, although I bet my share of the pizza it's phony."

"What did you mean by additional charges?" Sidney asked.

Sullivan stepped away from the desk. He smiled. "It's why we're going to Lorton. The woman on the desk said one of the house-cleaning staff mentioned there were Do-Not-Disturb signs on the door handles of the two adjacent rooms. She reported she would clean the rooms later in the day. Then she said she heard a child crying in one of them, so the occupants would probably go out for lunch. I was curious if having a wife and child with you increased the room rate, a reason many parents might not register more than one person."

"Does it?" Mullins asked.

"No. There might be other reasons, like the kid was sleeping and carried through an outside entrance closer to the rooms. But, we've got three matches—arrival time, van model, and a kid."

"Good enough for me," Mullins said. "Who are you notifying?"

"No one. We'll be there in twenty-five minutes. I don't want the state police and FBI converging on people who might be a family on vacation. We'll check the van license plate and maybe get lucky with a visual confirmation." Sullivan looked at Mullins.

"I suggest you stay out of sight. If they were monitoring Luguire or Archer, you might be recognized."

"And I suggest you not pull into the Comfort Inn driving a Crown Vic, the most marked unmarked cop car in the country."

"They've seen your Prius." Sullivan turned to Sidney. "What are you driving?"

"A Ford Escort."

"I thought you had an Audi," Mullins said.

"My girlfriend's. I figured you saw my Escort when we first met at the ballgame."

"Consider your Escort commandeered." Sullivan pulled his pistol from the holster and checked the clip.

Mullins did the same with his Glock.

"What about me?" Sidney asked. "Got a spare gun?"

"The pen is mightier than the sword," Sullivan said.

"Fine. Except the bad guys stopped using swords a hundred years ago."

Sullivan's intercom buzzed. "Rob, did you order a pizza?"

"Yeah. I'll be right out." He gestured for Sidney to go first. "You can't carry a gun, but you can carry the pizza. No one ever shot himself in the foot with a pizza."

Sidney drove, Mullins sat in the front passenger seat, and Sullivan dispensed pizza from the back. They rode in silence down I-95, not only because they were eating but also because they had nothing to say. Any thoughts about what lay ahead in Lorton would be speculation and any other topic mindless chatter.

They were near Newington at the Fairfax County Parkway cloverleaf when Sullivan's cell rang. He dumped his pizza slice back in the box and grabbed his phone with sauce-coated fingers.

"What? Where? When?" he asked with intervals that allowed no more than a one-sentence response. Then he said, "Give me the details."

Sidney glanced at Mullins but the veteran agent signaled the reporter to relax.

"Could be another case," Mullins whispered, and returned to his slice of pepperoni.

Sidney repeatedly looked from the interstate to the rearview mirror. Sullivan held the phone tight against his cheek, his lips tight and eyes focused somewhere beyond the passing landscape. Sidney discerned no clues from the frozen expression.

"Okay. Thanks," Sullivan said after three long moments of silence. "No. I won't bother unless you want me to. I'm working something else." He hung up without a goodbye.

"Well?" Sidney asked.

Sullivan wiped his phone on the edge of the pizza box. "That was Miami. They got a call from Lorton."

"Damn it." Mullins turned in his seat. "Bodies?"

"The van. State trooper found it in the parking lot of the Lorton Auto Train station. The officer checked because the train comes in from Sanford, Florida. Cars are loaded on in Sanford and can't come off till Lorton. The vehicle would have come north without anyone seeing it."

"Sounds like a lot of planning," Mullins said. "Not a spontaneous action. Those car slots have to be reserved, don't they?"

"Yes. But there are cancellations. The van had to be at the station by 2 p.m. yesterday. They could have made it from Miami to Sanford in plenty of time. The train ran late and arrived at 9:50 a.m. this morning."

"That eliminates our Comfort Inn guests," Sidney said.

"No," Sullivan said. "It makes them even more plausible. There's no record of that van being on the train."

"So, they dumped it," Mullins said.

"Yeah. There were food wrappers, soda cans, and a crayon wedged in the seat."

"They're holding up at the motel," Mullins said. "The vehicle change is a safeguard."

"They'd all have to be out and about, right?" Sidney asked. "Two drivers are needed to drop the van and get another vehicle."

"They've probably got help in the area," Sullivan said. "That means we don't know how many are at the motel. They could have a lookout."

Sidney pressed the accelerator harder. "We're less than ten minutes out. What do you want me to do when we get there?"

"Park in front," Sullivan said. "I'll find the woman I spoke with. Showing up in person with my credentials will let me ask questions I couldn't over the phone. When we've got rooms and a name, then we'll have the front desk call and say maintenance needs to service the air conditioner. If someone answers, I'll call for backup, and you guys are out of it."

"If no one answers?" Sidney asked.

Sullivan laughed. "Then I guess I'll find a maintenance staff uniform and see what's wrong with the room's air conditioning."

"Are you worried about jurisdiction?" Mullins asked.

"To go in and fix an air conditioner? No. Are you?"

"It's not my pension," Mullins said.

Sullivan gave Mullins a hard stare. "But it is the little girl and her mother. You're not the only one worried about them."

"Maintenance." Sullivan rapped on the door of 306, the first of the two adjacent rooms that had been booked on the credit card of Enrique Cortez.

The motel manager hadn't argued with Sullivan's credentials or his request to call the rooms to say maintenance needed access. When there had been no answer, the homicide detective slipped on a pair of coveralls, grabbed a tool box, and rode the elevator to the third floor. Sidney and Mullins were positioned to watch the motel's front and rear exits.

Sullivan knocked again. The only sound returning was the hum of the air conditioner. Within its steady whir, a sporadic rattle rose and fell. Ironically, maintenance did need to check the unit. He inserted the electronic passkey in the lock, saw the light turn green, and slowly opened the door. "Maintenance."

The room was empty, not just of people but of any sign of clothes, suitcases, or toilet articles. Whoever occupied the room had cleared out. They weren't staying for the second night.

Sullivan checked the other room and found the same scene. There were fast food wrappers in the trash. He called Sidney's mobile and told him to get Mullins and come up.

"Something spooked them." Mullins rendered his verdict after walking through the two rooms.

"Maybe they're just being super cautious," Sidney said.

"No. You don't draw attention to yourself by disappearing. Something altered their plans."

Sidney walked to the window and looked down at the parking lot, hoping to see a silver van pull in. "I might have screwed up."

"How?" Sullivan asked.

"I googled Asu's name this morning. All I got were a string of state universities."

"What did you enter?" Mullins asked.

"Just the name Asu."

"I can't see that raising any flags," Sullivan said.

Mullins frowned. "What kind of firewall security do you have?"

Sidney shrugged. "The usual. Norton. McAfee. Stuff to keep out viruses and malicious cookies."

"Hacking through that would be child's play for someone who can manipulate the cyber-security of the Federal Reserve. The odds of someone picking up every search for Asu are long, but the odds of someone specifically monitoring your computer are much much less. Probably a certainty."

Sidney looked alarmed. "Why?"

"If you posted speculation on a link between Luguire and Archer, that combination is specific enough to trigger someone's tripwire. You said you got responses from a Roanoke and an alleged congressional insider. Someone else might be lurking in the cyber shadows whose response was to invade and monitor your computer."

"So I probably scared Asu off?"

"No. It's more likely the Miami alert to state police and the FBI was intercepted." Mullins looked around the room. "Maybe Zaina left us a clue."

While Sidney and Sullivan watched, Mullins walked between the two queen-sized beds. Only one was unmade. "I suspect this is the room where the mother and child slept. Someone sat in the chair and guarded them. Both beds in the other room have been used."

Mullins bent over, grabbed the mattress near the foot of the unmade bed, and hurled it aside. A folded sheet of paper and a bag were stuffed on top of the box springs.

Mullins took a handkerchief from his pocket and used it to pick up the paper. He shook it gently, then tugged at the corners to straighten it. It was a page from a child's coloring book. Printed in red block letters across the uncolored drawing of a princess in a carriage were the words, "Help us! Silver Windstar."

He set the page on the dresser. "Why don't you take charge of that," he told Sullivan.

Then Mullins straightened the paper bag. It was at least two-foot square and had a Toys "R" Us logo on the side. Mullins reached inside and extracted a receipt. The print was small and he walked closer to the window for stronger light. "It's from ten-fifteen this morning. Cinderella's Castle. Twenty-four dollars and ninety-five cents. Must be something you assemble. The store location is Telegraph Road in Woodbridge, not far from here."

"Somebody bought a present for the little girl," Sullivan said.

"There's also wrapping paper, Scotch tape, and a packet of bows. Total expense—thirty-six dollars and forty-seven cents paid with forty-dollars cash and three dollars and fifty-three cents returned in change." He handed his handkerchief and the receipt to Sullivan.

Sidney studied the receipt over Sullivan's shoulder. "So, the purchase was made before they left the motel. Either Asu or Chuchi went out alone."

"Probably brought the gift back to quiet the kid," Sullivan proposed.

"Then why the hell wrap it?" Mullins walked to the waste-basket by the small desk. "Do you see any paper?"

Sidney stepped next door and checked the second room. He returned a moment later. "Nothing there. Maybe they wouldn't let her unwrap it until she was in the van."

Sullivan looked at the large Toys "R" Us bag. "Just as easy to keep it hidden without the wrapping paper and bows. These aren't the kind of guys who fuss over social niceties. I need to notify Miami and the Virginia state police."

"However you want to play it," Mullins said.

"I should stay here and hand over the evidence. You guys head on. I'll work out a ride to Arlington."

Sidney turned to Mullins. "Where are we going?"

"To the toy store. I'd like to get a description of the person who made the purchase." Mullins glanced at his watch. "Not quite four hours ago. Somebody remembers something."

◇◇◇

"How can I help you?" The young cashier looked at Mullins with curiosity.

He stood without any item on the checkout counter. "Do you have Cinderella's Castle in stock?"

"I believe so. But I sold one earlier. That might have been the last one."

Mullins groaned. "Oh, no. I'm getting one for my granddaughter's birthday. I hope it wasn't someone buying her the same gift. Was it a man or a woman?"

"A man."

Mullins looked at her name badge. "Karen, right?"

She nodded.

"That could be her uncle. Hispanic?"

"I don't think so. He had an accent but it was different. He was about your height, maybe mid-thirties, dark black hair."

Mullins smiled. "Oh, well, maybe I'm in luck. That doesn't sound like her Uncle Chuchi. Did he mention if it was for a birthday party?"

Karen shook her head. "No. But he bought wrapping paper and bows."

Mullins' smile disappeared. "There's a party on Saturday. He might have a child coming. I'm sure my granddaughter told everyone she wants Cinderella's Castle."

"If the box is unopened and you keep the receipt, we'll be happy to exchange it."

"Okay. Fair enough. Better to be safe than have a disappointed birthday girl. Where would I find it?"

The cashier pointed to her right. "Halfway down aisle seven. Nicole should be in that section. She'll be glad to help."

Mullins discovered Sidney in the aisle holding a box about eighteen inches square.

"This has to be it," Sidney said. "Same price as on the receipt. It's not the Disney version, but I guess you can't copyright the fairy tale Cinderella."

Mullins took the toy. The box was heavy. The cover art showed Cinderella slipping her foot into the glass slipper with the handsome prince kneeling in front of her. A banner across the corner read, "Over 100 cutout pieces." Mullins flipped the box over and saw the assembled castle, Cinderella's house, and figures of the main characters including the evil stepmother and ugly sisters. "Kind of elaborate for a four-year-old," Mullins said.

"Did you find what you need?" A young woman with a cheery smile walked toward them.

Mullins read "Nicole" on her name badge. "Is this the only Cinderella's Castle you have?"

"The only one that creates a 3-D presentation of the story. We have a plastic castle that's bigger but it could belong to Cinderella, Sleeping Beauty, Snow White." She laughed. "Your basic princess starter home."

Mullins studied the box. "The cashier up front said another one was sold this morning. We're concerned it might be for the same party. Did the buyer specifically ask for this toy?"

"No. I was the one who suggested it. He said he needed a gift for a four-year-old girl." She looked at the box and frowned. "I told him this might be a little too complicated for a child that age. An adult would definitely have to supervise."

"My granddaughter's five and she wanted this particular castle."

"Then you should be safe. Not only is the age different, but I think he was more interested in the size of the gift."

Mullins tensed. "Really?"

"Yes. He said he wanted the little girl to get a present big enough to impress her."

"I know a guy like that," Mullins said. "Except if he's coming to my granddaughter's party, he'll want to show up the other parents. Was he tall with light brown hair?"

"No. Dark black hair." She pursed her lips. "I can't be certain, but he looked like he was Egyptian or from one of those other Mideast countries."

"Then I guess we're good," Mullins said. "I'll take it."

A few minutes later, he set the bag with the castle in the backseat of Sidney's car and got in the passenger's seat.

"Where to?" Sidney asked.

"Arlington police station. I'll get my car."

"What should I do?"

Mullins thought a moment. "If someone's hacked into your computer, then we should turn that into an advantage. Write your blog that you've concluded Luguire committed suicide. You've found no connection between Luguire and Archer, and then rant on some other issue. I'm sure it won't take much prompting to turn your followers onto a new conspiracy."

"What about you?"

Mullins glanced at the Toys "R" Us bag behind him. "I'm going to find Asu. There's a little princess that needs rescuing."

Chapter Forty

"I'm going to run an errand." Asu slipped on his pale blue linen sport coat, more to hide his shoulder holster than to be fashionable.

Chuchi looked up from the floor where he sat with Jamila. Pieces of cardboard lay around them.

The girl picked up one of the colorful squares. "It's Cinderella." She showed the drawing of the princess to her mother.

Zaina sat on the small love seat near the window. She forced a smile. "I see. She's beautiful."

Jamila handed the cardboard to Chuchi. "Make her free."

Asu headed for the door. "Play nice, Chuchi. I'll be back." He looked at Zaina. "Soon this will be over. What do they say? And everyone lived happily ever after." He turned to Chuchi. "Both of you have my word on that."

Zaina glared at Asu but said nothing.

"Thank you," Chuchi said, and for the first time since Zaina spoke Asu's name, he relaxed. He carefully punched out the perforated outline of the cartoon character while Jamila searched through the cards for Prince Charming.

Asu walked out of the Harpers Ferry Comfort Inn into the bright sunshine of July Third. Even the hilly, wooded terrain of West Virginia didn't escape the brutal heat.

Asu needed a place to work, but he didn't want to bring the materials into his room. Chuchi would ask questions, and at this point, Chuchi knew only that they were supposed to meet Fares Khoury the next day.

The new rental van was a dark blue Honda Odyssey. The police might have found the Windstar by now, but Asu was sure it would take them a while to sort through rental company records. He'd picked up the Honda at Reagan International where cars are turning over constantly. He had to use the last of his false identities for the paperwork, the name that would get him out of the country, the only identity important to him now.

He drove the van a short distance from Union Street down Highway 340 to the Harpers Ferry National Historic Park and paid the six dollar entrance fee in cash. The parking lot was fairly crowded for the start of the July Fourth weekend, and he found a spot farthest from the information station. He wasn't interested in taking a tour or hiking to a vantage point where he could see the scenic confluence of the Shenandoah and Potomac Rivers. He wasn't aware of John Brown's raid over a hundred and fifty years ago that led to the abolitionist's execution and the immortalization of Harpers Ferry.

Asu wanted a place where he would be lost among a crowd of cars, vans, and buses. He needed an uninterrupted half-hour in the passenger's seat with the motor running and the air conditioning circulating cool air. That would be enough time to pack the three bricks of C-4 plastic explosive into a box about the size of Cinderella's Castle. The weight should be comparable. Approximately five pounds including the modified keyless remote receiver.

Asu had to admit his clients had thoroughly thought through the operation, and, as circumstances changed, quickly and effectively altered plans to take advantage of evolving situations. He was impressed with the detonator, an enhanced keyless remote transmitter with a two-hundred-foot range. Asu's experience with bombs had been limited to detonation by cellphone, a scary prospect once the bomb was armed. Even though the odds were long, the possibility of a misdialed phone number made the final stages extremely nerve-wracking. The odds of a keyless remote code accidentally triggering the C-4 were approximately one in a trillion, better odds even if every man, woman, and child on the planet unlocked their cars at the same time.

He would take the chance and activate the bomb today. And he would wrap the package as smartly as he could. Jamila would be careful with it, excited to learn she was bringing a present she already enjoyed. Excited to see her father.

An hour and a half away, Sidney Levine went down the back steps to his basement apartment in Georgetown. As he entered the hallway, he remembered he was supposed to call Colleen. Mullins had been worried about those closest to Sullivan and him, although Sidney found it doubtful that any danger extended to his friends. He'd reach Colleen while he was thinking of it and before he made his blog posting. Maybe he'd invite himself to her place on the off chance that Mullins' concerns were valid.

He inserted the key in the lock. Strains of Wagner's *Ride of the Valkyries* sounded from the other side of the door.

The apartment was dimly lit by the lamp next to the stereo, exactly the way he'd left it that morning. He stepped inside and felt his shoes sticking to the floor, the first sign that something was amiss. He turned on the overhead light and saw the second sign. A brown grocery bag lay split open at the base of the kitchen counter. Broken glass from a bottle trailed from the bag to the third sign. Colleen, sprawled halfway into the kitchen, her head propped against the base of the refrigerator, and her white blouse soaked in a hideous Rorschach blot of wine and blood.

Chapter Forty-one

Mullins knew trouble had struck as soon as he saw Detective Sullivan's cellphone number on his caller ID.

"What's up?" he asked.

"Where are you?" Sullivan barked the question like Mullins was an AWOL private.

"In my apartment. I decided to hell with the cloak and dagger bit. I'm keeping this pre-paid a secret but using my landline to call motels. I think Asu's still in the area."

"Well, there's a new development. Sidney just called. The guy was nearly hysterical. He found his girlfriend shot in his apartment.

"Oh, Christ. Dead?"

"He said she had a pulse. He called an ambulance and the police. Then he called me. I'm on my way. I don't have any jurisdiction, but I'll be on the scene."

"I'll be there too." Mullins hung up before Sullivan could argue.

"What have you got for me?" D.C. Detective Steve Leonard asked. He stood at the top of the basement steps on the other side of yellow crime scene tape, his dark eyes tired from seeing too many shooting victims.

Mullins looked past him to the bottom of the steps where Sullivan stood in the doorway, wearing paper shoe covers and latex gloves. Obviously, the Arlington detective had been extended the courtesy of entering the apartment. But, in a city crawling with federal and ex-federal law enforcement, Mullins knew his credentials as a former Secret Service agent wouldn't even get him a free cup of coffee in a D.C. squad room. Leonard had no reason to accommodate Mullins, unless he had something to trade.

Sullivan shook his head, signaling Mullins not to bother.

"I was with Sidney Levine earlier," Mullins said. "Detective Sullivan called me after he heard. If you're establishing a time-line, I can vouch for Levine's whereabouts for most of the day."

"Fine," Leonard replied. "Give Davidson your statement and your contact information." He glared at the young uniformed officer who had relayed Mullins' request to see the detective in charge. "And don't disturb me again." With that parting rebuke of Davidson, Leonard descended the stairs and brushed past Sullivan.

The Arlington detective smiled. "Impressive, huh? The guy should have his own TV show. I'll be up in a few minutes. See if you can find Sidney." Sullivan disappeared into the apartment building.

Mullins turned to the uniform. Officer Davidson had taken a notepad from his pocket.

"The timeline?" he asked.

Mullins looked past him to one of the patrol cars angled up on the curb. He thought he saw Sidney in the backseat.

"Sir? You said you had a timeline?"

"Yeah." Mullins took a deep breath. "Sidney Levine was with me from nine this morning until about an hour ago. Say, approximately three o'clock. He dropped me off in Arlington. I returned to my apartment in Shirlington and got the call from Detective Sullivan shortly thereafter."

"Anything else?"

Mullins knew the patrolman wasn't a trained interrogator. Leonard had given him the task to get Mullins out of his hair. If whatever Mullins offered contradicted Sidney's story or rein-forced something Sidney said that forensics cast into doubt, Detective Leonard would be all over him.

"No. Other than this is a terrible shock. Can I speak to my friend?"

"If Detective Carlton is finished with him. We put Levine in a car, but won't take him downtown unless circumstances warrant."

Like he becomes the chief suspect, Mullins thought. He headed for the patrol car.

"Hold up," Davidson ordered. "Can I have an address and phone number?"

Mullins gave him his residence and home phone.

"Cell phone?"

"I lost it," he lied.

"Wait here. I'll check on Levine's status."

Five minutes later, Sidney and a man in plainclothes emerged from the vehicle. Mullins assumed the second man was Detective Carlton, Leonard's investigative partner. Carlton glanced at Mullins but made no effort to speak with him.

Sidney took small wobbly steps, like a child learning to walk. As he came closer, Mullins saw the reporter's skin had turned to chalk and the knees of his jeans were smeared with blood. Sidney probably had covered crime scenes before, but that's not the same thing as finding your girlfriend shot in your own home. Mullins doubted if Sidney would be considered a suspect. Such obvious signs of shock are impossible to fake. At least, Mullins had never encountered someone able to drain the blood from his face at will.

"Oh God, Mullins. They shot her right in the kitchen. She didn't take more than four steps into the apartment. What have we done?"

Mullins grabbed Sidney's arm and steadied him. "Let's sit in my car. I parked in front of the dumpster." Mullins kept a gentle hold on Sidney's elbow and steered him to the Prius. When he had Sidney safely in the passenger's seat, he slid behind the wheel and rolled down all the windows for ventilation.

"You told me to warn her." Sidney choked on the words and wiped his eyes with the back of his hand. "You told me and I didn't do it. I'm the reason she's fighting for her life."

"No. It's because some son of a bitch shot her. Your warning might have prevented nothing."

"You don't know that."

"I don't," Mullins agreed. "But what would you have told her to do?"

Sidney thought a moment. "Go to her apartment and not let anyone in till I got there."

"Then these people would have tracked you there through your phone. I'm the one who screwed up. I should have considered that the information I had you post would bring them after the source."

"My laptop's gone," Sidney whispered. "And three external hard drives."

"Tell me what happened. Take it as slowly as you need."

"Okay." Sidney swallowed and then moistened his lips with his tongue. "I came straight here from Arlington." He glanced at the stairs to the basement. "When I stepped into the hall, I remembered that I needed to call Colleen. Maybe a premonition, because I was suddenly afraid for her. Then I relaxed when I heard classical music coming from my apartment. I leave an FM station on so people will think I'm home. When Colleen's here, she changes it to rock. I let myself in and planned to call her immediately. The floor was sticky. I turned on the overhead light and saw a bag of groceries split open. A bottle of wine had shattered. The apartment floor isn't level and the liquid had pooled by the threshold. Then I saw her leg."

Sidney's breath caught in his throat.

"So, she'd just come in," Mullins said. "Didn't put away the food, didn't switch stations."

Sidney nodded. "There was no sign of a break-in."

"Means they were professionals. I easily picked your lock the other day. She must have surprised them."

Sidney shook his head. "The blood on her shirt. I'll never get that image out of my mind. The paramedic said he thinks the wine bottle might have saved her life. Deflected the bullet just enough to miss her heart."

"I'm going to find whoever did this," Mullins promised. "You want me to take you to the hospital?"

"No. I've got my car." Sidney looked at Mullins with a hard resolute glint in his eyes. "But then I need something to do, god damn it. When she's out of danger. I'm going to do something to make this right."

"Okay. I want you in the game. We don't know who to trust. The attack on Colleen proves I can trust you."

Sidney's mouth dropped open. "You still thought I was part of the conspiracy?"

Mullins smiled. "Ninety-five percent sure you weren't. But five percent's nothing to ignore when lives are on the line. What did you tell the police about the stolen computer and drives?"

"That I was doing an investigative story on bank fraud. It's such a broad topic that I don't think they were particularly interested. They're working on the hypothesis that Colleen interrupted a burglary. There have been several in the neighborhood."

"Don't say anything to lead them elsewhere. Tomorrow federal law enforcement's anti-terrorism sweep will bring everything out into the open. Then we can give them the whole package. And, I hope Khoury's wife and daughter will be alive to testify."

"But Asu gave us the slip."

"For now. But he has a destination, and I plan to be there when he arrives."

"Where?"

Mullins shrugged. "I don't know. But I will. Your job is to monitor what happens. I need you covering the story as a reporter and I need Sullivan ready to make an arrest for Paul Luguire's murder. There's a briefcase in the seat behind you. Take it with you but don't open it in the hospital. After you get an update on Colleen's condition, you should check into a motel tonight. The briefcase has instructions and the equipment you need. No more contact with me until this goes down. Understood?"

"Honestly? No." Sidney took a deep breath. "But if you're trusting me, then I have to trust you."

"I'll cover Sullivan and he'll be in touch." Mullins reached in the backseat, grabbed the briefcase, and held it out to Sidney.

The reporter hesitated, suddenly aware of the dry blood coating his palms.

"Take it," Mullins urged.

Sidney clutched it to his chest. "The story of a lifetime. Every reporter's dream. God, look at the price being paid."

Mullins said nothing. He knew the price was a long way from being totaled.

Chapter Forty-two

With the Fourth of July falling on a Saturday, the business holiday would be celebrated on Monday. Most of Washington took that as clearance to bolt out of town Friday afternoon, getting a jump on the traffic and thereby guaranteeing traffic gridlocked several hours earlier than usual.

Amanda Church remained in her office until five-thirty. Then she locked her door and exited through the lobby of the Federal Reserve building. The photography exhibit of one hundred fifty years of July Fourth celebrations lined the walls. Extra security screening stations were being set up inside the main entrance. In short, the Federal Reserve was becoming an airport terminal, complete with body scanners and random pat downs. She felt confident no hand-carried bombs could make it through that perimeter of defense, and she'd recommended that vans and trucks be rerouted or screened before coming down the adjacent blocks of 20th and 21st Streets. Whatever happened, she wanted her ass covered. Now she just needed the final briefing with Mullins.

The plan was to meet him at her apartment at six-thirty. She could give assurances that the threat had been defused across the nation without a word leaking to the press. Eleven of the twelve terrorist cells had been identified. Federal agents were set to move in at the first sign that the attacks were being executed.

But she'd admit two remained undetected—the Richmond branch and Washington, D.C. Amanda would tell Mullins that Richmond might have been thwarted by the death of Fares Khoury, and his co-conspirators scattered to the four winds. Washington, if it was the thirteenth target, was being protected the best way possible. The next day, she and Mullins would monitor that operation together.

At five after six, she arrived at her co-op on Connecticut Avenue NW. Mullins would be prompt. The wine would need to breathe and the appetizers warmed. They would toast to breaking up the greatest terrorist plot since 9-11.

Curtis Jordan watched his wife's BMW turn into the alley for their underground garage. He sat in a rented black Chevy Tahoe on Appleton, the side street next to their building. The SUV's tinted windows concealed his identity, and no one gave the vehicle a second glance. There were only a million of them in the city.

He considered letting Amanda know he'd flown back from Paris. But she'd take it as a sign that he thought her collaboration with Mullins wouldn't succeed and that he came to pick up the pieces. In her mind, his lack of confidence in her was tantamount to being unfaithful. And he understood her logic. It was Mullins who worried him.

Twenty minutes later, Jordan saw the blue Prius drive by. Reflexively, he turned his head from the window. If Mullins recognized him, the encounter would be awkward. He was supposed to be out of the country.

The Prius continued half a block before finding a parking space. Jordan's first inclination was to drive off, make a U-turn and head in the opposite direction. But Mullins might notice the vacant spot and recall the missing vehicle. Jordan knew memory hinged on little things and drawing Mullins' attention was the last thing he wanted to do. Better to stay put. So, not trusting the tinted windows, he slid down below the windshield line and waited five minutes, plenty of time for Mullins to walk past.

Mullins eyed Amanda's building with appreciation. The five-story brick structure, known as the Ponce de Leon, was on the National Register of Historic Places. Mullins had been in the co-op only once. Amanda had invited Laurie and him to a private party celebrating the launch of one of her husband's thrillers. It was the last event Laurie felt well enough to attend. She'd been impressed with the high ceilings and overall spaciousness of the three-bedroom residence. Curtis Jordan had told them Alben Barkley once lived on the top floor. Alben Barkley, Truman's vice president. How obscure could you get, Mullins thought.

He stopped at the corner of Connecticut and Appleton and looked back up the side street for any sign that another vehicle had been following him. The road was quiet. The only sign of life, a man walking a schnauzer puppy along the opposite sidewalk.

Mullins turned to the building's entrance. For the second time, his wife's voice rang in his head. "Upside down." He knew Laurie's words were only in his mind, but the message was clearly coming from somewhere. Whether generated by his subconscious or beyond the grave, Mullins couldn't ignore it. "Give me strength, Laurie," he whispered, and ascended the front steps.

Amanda's co-op was on the fourth floor close to the elevator. She heard the knock on her door as she pulled a tray of feta cheese and caramelized onion appetizers from her oven.

"What's wrong? Can't you pick the lock?" Amanda crossed the foyer and undid the deadbolt.

Mullins hesitated, sniffing the air that drifted across the threshold. "You're cooking?"

"Why not? We have to eat." She reached out and took his hand. "Come in before someone sees you. In that suit you look like a damn IRS agent. The neighbors will think I haven't paid my taxes."

As he stepped by her, she slid her hand under his lapel. "Let me hang up your jacket. And do you want to check that shoulder holster along with it? We can talk about work without looking like revolutionaries."

"Okay." He let her slip the coat off and then he unsnapped the holster and handed it to her. She arched her eyebrows as he removed his Glock and held it by his side.

"Expecting company or are you afraid of me?"

He smiled. "Yes."

"Yes what?"

His smile vanished. "Do you know Sidney Levine?"

The question startled Amanda. She recalled her husband mentioning Sidney Levine the day before. She realized that her recognition had been seen by Mullins, a man trained in reading faces.

"The name sounds familiar. A reporter, right?"

"Yes. Freelance. He wrote a book taking the Federal Reserve to task."

Amanda nodded. "That's probably where I've heard of him. Why?"

"He tracked me down last Saturday. He wanted to know if I thought Luguire had been murdered."

"What did you tell him?"

"That I'd been surprised by the report of suicide, and I told that to the Arlington police. I was very interested to see what their investigation uncovered."

"So, this guy was fishing for a story." Amanda gestured for Mullins to follow her into the living room. "Can I bring you a glass of wine? I have a nice Pinot Noir, California. I stock it just to piss off my husband who's an irrational Francophile."

"All right." Mullins sat on the white sofa and laid his pistol on a marble end table. He looked around the well-appointed room. "I don't know, though. Red wine in this room could be dangerous."

"This coming from a man who needs to keep his loaded gun beside him at a friend's house?"

"I hadn't finished telling you about Sidney Levine. He left a message on my home machine that I retrieved on my way here. This afternoon someone broke into his apartment and shot his girlfriend. We don't know whether she'll make it."

Amanda's face drained. "Jesus. You think it has to do with tomorrow's attacks?"

Mullins saw she was genuinely shocked. He motioned for her to sit beside him. "Sidney posted speculation tying Luguire and Archer together. You and I know there's a connection. I assume the only person you've told is Rudy Hauser."

"Yes. I saw him alone at his office at Treasury. But I expect the Archer-Luguire link got passed up the coordinating chain as the anti-terrorism units were briefed."

"Somebody saw Sidney as a threat," Mullins said. "They stole his laptop and his hard drives. I think his girlfriend just walked in at the wrong time."

Amanda sighed. "So our secrecy successfully kept the plotters from learning we were on to them. As far as they know, there's still a secret to protect, a secret that got the woman shot."

"Yeah. Hell of an irony, isn't it?"

She cocked her head and studied him closely. "You haven't told me the whole story, have you?"

Mullins got to his feet. "You said something about wine." He picked up his gun. "This white sofa makes me nervous. Why don't we sit at the dining room table?"

Amanda brought two crystal glasses and a full bottle of Pinot Noir, gave each of them an abundant pour, and then returned with trays of fruit and the warm Pastry Bites. "Trader Joe's finest," she said. "I've probably let them get too cool."

Mullins sampled one. "Very nice. I could eat them all."

"I also have two small steaks. Those and a salad will be dinner." She sat in the chair directly across the table width. "After you tell me what's going on."

He took a sip from his glass and then ran his finger around the base. "I've had more than one conversation with Sidney Levine. He followed me to Roanoke."

"What?" Amanda's hand trembled so hard a trickle of wine fell across her fingers. "He knows you talked to Archer?"

"He suspects I did. Archer logged my appointment under a false name. I guess he didn't want anyone knowing he was meeting with the Federal Reserve."

Amanda's eyes narrowed. "Why the hell didn't you tell me?"

"Because I just found out about it." Mullins said the lie with just enough defensive tone to aid its credibility. He didn't want to get into an explanation of his parallel investigation into the disappearance of Khoury's family or his collaboration with Sidney and Sullivan.

Amanda made the mental leap. "Your name is on that computer."

"Yes."

"What about me?"

"He has no knowledge of you or the information you gave me." Mullins hesitated. "At least, if he does, it didn't come from me."

"Well, that's not reassuring. Especially given the number of people who know we're close."

"Where do things stand on your end?"

Amanda gave him an encouraging account she said came straight from Rudy Hauser of the Secret Service. Eleven terrorist cells identified and monitored, Richmond's was probably disrupted but the Reserve branch was under tight security, and an impenetrable net had been drawn over the Federal Reserve building in D.C. "If that's the thirteenth target, there's no way they'll get close enough to execute an attack."

"What's the common denominator?" Mullins asked. "Al Qaida? Iranians? Syrians?"

"That's the odd part. We've got Khoury a Lebanese, Asu a Syrian, and the other cells seem to be linked to the more extreme elements arising from the Occupy Wall Street protests."

"Domestic? Who's infiltrated whom? Are the protesters unwittingly harboring these terrorist cells?"

"We don't know. At this point, we're set to stop eleven of thirteen. Hauser's betting noon for the trigger time."

Mullins nodded. "Nine in the morning in San Francisco. Once one Federal Reserve Bank is hit security will clamp down on all of them. It has to be a nearly simultaneous attack. But strike too early and there's not enough traffic or pedestrians."

"Not enough casualties, you mean." Amanda took a sip of wine and then shivered. "I'm scared, Rusty. I was confident until you told me about the reporter's girlfriend. Their tentacles seem to be everywhere. What about your daughter? Is she safe?"

"Kayli and my grandson are away from their apartment. They're to lie low until this is over."

"A wise precaution." She rose from the table. "Keep your seat. You can talk to me while I make our salads." She headed for the kitchen. "Finish those appetizers."

"Why do you think Asu would buy wrapping paper?"

Amanda froze in the doorway. Then she turned slowly. "Wrapping paper?"

Mullins popped one of the Pastry Bites in his mouth, chewed and swallowed.

Amanda stared at him, her forehead creased with furrows. "What the hell are you talking about?"

"Asu bought gift-wrapping paper at Toys "R" Us in Wood-bridge this morning. He also bought a cardboard cutout set called Cinderella's Castle. I can understand him getting that for Khoury's daughter but why the paper?"

"You should have told me at once."

Mullins picked up his wine and shrugged. "Virginia state police found the receipt in a motel room Asu rented. I'm sure it went up on the network where Hauser's people saw it."

"You don't know that."

"There's a lot of things I don't know. And right now wrapping paper is top of the list."

Amanda marched past him. "I need to call Hauser. My phone's in the bedroom."

"Does that mean you don't have a theory?"

"My theories would be just that. Theories. Hauser and Homeland Security have the analysts in place to make real headway." She left him alone in the dining room. He refilled their wine glasses.

Five minutes later, Amanda returned. "Sorry I snapped at you. Hauser had the information. They're working on it."

"That's okay. I shouldn't have assumed the Virginia report crossed to the feds. I thought the news about Sidney Levine's girlfriend was more important."

"And more of an immediate threat." Amanda rested her hands on Mullins' shoulders, and then gently massaged them. "That's got me uptight."

Mullins leaned forward out of her grip and picked up her wine. "Here. A second glass always works for me."

She took it. "I'll take out my frustration on the salad. Toss it without mercy."

Mullins laughed. "You do that. Where's the restroom?"

"Down the hall to the left past the middle bedroom."

He looked in the first bedroom and noticed it had a distinctly feminine flair. A mirror above the bureau on the far wall reflected the doorway on the other side of the queen-sized bed. The bathroom for the master bedroom. Atop the bureau, he saw Amanda's open purse. Quickly he crossed the floor and pulled the cellphone clear. He called up the log of outgoing calls. Within the previous hour only one number appeared, a 202 area code. He committed the Washington number to memory. Satisfied Amanda had made only the one call, he replaced the phone and returned to the hall.

The middle bedroom had a king-sized bed. Prints of Paris landmarks decorated the walls and an impressionist painting hung over the headboard. Mullins didn't know much about art but the work looked like an original.

The third bedroom had been converted into an office. Bookshelves lined two walls. A chrome and glass desk faced double windows. A leather recliner sat where the bookshelves came together. The layout suggested a private office for writing and reading. There was no client chair or conference table. It had to be where Curtis Jordan created his thrillers when he wasn't traveling around the globe or ensconced in his beloved Paris.

Mullins stepped into the hallway bathroom, flushed the commode, and braced himself for the ordeal ahead.

They ate slowly, first the salad of mixed greens, walnuts, and crumbled bleu cheese. Amanda seemed to be drawing out the evening, talking about old times at Treasury, asking Mullins about presidents and memorable assignments, and liberally refilling their wine glasses.

She had him stay at the table while she broiled the steaks, keeping the conversation going through the kitchen doorway.

When she rejoined him, Mullins tried to shift the conversation away from himself, although he understood Amanda's need to prattle about anything other than the next day's operation.

"What's your husband's next book about?"

"Four hundred pages." She cut into her steak with undisguised ferocity.

"It's set in Paris?"

"Maybe. At least one scene for sure so he can write off his living expenses. He spends almost as much time at the Odéon Saint-Germain as he does here."

"I see his books everywhere."

"Yeah. Especially on the remainder tables in front of the bookstores."

Mullins looked puzzled.

"Remainders," Amanda repeated. "When a book goes out of print and the publisher doesn't even want to spend the money for warehouse space. The inventory is dumped on the market and the author receives no royalties for the bargain-basement clearance sales."

Mullins chewed his steak. His mind jumped back to his book conversation with Sidney Levine. He swallowed, and then asked, "Shouldn't they print fewer and then do POD?"

Amanda looked up in surprise. "POD? Print-on-demand? Where'd you learn that term?"

"Kayli researched it," he lied. "She wants me to write my memoir. I figure a print run of two—one for Kayli and one for my grandson Josh."

Amanda laughed. "Put me down for a copy. Unless you say bad things about me."

"Never. So, your husband's publisher doesn't do print-on-demand?"

She shook her head. "They sell enough that even with a large number going to remainder, it's still more cost-effective. And Curtis considers the remainders loss-leaders. Get readers to sample his writing for five bucks and then they might pay regular price for the next one. But POD eliminates impulse buys."

"How?"

"They're usually not in stock. Might be a five to ten day lag time."

"Even for the big chains?"

"Curtis says they're notorious for not keeping POD titles on the shelves."

"How long's he planning to be in Paris?"

"Your guess is as good as mine." She cast her eyes down at her half-eaten meal. "I'm afraid we've grown apart the past few years."

"Sorry." Mullins took another bite of steak, signaling he would ask no more questions about Curtis Jordan.

Later, he stood in the solarium off the living room with a cup of decaf in his hand. As he stared down at the traffic on Connecticut Avenue, he thought somewhere within easy driving distance, Asu held Zaina and Jamila Khoury hostage. Why?

Light footsteps sounded behind him. He felt an arm reach around his waist.

"Stay with me, Rusty," Amanda whispered. "You can have Curtis' room. I'll find you a clean shirt in the morning."

"I really shouldn't."

Amanda stifled a sob. "I don't want you to be alone. Not tonight. Not until this is over. You're safe here. You said the reporter had you on his computer. I feel responsible for getting you in this mess."

"You? I'd have gone after Luguire's murderer anyway."

"No. I'm responsible because I recommended you as Luguire's bodyguard. I thought you'd get along."

"You know me too well." Mullins took the final sip of his coffee. "All right, Amanda."

She stood on her tiptoes and kissed his cheek. "Thank you."

On the sidewalk below, Curtis Jordan waited in the shadows. He saw the two silhouettes in the window four stories above him. Betrayed by a kiss, he thought.

He walked up Appleton to his SUV. Mullins was going nowhere and Jordan would spend the night at the Hay-Adams Hotel on Sixteenth Street. But first he would pay a visit to Mullins' apartment. Turnabout was fair play.

At eleven, Mullins said good night and retired to the second bedroom. Amanda would make sure he was up by five-thirty so that they'd be at the Federal Reserve building by seven.

Mullins stripped to his boxers and crawled between the cool sheets. Maybe it was thirty minutes, maybe forty-five before he began drifting toward sleep.

He heard footsteps, bare this time on the hardwood floor. The bedroom door rattled, but he'd locked the knob. Two gentle raps, then silence for a few seconds. Mullins kept his breathing rhythmic, adding a light snore.

The sound of departing footsteps faded down the hall.

Chapter Forty-three

Mullins let the hot water pound the back of his neck. He showered to stimulate circulation to his brain more than to wash his body. For the final two minutes, he turned off the hot water and stood under a cold spray till the invigorating assault took his breath away.

Refreshed and revitalized, he wrapped a towel around his waist and returned to the bedroom. Amanda sat on the edge of the mattress. She wore a powder blue bathrobe cinched tightly at the waist. Mullins crossed to the opposite side of the bed.

"Why didn't you wake me?" she asked.

"It wasn't five-thirty yet."

"That's when I was going to wake you." She laughed. "I wanted to see if you slept with your gun."

He nodded to the Glock on the nightstand. "Not exactly in the bed, but close enough for pillow talk."

She stood and faced him. "While you were in the shower, I hung your suit pants in the closet hoping some of the wrinkles might fall out of them. You'll find a clean white shirt beside them. I folded your dirty one and left it there." She pointed to the shirt on the corner of the rosewood dresser.

"Thanks."

An alarm sounded from the front bedroom.

"Five-thirty," Amanda said. "So it begins, and God only knows how long it will last."

When he heard the shower running in the master bathroom, Mullins pulled his suit pants from the closet. He checked through all the pockets, the waistband, and the cuffs. Nothing was amiss. He examined the dress shirt Amanda had pulled from her husband's wardrobe. It was still in the protective covering of the cleaners. The sleeves were crossed over the front and held in place with a plastic clip. Mullins looked under the collar. Insertable stainless steel stays kept it firmly in place. He scrutinized each of the two stays carefully but could see no sign they were more than they appeared.

His dirty shirt still had his cheap plastic stays. He removed the metal ones from the clean shirt and went to the corner of the bedroom where he'd left his shoes. They had been moved slightly. He took a deep breath and then picked them up one at a time. To his relief, the fresh glue of the soles was undisturbed.

Zaina felt Jamila's bony elbow jab her in the back. The child pushed away, whimpering in her sleep. She'd tossed and turned most of the night, keyed up by the promise of seeing her father.

Asu had made Zaina lay out Jamila's best dress. He said Fares was meeting them at a special event the next afternoon. A Fourth of July celebration with other families whose homes had been returned. The children were bringing gifts to exchange.

Zaina opened her eyes. The digits on the bedside clock read 5:35. Without moving her head, she shifted her gaze to the figure in the chair by the motel room door. Asu sat motionless, staring at her through half-closed eyes.

He smiled and the glow of the clock tinged his teeth red.

Sidney Levine sat in his room at the Courtyard Marriott in Crystal City just across the Potomac from D.C. He'd checked in after midnight, after Colleen had left the recovery room following a four-hour operation. The surgeon said she was lucky. The bullet barely missed the heart and aorta, and if Sidney had arrived ten minutes later, she would have probably bled out. Sidney heard only one thing: Colleen had been saved by luck. There was no question in his mind that the intruder had intended to kill her.

Sidney channeled his anger into the assignment Mullins gave him. He studied the electronic gear on the desk in front of him. The GPS device seemed straight forward enough. The audio monitor would have to be adjusted on the fly, although the automatic gain was supposed to respond to voice-level changes within a few milliseconds. Despite the trauma of the previous day and only three-hours sleep, Sidney's reservoir of energy had never been stronger. He was actually going to do something that would have an impact, something that would provide him with the greatest story of his life.

He rechecked the charges on both installed batteries and the spares, and then he repacked everything in the briefcase. He checked his watch. 5:45. Detective Sullivan would pick him up in fifteen minutes. Sidney was ready.

◇◇◇

In the same Courtyard Marriott two floors higher, Kayli Woodson lay with her arm draped around Josh. The toddler slept soundly. She'd let him stay up and watch The Cartoon Channel till nearly ten the night before, knowing he'd sleep later in the morning.

Now she wanted to get up and pace around the room. Like her father, she thought better while moving. But she dared not wake Josh or the morning would become unbearably long trapped with a two-year-old. Kayli was agitated not only because she knew her father was in danger, but also because she was cut off from all communication. She'd removed both the battery and SIM card from her cellphone. Her dad said he'd contact Allen through military channels and tell him Kayli wouldn't be reachable until Sunday. And she wasn't to worry. She'd know when it was safe to emerge from hiding.

That meant his investigation would have a very public resolution. She would have to negotiate TV time with Josh. The Cartoon Channel wasn't known for its news coverage.

Her one regret was leaving the condominium without letting Sandy Beecham know. The two mothers often went to the Saturday morning Eastern Market in the historic Capitol Hill neighborhood of D.C. They'd buy fresh produce from local farmers and the occasional handmade craft from a favorite artisan. Kayli suspected Sandy had tried to reach her. On the morning of the Fourth of July, Eastern Market would be brimming with bargains.

What harm could possibly come from talking to Sandy just long enough to let her know she and Josh were away for the weekend.

With that thought in mind, she drifted back to sleep.

Detective Robert Sullivan sat at his kitchen table and finished his first cup of coffee. Even though his wife was out of town, he'd changed into his street clothes in the guest bedroom. He'd followed the same routine thousands of times, but never when the stakes were so high.

Sullivan had been a policeman long enough to understand something went wrong with every plan. Success usually depended upon how you reacted to the unexpected. Rusty Mullins was a smart agent, one of the best Sullivan had met. Like Mullins, Sullivan believed what they didn't know that they didn't know created the greatest vulnerability. And Sullivan was confident there was something they didn't know that they didn't know.

Would they discover it in time? If not, what would be the cost of their ignorance?

He rinsed his cup in the sink, slipped on his suit coat, and left the house. As he locked the door behind him, he wondered if the world would be changed when he returned.

Chapter Forty-four

The Federal Reserve building in Washington, D.C., was an imposing structure. The white marble exterior projected a palatial presence, a rock-solid metaphor for the power and strength of the U.S. monetary system. Even the bruising financial turmoil of the global economic crisis couldn't dislodge or even blemish a single stone. High above the mammoth doorway facing Constitution Avenue, a carved eagle perched under the Stars and Stripes, its wings extended and its gaze ever vigilant.

On Saturday morning, the Fourth of July, the Federal Reserve stood ready to receive the American public. U.S. flags lined the block—Constitution Avenue in front, C Street behind, and 20th and 21st Streets on either side.

Mullins took in the spectacle from the passenger's seat as Amanda Church drove her BMW to a reserved spot in a nearby parking garage. Mullins noted the beefed-up security; 20th and 21st streets were blocked at their intersection with Constitution Avenue. Amanda had to flash her ID in order to access 20th Street.

Constitution was such a main thoroughfare that traffic normally couldn't be rerouted, but the Federal Reserve's expanse of lawn and grounds was greatest on that side. What looked like dark copper or bronze posts rimming the sidewalk were actually barricades against any vehicle attempting to crash through the building. Security on Constitution Avenue had another advantage. The Independence Day Parade would begin at 11:45 a.m. and proceed down Constitution from 7th Street to 17th Street NW, only a few blocks away. Thru traffic would be blocked for over two hours.

Along the side streets, only the width of the sidewalk separated traffic from the marble walls. A car bomb could get close enough to inflict tremendous damage. And C Street was no better. It ran between the main Board of Governors building and a second Federal Reserve office building. Guards were posted at either end of that block, allowing only authorized vehicles to enter.

"What size crowd are you expecting?" Mullins asked.

"We honestly don't know. Since we only do group tours that have been arranged in advance, we're not on the popular circuit of tourist attractions. The parade could generate more visitors, or siphon them off. People stake out viewing spots hours ahead of time.

"The ones who walk down here will be coming specifically for the Federal Reserve or the Vietnam War Memorial across the street. Regardless, we'll be controlling admittance so that the lobby and cafeteria don't get too crowded."

Mullins turned in the seat to face her. "Cafeteria? You're feeding them?"

"No. That's the site of the main photographic exhibit. Guests will come in from Constitution Avenue."

"That's gotta be the first time that door's been opened in a while."

Amanda maneuvered into her parking spot. "Yeah. They probably had to make sure the hinges hadn't rusted shut. But it's the most impressive entrance and provides a better staging area on the lawn. We'll have water and lemonade stations set up in case the wait gets too long. Be our luck to make the efforts for good PR and then have someone die of heat stroke."

"Better than a bomb going off in the middle of the crowd."

Mullins followed Amanda as she walked to C Street. He saw twice the usual number of security police at the crosswalk. "Will you have to re-screen everyone going from building to building?"

"No. They'll come through the tunnel. The elevators to the top floor are the potential bottleneck so we'll not only control the crowd entering the lobby, we'll also control the number of people walking underneath C Street. When guests come down from the cafeteria, the elevator will stop to let them out at street level before descending to pick up a new group. Access to all the other floors has been blocked."

Mullins liked the arrangement. The Federal Reserve security team had done a good job. One way in, one way out. The photographic exhibit would line the route without anterooms or separate display areas that turned a museum into a maze more difficult to monitor. The only problem he foresaw was getting the public to leave the top floor. The cafeteria had a wall of windows and stood higher than the original Federal Reserve building in front of it. One could see across Constitution Avenue to the open land containing the Vietnam Veterans Memorial, the Reflecting Pool, and then beyond to the Jefferson Memorial.

Mullins nodded to the newer building fronting C Street. "Is there a time limit for staying up there?"

"No. But there's also no food or water available. We figure people will finish the exhibit, admire the view for a few minutes, and then leave. The door on Constitution Avenue will close at three. The public exhibit will close at four."

"Will security sweep the building afterwards?"

"Yes. But staff will be returning to the cafeteria at six."

"Why?"

"For the Fourth of July party."

Mullins stepped closer to her. "What party?"

Amanda looked at him with surprise. "There's always a Fourth of July party for staff and families. The fireworks are set off on the Mall and the cafeteria offers the best seat in the city."

"I didn't know that. I'm not a staff member. Are there presents at this party?"

"No." Her eyes widened. "You think the attack might be tonight? At the staff party?"

"Everyone's so focused on this public event that when it goes off without a hitch, you're back to business as usual."

"The terrorists would still have to gain access."

"But if it's for families, there will be children. Unfamiliar faces. Children like Jamila Khoury."

"I still don't see it," Amanda argued. "Staff and their families also come in through screening."

Mullins nodded. "Unless they're already here. Hiding from when they came in with the public three hours earlier."

For a moment, Amanda stood quietly thinking. "Okay. I know we can't dismiss the possibility. I'll pass the word. Our job doesn't change."

"That's right," Mullins said. "We stay focused on finding Zaina and Jamila. The scenario of an attack happening at a Federal Reserve family event creates roles for them, roles that might be the heart of the terrorist plot."

Amanda glanced at her watch. "It's seven-fifteen. I expect the curious who really want inside to start arriving soon. I doubt that will include Asu. He'll want to melt into a crowd, especially if he's forcing Zaina and Jamila to accompany him."

"Don't forget Chuchi," Mullins said. "They might split the mother and daughter up and try to come in separately."

"Good point. You're much better at this real world security than I am. How do you think we ought to position ourselves?"

"Let's check the setup on Constitution." Mullins headed down 21st Street.

They stopped on the sidewalk directly in front of the raised lawn terrace and the steps ascending to the great door beneath the carved eagle. Adjacent to one of the four square columns of the front facade, two technicians were setting up a podium and a PA system.

"Is there some sort of program?" Mullins asked.

"Chairman Radcliffe is going to make some welcoming remarks a few minutes before nine. Then the door will open."

Mullins frowned. "Just that once or is he welcoming people throughout the day?"

"Just the opening. He'll do the chat and greet in the lobby for a while, and then he's going to watch the parade from a viewing stand a few blocks up Constitution."

"Parade crowd control," Mullins said. "Now there's a nightmare."

"The National Park Service and D.C. police check every float and you can bet Homeland Security is walking through the crowd. The good thing is that once the parade starts, spectators might be five or six deep along the sidewalks. Hard for anyone to move without drawing attention."

"Is Radcliffe coming back for the fireworks tonight?"

"Yes. And he'll have his personal security team in place all day and through the evening."

Mullins turned his back to the Federal Reserve and surveyed Constitution Gardens, the tree-dotted land across Constitution Avenue. The space was open enough and the vegetation sparse enough that any sniper would be easily spotted. Maybe from a vehicle would be a threat, but there were no parking spaces offering a line of fire. Food and souvenir vending carts on the sidewalks had all been screened.

"Have the security teams seen pictures of Chuchi and the Khourys?" Mullins asked.

"Yes. Everyone was briefed yesterday, and they've been instructed not to flash the photos around. Not worth the chance Asu could be tipped off."

Mullins faced the building again. "Okay. I'll stay out here. Less chance of running into any of my Prime Protection colleagues. Why don't you float near the tunnel? If I miss them outside and the screeners don't pick them up inside the door, you'll be where the narrowing passageway should make it easier to spot them."

"And how should we stay in touch?"

Mullins pulled the pre-paid cellphone from his pocket. "At this point, I may as well burn the minutes. You're supposed to be here anyway, so if they track your location, it won't cause an alarm. We'll talk only if there's a major development."

"Don't be a hero. Call for help at the first sign of something suspicious."

"You too."

By eight-thirty, the temperature had climbed into the eighties. Mullins felt perspiration trickling down his back and under his arms. He wanted to remove his suit coat and sling it over his shoulder, but the holster under his left arm would be visible and unnerve the security officers more than it would the tourists. They'd just think he was some kind of guard.

The crowd around the Federal Reserve steps numbered between one hundred fifty and two hundred. A greater number strolled past on their way to secure prime spots for the parade. Watching little Tommy from Nebraska march by playing his trombone was a greater priority than entering the hallowed halls of the U.S. monetary system.

Mullins stood off to the side near the sculpture of what he took to be a large greenish bowl. The artwork and bordering shrubbery gave him some shade and some cover.

He tensed as he saw Chairman Radcliffe emerge from the door and walk to the podium. Mullins made a quick visual sweep of the area, reverting instinctively to his mode of presidential protection. His rule was not to watch the president but watch the people watching the president. Scan the faces for any sign that called for a split-second reaction—a split-second between life and death.

He noticed others do the same—turn away from the podium and search the crowd and nearby tree line. Radcliffe's security team stood on full alert, and Mullins had no doubt it included a number of ex-Secret Service agents.

He let them do their job and returned his attention to Chairman Hugh Radcliffe.

"Good morning." Radcliffe's baritone voice echoed across the lawn.

At six-three, with steely gray hair and wearing a dark blue suit and muted gold tie, Radcliffe looked as solid and reliable as the building behind him. He could have had a successful career in politics. He was a Vietnam War veteran who led his platoon through a hellacious firefight and the return trek to safety, without leaving the wounded or even two dead comrades behind. Mullins smiled to himself. Hell, who was he kidding? Radcliffe was in politics. Like everyone else in this town.

"Welcome to your Federal Reserve. On behalf of the Board of Governors, the twelve regional Federal Reserve Banks, and our entire staff, we are honored to share this special Fourth of July celebration with you."

Polite applause broke out. Mullins looked for groups of four, three, or two, hoping Asu, the one person without visual reference, wasn't here solo.

"I'd like to introduce two special people in my life—my daughter Katrina and granddaughter Helena."

Mullins took a closer look. He'd noticed the attractive brunette standing beside Radcliffe but hadn't seen a little girl. He still couldn't find her.

"Today is a very special day for Helena. Her fifth birthday. Yes, she was born on the Fourth of July. So, in honor of our country's birthday, I've asked Helena to open the door for us all."

Mullins saw that during the chairman's remarks the door had been closed again.

"I'll admit that the door looks imposing," Radcliffe continued, "but our goal is to open the door of financial opportunity for everyone."

The second round of applause was louder. Radcliffe stepped toward the door. A girl in a flowery print sundress clung to his hand. Mullins realized she'd been blocked from his view by the angle of the podium. She grasped the latch, and by pre-arranged signal, the door swung open. As she, her mother, and the chairman entered, security officers fanned out to shepherd the visitors inside to the screening devices ready to clear them through.

Mullins relaxed. If an exterior assault was planned, the best opportunity had passed.

He mingled with the crowd on the lawn and checked new pedestrians as they came from the sidewalks. After the first thirty minutes, one of the Federal Reserve security officers grew suspicious that Mullins didn't join the line. As the man approached, Mullins broke his promise to his boss and flashed his Prime Protection ID. The man nodded, and from then on, no one bothered him.

The time neared eleven-thirty. If the theory of a coordinated attack at noon Eastern time was true, then some element, a truck, a van, a suicide bomber must be moving into place. The stream of visitors was steady, but not overwhelming. The lemonade and water stations kept people hydrated, and the wait to enter hovered between fifteen and twenty minutes. That meant the perpetrator of an interior attack would need to be in line within the next five to ten minutes.

His cellphone rang.

"Something's happening. Meet me at the car now." Amanda spoke the two sentences calmly, but her understated tone made them all the more ominous.

Mullins headed toward C Street. "Copy that." As he dropped his phone in his coat pocket, he noticed the exterior security team still patrolling the lawn. He could see from the signs in their posture and movements that there was no heightened alert. "I'm meeting Amanda at her car," he said to no one around him. "Whatever's going down must be offsite. Repeat, offsite."

Amanda intercepted him at the entrance to the parking garage. She hooked his right arm with her left and steered him to a different row of vehicles. "It's Radcliffe. He's the thirteenth target. We're taking a Federal Reserve car."

"Why?"

Amanda opened the driver's door to a white Ford Taurus. "Get in. I'll explain on the way."

"Tell me now or I'm not going."

Amanda's face hardened. She looked across the roof to a gray cargo van parked behind Mullins.

Mullins turned as a slender man in a pale blue linen sport coat stepped around the van's rear bumper. He had jet black hair and dark, piercing eyes.

"You heard the lady, Mr. Mullins. Get in the car."

Mullins heard the accent, Mid-Eastern and probably Syrian. He saw the semi-automatic pistol leveled at his chest.

He smiled. "Hello, Asu."

Chapter Forty-five

Mullins turned to Amanda. "So, you're a traitor. That doesn't surprise me as much as seeing you hooked up with this piece of shit."

"We're doing what we're doing to save this country." Amanda drew her own pistol. She looked at Asu. "He's got a Glock under his left arm. That's it."

"What about a wire?" Asu asked.

"No. I made sure he's clean."

"Stripping me down to a towel and hanging up my clothes," Mullins said. "How far were you willing to go, Amanda?"

"As far as I had to."

Asu stepped closer. "Arms out to the side."

Mullins obeyed.

Asu snatched the Glock from Mullins' holster and stuck it in the waistband in the back of his slacks. "He's been out of your sight this morning. I'm patting him down." Asu ran his hands across Mullins' chest, sides, and the inseam of each leg.

"You're wasting time," Amanda urged. "We can't stand here all day. Someone will see us. Radcliffe will be on the move soon."

"Sure we can," Mullins said. "I'm not getting in the car."

"I think you are," Amanda said. "Unless you not only want to sacrifice your life but also the lives of your daughter and grandson."

Mullins felt his knees tremble, and he knew as calm as he tried to be, the telltale pallor of his face convinced them they'd gained the upper hand. "This is what you did to Luguire, isn't it? Threatened his family. Well, I don't believe you. I sent Kayli into hiding."

"Right. And I'm sure you told her not to say a word to anyone. But, she did worry about disappearing without telling her neighbor and best friend Sandy Beecham. And you know Don Beecham. He works at the Federal Reserve with me. He also works for me in what you might call extracurricular activities."

"You're lying," Mullins said.

"Is that a risk you want to take? Asu, give him back his phone. If he says anything, shoot him."

Mullins took the phone.

"Call your daughter, but don't speak."

Mullins scanned the recent dials, highlighted her cell number, and pressed send.

A man answered. "Mr. Mullins, we have your daughter and grandson." His high voice sounded strained, like he was nervous. The inflection of the words had all the naturalness of a bad actor cold-reading a script.

Mullins pulled the phone from his ear and activated the speaker. He turned it around so that Asu and Amanda could hear.

"They are all right and will stay that way as long as you do exactly as you're told."

"I want to talk to Kayli," Mullins silently mouthed to Amanda.

She shook her head. "The word ketamine should explain why. Evidently your daughter was quite feisty."

Mullins heard the click as the connection broke.

Asu grabbed the phone. "Now get in the car."

"All right. But a Taurus is quite a comedown from a BMW." Mullins opened the passenger door without taking his eyes off Asu. "So, where's the party?"

Mullins saw Asu's eyes flicker with surprise, the first visible emotion during their encounter.

"The wrapping paper," Amanda told Asu. "Just one of your screw-ups."

Asu took the backseat behind Mullins. He pressed the muzzle of his pistol against Mullins' ear. "Look straight ahead. Any sudden move, any attempt to signal for help and you're a dead man."

"You still haven't answered my question. Where's the party?"

"You'll know when you need to know."

Amanda backed the Taurus out of the space. "Relax, Asu. He's not going anywhere, and he's not going to cause any trouble." She exited the garage and skirted the security checkpoints by looping away from Constitution Avenue.

Mullins sat motionless, waiting for Amanda to fill the silence. He knew she'd have to justify her actions.

"Our country is facing the greatest crisis since the Civil War. And only a few of us know it."

"So, you infiltrated the Federal Reserve in an attempt to destroy it," he said.

"No. To save it. These lunatics who want to abolish the Federal Reserve have no idea of the consequences. Can you see us going back to the gold standard? Can you see Congress dealing with international monetary policy? Those assholes can't even agree on a domestic budget let alone make the decisions that safeguard Western Civilization." Anger rose in her voice and she turned to glare at him. "In 2008 our country nearly collapsed while Congress played partisan politics. Decisions were made fast because they could be made fast and had to be made fast."

"Would you watch the road," Mullins said. "A wreck on 23rd Street isn't a good idea, not with Mr. Trigger Finger behind me."

"Sit back, Asu," Amanda ordered. "And keep your gun down."

Mullins loosened his tie. "You expect me to believe proponents of the Federal Reserve sanctioned an operation to blow up the regional banks?"

She smiled. "You disappoint me, Rusty. Why would we totally destroy an institution we're trying to protect? Richmond will be enough."

"There are no other bombs?"

"We just needed you to think there were. You were a good agent, and if you believed a nationwide plot existed, you'd understand the need for secrecy, particularly if I told you I was coordinating everything with Rudy Hauser and Secret Service."

"You never spoke to Hauser? You never alerted him to a bombing plot?"

"No. I did my job helping troubleshoot security here. And it was excellent, don't you think?"

"Are we headed to Richmond? Do you need me in proximity?"

"We'd never make it. The timer's set for noon. About twenty minutes. And you'll be busy here. Don't worry. We're not monsters. It's a holiday so casualties in Richmond will be light."

"Where's the bomb?" Mullins asked.

"Where it needs to be. Khoury will be linked to it. He brings the right credentials, a disgruntled Muslim victimized by the subprime mortgage meltdown. An Islamophobic nation will see him as another Arab terrorist with links to Al Qaida. His journal will be discovered detailing his acquisitions for a bomb."

"Why kill him?"

"He was too unstable to do more than create a paper trail. Khoury's body will never be discovered, and the country will be consumed with tracking him down."

"And then there's me. I feel flattered. Am I to be the mastermind?"

"I also knew you'd not turn loose of Luguire's death until you had answers. Better to have your motivation working for us rather than against us. Your investigation created a trail that can be read as if you were leading the parade, not following it."

"And the money flowing through Laurel Bank and Craig Archer?"

"They'll be traced to an account with ties to funding for Occupy Wall Street and, of course, a big payday for you."

"Creative. Associate the protesters with Al Qaida and an attack on an American institution on the Fourth of July."

"If you want to unite people, give them a common enemy. An attack on the Fed will snuff out the cries to abolish the Fed. Otherwise, you're suddenly un-American."

"And snuff out a voice for moderation and transparency," Mullins added. "Chairman Hugh Radcliffe is your sacrificial lamb, isn't he?"

She shrugged. "You know what has to happen when you're making an omelette."

"Breaking shells is one thing, murder is something else. And Asu is nothing more than a glorified hit man. For whom? This is no dark ops mission, no matter how desperate some American government officials or financiers might be. And it's too well planned. Multinational, I assume."

"The nation-state is an antiquated concept, Rusty. It's like rooting for a sports team. You can be a player, you can be a coach, or you can be in the stands, but it's the owners who are in control. There are owners, so deeply buried in the fabric of their societies as to be virtually invisible and thereby untouchable."

"Absolute power corrupts absolutely."

"Maybe. When it's power for the sake of power. But when it's for the cause of political stability, for the semblance of economic vitality, and for the maintenance of social order, then in the grand scheme how can actions be corrupt when the consequences are for good?"

"And you've been working for these consequences for how long?"

"Since before I joined Treasury. We didn't know how the story would play out, but we knew we needed to be in position to control the ending."

Amanda exited off the Lincoln Memorial Circle onto Henry Bacon Drive NW.

"Henry Bacon? Are we going right back to the Fed?"

"No. We have some reserve parking. I made arrangements although the request will be backtracked to Prime Protection." She maneuvered around traffic cones set up on the shoulder of the road. "Supposedly for security vehicles as back up to Radcliffe's protection. The investigation will conclude you requested them."

"You're going after Radcliffe where? The parade?"

"Too far away. Too unpredictable. Too crowded for our courier to get close."

Mullins noticed they'd parked just off the Lincoln Memorial Circle behind a blue Honda van. He saw a stocky Hispanic man get out and open the side door for a woman and little girl. The Hispanic man then grabbed a cloth bag from the passenger's seat. Protruding over the edge were several rosebuds and the corner of a box wrapped in pink and green paper.

"Khoury's family," Mullins said. "You're using them." His mind raced. "The Vietnam Memorial Wall. The names of Radcliffe's men killed in action. My God, Amanda, it's monstrous."

"No. It's regrettable. But your daughter and grandson will be all right. You have my word. Killing them would gain us nothing."

"Only because it would go against my motivation. A mercenary killing for money reads better to a paranoid public than a man who was trying to save his family. That theme's a little too common in this drama. First, Luguire. Then, Fares Khoury. And now me."

"This is maximum impact. A controlled explosion with a specific damage radius. The wall will project the blast in one direction only. No more collateral damage than necessary. Something our military negotiates every day. The stakes here are even higher."

Asu opened the rear door. "I've got to give Chuchi final instructions. Keep him here until you see them head for the memorial."

"Amanda," Mullins pleaded.

"Shut up."

"How do you know Radcliffe will even come? The Richmond bomb has to create some kind of lockdown."

"Give me some credit, Rusty. Timing is everything. Radcliffe will be here first. Even if the Richmond bomb is discovered, the Fed's confident of their D.C. security measures. Radcliffe might be convinced to skip the parade, but he'll never skip honoring his comrades. And he wants his granddaughter to see what sacrifice and courage are all about. No press or photo op. Just a private moment. And all we need is ten seconds for one little girl to give another little girl a birthday present."

"And Chuchi?"

"He thinks Fares Khoury is going to show up. Asu believes Chuchi's feeling sympathy for the mother and daughter. Better to give him the same story."

◇◇◇

A few blocks away on 23rd Street between Constitution and the Lincoln Memorial Circle, Sidney Levine looked up from the digital audio recorder and radio receiver in his lap. "What the hell do we do?"

"Now that Richmond's alerted we get to that bomb." Sullivan slapped his two-way mike into the holder. He wheeled his Crown Vic in a sharp left turn, jumped the concrete divider and cut in front of two lanes of oncoming traffic. He drove over the curb and churned across the open park grass toward the intersection of Henry Bacon Drive and Constitution Avenue. He grabbed a magnetic-based blue police light from under the dash and slapped it on the roof. Pedestrian tourists sauntered along, forcing Sullivan to lay on the horn.

"Jesus, man," Sidney shouted. "If Asu sees us, he'll detonate."

"They're at the other end. Mullins will keep them distracted."

◇◇◇

Mullins never took his eyes from the front of the van where Asu spoke to Chuchi while the mother and little girl waited. After a few minutes, the three started walking across the grass toward the memorial. Mullins had no doubt Chuchi carried a gun in the pocket of his tan sport coat. He heard band music in the distance. The parade had begun. The music would grow louder as bands and floats from across the nation honored the spirit of America, unaware that on nearby sacred ground a new sacrifice was only moments away.

Asu hurried back to the Taurus.

"Let's go. We need to move him to the van."

"What's in the green and pink box?" Mullins asked. "C-4?"

"Get out of the car now!"

Mullins stood. Amanda emerged from the driver's side and walked around the front of the car to join them.

Mullins turned to face her. "It's over, Amanda. You should have let Asu do a better job of searching me."

"What are you talking about?"

"I'm wearing a wire."

Asu shifted nervously. His left hand went into his coat pocket and he pulled out an electronic car key without a real key attached. "You said he was clean."

"He was. I went through his clothes."

"But you missed two collar stays hidden in the sole of my shoe and a GPS tracker in the heel. Very careless."

"He's bluffing," Amanda said.

Mullins studied Asu's face. A slight twitch appeared in his temple. The ice blood in his veins started heating up.

"No," Mullins said. "You're the ones bluffing. I trust that my daughter never disobeyed my instructions. I'm betting you've set up an intercept on her number. You certainly have money to buy whatever resources you need."

Asu shot a glance at Amanda. Mullins felt the knot in his stomach relax. He had guessed correctly.

"So, sacrificing the little girl who thinks she's bringing a Cinderella Castle to a celebration is quite pointless. It will only guarantee your execution."

Amanda glared at Asu. "You idiot. They've been following you."

The Crown Vic came to Henry Bacon Drive. Vehicles were bumper to bumper, backed up from the light at the intersection with Constitution and blocking Sullivan's cross-country shortcut. He slammed on the brakes and grass tore free under the skidding tires. With the car still in motion, Sidney jumped from the passenger's side and nearly tumbled head over heels as he fought to keep his balance. Then he darted into the traffic.

◇◇◇

Over Amanda's shoulder, Mullins saw a Crown Vic brake to a stop on the grass near the far end of Henry Bacon Drive. Sidney Levine sprang from the passenger seat. Then Detective Sullivan started driving toward them. "Stay back," Mullins said.

As Sullivan's car stopped, Asu stepped forward. "No. I'll see for myself." He reached under Mullins' chin and ripped the collar open. Two metal stays fell out. A thin wire stretched between them.

◇◇◇◇

Sidney darted between the bumpers as he squeezed across the four lanes of Henry Bacon Drive. He headed toward the north side of the Vietnam Memorial, nearest the Federal Reserve. If only he could intercept Radcliffe first and then take care of the bomb. He jumped over the permanent chain and stanchion barrier beside a sign reading, "Honor Those Who Served. Please Stay On Sidewalk." Ahead of him in the distance rose the Washington Monument. He angled across the grass to where the Wall rose to ground level. He jumped three feet down to the memorial's walkway, startling those searching for names engraved on the tapered end. A man cursed his disrespect, but Sidney hurried on. He saw flowers strewn along the downward sloping base and veterans stooping as they sought to touch the names of fallen warriors. Toward the center where the two black granite wings met at their deepest point, he saw the back of a tall man walking slowing along the litany of the dead, holding the hand of a small girl beside him. The man and girl stopped. Other men Sidney took for protective guards backed away, offering a small degree of privacy in the very public place. No one else at the Wall paid the man and girl any attention. They were lost in their own memories.

Then Jamila stepped from behind her mother, her thin arms extended as she walked forward, shyly holding the package in front of her.

◇◇◇

Mullins stepped back against the car. "In case you can't see, Amanda, it's a microphone, battery, and transmitter. Prime

Protection's first class when it comes to electronics. You'll remember I mentioned each road as we doubled back here."

Asu stared at the collar stays, eyes wide as he replayed their conversation in his mind.

"Give me the detonator, Asu. There's no money for you. You can bet as soon as you detonate that bomb from the van, Amanda shoots you, and then me. She bags the Syrian terrorist and the mastermind. And she'll be so upset that she arrived a split-second too late to avert the tragedy."

Helena let go of her grandfather's hand, her eyes on the present. It was her birthday. Was this a surprise party? Her grandfather said he was showing her a very special place. Without hesitation, she stepped toward the younger girl.

Chuchi saw the man running down the walkway toward them. He was coming too soon. Asu said Fares Khoury would make his appearance when the granddaughter of the man who helped him received the present from Jamila. Chuchi was supposed to text the cue. But this wasn't Zaina's husband. He wasn't Lebanese. Instinctively, Chuchi stepped in front of Zaina, protecting her as Jamila handed the package to the other girl.

Sidney ran past one of the security detail who hesitated, unsure what to do. As Helena reached for her gift, Sidney snatched it from the hands of both girls. "Bomb," he gasped, and then struggled to refill his lungs. He ran up the second wing without changing direction, ran as fast as he could, desperately looking for any place clear of people.

"Bomb." Chuchi heard the word and knew the truth. He reached for Jamila, yanking her backwards.

"Get down," he yelled, and forced Jamila and Zaina to the ground. He spread his body over them. Just before he closed his eyes, he saw other men shove the man and his granddaughter down beside them.

◇◇◇

Time slowed for Mullins. While Asu stared down at the wired collar stays, Mullins saw Sidney run from behind the Wall, the package in both hands. He saw Sullivan jump out of the Crown Vic and yell something that was swallowed up by the sound of brass and drums rolling across the Mall. From the corner of his eye, Mullins saw the giant head of Uncle Sam, a parade balloon floating above the trees. He watched Sidney turn toward Sullivan and run for a spot where the detective pointed. Sullivan continued yelling, and people in the vicinity scattered for safety.

"You stupid bitch!" Asu's scream jerked Mullins back to the fury of the man in front of him.

Asu pulled his pistol from his pocket.

Amanda brought her gun up and fired. The bullet struck Asu in the left side of his chest, spinning him around as he was knocked backwards. He landed facedown, his left hand trapped under his body.

◇◇◇

Sidney stumbled off the curb and crouched by the storm drain. He shoved the package into the hole in the curb. Then he jumped up and turned toward Mullins.

◇◇◇

The ground shook. A fireball blew upward and manhole covers along the road flew into the air like giant Frisbees. The concussion from the explosion hit with the force of a sledgehammer. Mullins and Amanda fell to the ground. Amanda twisted around to see what might be hurtling toward them.

Mullins grabbed his pistol from Asu's waistband.

Amanda turned back to him.

Mullins shot her through the forehead.

Part Three
The Clean-Up

Chapter Forty-six

Mullins rolled Asu's body over. Not trusting the open eyes, he felt the Syrian's carotid artery for a pulse. No trace of a heartbeat. The breeze blew a cloud of concrete dust from the explosion and created a mini sandstorm in the heart of Washington. Mullins squinted against the grit and crawled to Amanda. The lack of blood flowing from the head wound told him death had been instantaneous.

He left the gun in her hand and searched her pockets. All he found was her cellphone. It was all he wanted.

He staggered through the blinding cloud, dodging chunks of pavement and cement spewed along the ground. Halfway to the epicenter of the blast, he discovered Sidney Levine's body. The explosion had hurled him at least fifty feet. The back of the reporter's head had been crushed, probably by a piece of flying concrete. Mullins knelt beside him. There was nothing to be done. "You did more than something to make it right, Sidney. A hell of a lot more."

Mullins found Detective Sullivan sitting on the road beside the Crown Vic. The car's front windshield had been blown out. Miraculously, the stoplight had changed at the intersection of Henry Bacon Drive and Constitution, allowing the jammed street to clear only seconds before the explosion. The detective struggled to get up, and Mullins suspected he'd been momentarily stunned by the blast.

Mullins helped Sullivan to his feet. Blood flowed through his thin gray hair and from his right cheek and forehead. The wounds appeared to be superficial cuts from the debris.

"Richmond," Mullins yelled, his ears still ringing from the blast.

Sullivan took a deep breath and then choked on the dust. "I radioed as soon as I heard," he managed to say. "Sidney?"

Mullins shook his head. "No. He was too close. But he saved a lot of lives."

Sullivan coughed again and grabbed the open car door for support. "We heard everything up until they found the wire."

"Was it recorded?"

"Yes." Sullivan looked back at the front passenger seat where a Zoom H4 recorder sat covered with shards of safety glass. "Sidney bolted for the package as soon as we arrived. I couldn't stop him. He was a man possessed. An unlikely hero, but a hero all the same."

"We'll see he gets the credit he deserves. Now listen, is your head clear enough to follow instructions?"

"Yeah. I'm okay."

Mullins pushed past Sullivan, reached across the steering wheel, and picked up the recorder. In the distance, the sounds of wailing sirens grew louder.

"I'm going to take this. The situation's still dangerous and I need to make copies as soon as I can."

"Okay."

"You got a pen and paper?"

Sullivan fumbled in his suit coat pocket. "Yes."

"Give them to me."

Sullivan handed Mullins a notepad and ballpoint.

Mullins started writing. "This number is for my daughter's cell phone. I believe they've routed it to a phone on Chuchi. He probably escaped and is now one of a hundred thousand on the Mall. But the techs should be able to use the signal to locate him."

"Okay."

"I want you to tell the authorities, whether it's FBI or Radcliffe's security detail that you need to speak to Rudy Hauser, Deputy Director of the Secret Service, and you'll talk to no one else. Tell them you, Sidney, and I uncovered a plot against the Chairman and the Federal Reserve that we only disrupted at the last moment. It involved a rogue Federal Reserve employee, Amanda Church, and a terrorist network. Amanda shot her partner, and then I killed her in self-defense. The scene matches those facts. That story should get you to Rudy Hauser immediately, but don't tell him about the recording."

"What do I say about you?"

"Tell them I'm pursuing Chuchi."

"What are you really doing?"

"Cleaning up. And I don't want to be inconvenienced by things like the law." He pointed across the devastated street to the blue Honda minivan. "Stand guard over Amanda and Asu's bodies. I'm sure Radcliffe's protection detail is holding Khoury's wife and daughter. I'll be back in touch."

Mullins ran to the white Taurus. The Honda had shielded it from the worst of the explosion. Mullins saw blue and red lights flashing as emergency and police vehicles raced toward him. He found the keys in the ignition. The engine roared to life. He backed up, swung the car in a tight circle, and headed toward the Lincoln Memorial. To his right, he saw a black SUV cut across the grass toward the Rock Creek and Potomac Parkway, the opposite direction from every other government and emergency vehicle.

Mullins reached Memorial Bridge and sped across the Potomac to Arlington, leaving chaos and confusion in his wake.

Chapter Forty-seven

Kayli Woodson saw the "Breaking News" banner flash on the screen of the television in the Courtyard Marriott's lobby. She and Josh were returning to their room after lunch at Cafe Pizzaiolo in Crystal City a few blocks away. She stopped and lifted Josh, clutching him tightly as she stepped closer to hear the report.

A newsman stood in front of the Vietnam Veterans Memorial in Constitution Gardens. The polished black granite wall seemed dull and tinged with grime.

"First responders state a bomb exploded in a storm drain in Henry Bacon Drive just blocks from Constitution Avenue and the Independence Day parade." The reporter practically shouted the words into his microphone, he was so excited. "The blast left one person dead and fifteen injured with multiple cuts and lacerations. Three of the fifteen are listed in serious condition. Fortunately, the area at the far edge of Constitution Gardens was relatively clear, with the majority of tourists concentrated along the parade route that ends more than five blocks away. However, I've learned that at the time of the explosion, Federal Reserve Chairman Hugh Radcliffe and his granddaughter were placing flowers at the Vietnam Veterans Memorial behind me. Early speculation suggests Chairman Radcliffe might have been the target, but the shelter of the Wall actually shielded him and others from the brunt of the blast."

Radcliffe's name and words "one dead" sent an icy chill to the pit of Kayli's stomach. "God, no. Not Dad." She stepped closer.

"It's believed that the fatality was a citizen who raced away from the Wall carrying a wrapped package. Why he suspected the package isn't known, but there's no doubt many families owe this courageous man a debt of incalculable gratitude."

Kayli felt hot tears on her cheeks.

"His name is being withheld pending notification of next of kin, but witnesses describe him as Caucasian, slightly overweight, and in his late thirties or early forties."

Relief poured through Kayli's body. She nearly collapsed as the tension that had been holding her erect dissipated.

"The unknown hero might have been accompanied by two other men, at least one of which is rumored to be in law enforcement. Whether local or federal is not clear, but he was seen talking to authorities and then driven away. There are also unconfirmed reports that a bomb was discovered in a van near the Federal Reserve Bank in Richmond, Virginia, and defused only moments before a timed detonation. As I stated earlier, two gunshot fatalities were also found at the scene, a man and a woman, and their deaths are considered a part of what appears to be a coordinated terrorist attack."

Kayli's fear rushed back tenfold. An unidentified man shot. She heard her father's voice. "I've got two sidekicks, a detective hours away from retirement and a washed-up reporter." The reporter had to be the bomb victim, the detective was the man driven away, and the man shot to death?

She struggled to breathe as she carried Josh to the elevator. She had to call her father. His orders didn't matter now.

Mullins took I-395 South to his Shirlington exit. As anxious as he was to confirm that Kayli and Josh were safe, he dared not call if her number was routed to Chuchi. Instead he set the pre-paid on the seat beside him, ready to grab it on the first ring. Only Kayli and Sullivan had the number.

He parked the Taurus in the lot of his apartment building and sat for a few minutes, collecting his thoughts. The news on the radio was devoted exclusively to the Constitution Gardens explosion and Richmond bomb. Thankfully, only Sidney had died. It sounded like Sullivan successfully contacted federal authorities on the scene and had been taken into protective custody. Mullins knew the search would begin for him if he didn't surface soon. He didn't have much time.

The phone rang. He didn't recognize the number.

"Yes," he answered.

"Dad!" Kayli broke down, unable to control her sobs.

"I'm okay, dear. Are you all right?"

"Yes. I was so worried."

"It's almost over. Are you calling from a room phone?"

"Yes."

"I want you to stay there till I call again."

"Okay."

"Don't let anybody in."

"I understand."

"Kayli, did you speak to Sandy Beecham?"

"No. I thought about it, but you said no contact."

"Good girl. Do you know what they were doing today?"

"Yeah. Having a picnic this afternoon with friends in Reston. Then they were coming into D.C. to the Federal Reserve to watch the fireworks."

"Glad to hear it."

"Why?"

"Nothing, dear. Just trying to account for everyone who's close to us." He thought a moment. "The news of the explosion has probably gone international. Use the house phone to contact Allen and tell him we're all right. And tell him to check his email several times over the next hour."

"For what?"

"Just give him the message. I'll explain later. I've got to go. Tell Josh I love him, and I love you."

"Love you too, Dad. Please be careful."

"Always."

He got out of the Taurus and looked around the parking lot. There were plenty of spaces since many residents were gone for the holiday weekend. His Prius was probably still on Appleton at Amanda's co-op. Part of the plan would have been to move it, probably back to his apartment so the authorities would assume he'd been dropped off at the Federal Reserve building by Asu. Amanda would have claimed to have seen him and become suspicious. She'd followed him to the Honda but been unable to stop the attack in time.

Mullins walked through the lot, double checking for his car. If it was already there, then Mullins knew additional conspirators were involved in D.C. because too many vehicles were being shuttled for just Asu and Chuchi to handle. The Prius was nowhere to be found.

Mullins took the back entrance to his building and climbed the stairs to the fourth floor. He stopped at his door and examined the deadbolt. Minute scratches were visible around the key slot. Someone had used picks not unlike his own to gain access to his apartment.

He found the gun under a cushion of the sofa. The blood-splattered manila envelope lay on a shelf in his bedroom closet and Khoury's journal was buried beneath a ream of paper by his printer. Mullins donned a pair of gloves and put the three incriminating items in a paper bag.

The planted evidence would have worked. The blood on the envelope was no doubt that of Craig Archer. The gun would match a ballistics test with the bullet that killed him, and if Fares' body was ever discovered, that bullet as well. Mullins didn't know how they planned to get his prints on the gun, but that didn't matter. If the gun was wiped clean, that would be suspicious, and Archer's blood would cinch the case.

Mullins removed his gloves and took the Zoom H4 recorder to his computer. He connected the two with a USB cable and saw only one mp3 file on the recorder's data card. Sidney hadn't stopped the recorder once it started. In less than thirty seconds, he copied the audio onto his hard drive, disconnected the cable, and extracted the H4's memory card. He compressed the mp3 file on his computer, uploaded it to the Dropbox account he shared with Kayli and Allen, and sent Allen an email with instructions. Then he sent the compressed file to his secure folder on Prime Protection's FTP site. Finally, he transferred a duplicate copy onto a flash drive.

He took a quick shower and put on a clean suit. Mullins felt business should always be conducted in a professional manner.

Chapter Forty-eight

Mullins figured the full ramifications of what had transpired would take a few hours to circulate through the corridors of power. When Sullivan told Rudy Hauser that a former Treasury agent had gone rogue, Hauser would want to proceed cautiously. Mullins liked Hauser, thought he was a good guy, but also knew the deputy director was an administrator whose first reaction would be to protect the president and second reaction would be to protect the Secret Service. When Hauser learned Mullins had a recording of Amanda en route to the assassination attempt, he would love to cross paths with Mullins first and to hell with the investigative jurisdiction of the FBI and Homeland Security. Mullins was banking on Hauser wanting to give him some time to pursue his leads, knowing if Mullins had sent Sullivan to him, then Mullins himself would likely follow.

Both the FBI and Homeland Security would be clamoring to question Sullivan. Hauser might be able to hold them off for a while, but he had no chance of winning. In the meantime, Hauser would immediately tighten security on President Brighton and gain access to Brighton's ear. If no further danger appeared imminent, Brighton would also agree they needed to proceed carefully if conspirators were within the government, especially the Executive Branch. The only thing more important than information was the control of that information.

Other than the existence of the recording, all these maneuvers could be anticipated. Mullins would be in place and in time because everything depended upon the desire to appear innocent.

Mullins cruised up Appleton for two blocks. He passed his Prius where he'd parked it. He was relieved that moving it away from Amanda's apartment had been planned for after the bombing. Their number of operatives was limited. He didn't see the black Tahoe he'd noticed the night before, the same model he'd seen leaving the bomb wreckage at Constitution Gardens.

He parked the Taurus around the block and walked down Albemarle Street, carrying the paper bag from his apartment. The route brought him to the alley where he could approach the entrance to the underground garage with less chance of being seen. The door stood open and he walked among the cars to the rear of the garage. No Tahoe.

A Volvo sedan pulled in and parked in a spot just inside the garage door. A young African-American woman with a large Neiman Marcus shopping bag got out. Mullins timed his walk to draw near as she opened the building's door.

"Here, let me hold that for you." Mullins grabbed the side of the door and pulled it open wider. "Your bag's bigger than mine."

She jumped at the sound of his voice, but relaxed when she saw his smile and neatly pressed suit. He let her walk on ahead and when she stopped in front of the elevator, he passed it for the stairs.

"I need the exercise. Big picnic tonight."

"Enjoy your Fourth," the woman said, and entered the elevator.

Mullins stood in the stairwell a few minutes, allowing time for the woman to reach her unit. He didn't want to run into her again.

Amanda's floor was quiet. At two in the afternoon, most people were away on holiday or inside enjoying their air conditioning. Mullins placed his bag on the floor, took his set of Peterson lock picks out of his pocket, and went to work.

◇◇◇

Curtis Jordan wheeled his suitcase across the threshold and closed and locked the door behind him. His brain raced at a speed that happened only when he was in his best writing zone, the ideas coming so fast that he didn't worry about spelling or punctuation. He just held on for the ride. Usually that occurred at the climax of a novel as events and characters cascaded to their inevitable conclusion.

But this time the challenge was greater because to be believable, his mind had to go completely blank. The shock would have to overwhelm him, leaving him speechless and nearly helpless. The irony was he had been shocked, speechless, and nearly helpless. Now he had to recapture that moment and play it back fresh.

He decided to leave the suitcase in the foyer, throw his coat over a living room chair, and forego a glass of wine for a stiff bourbon. He dropped two ice cubes in a crystal glass and went to the bar in the solarium. He poured himself a healthy shot of Maker's Mark and stirred it through the ice with a swizzle stick. He took a long drink.

"You might want to make it a double."

Jordan froze. He used the moment to transform fear into grief. Then he turned around.

"I know. I just heard about Amanda. I'm at my wit's end. Is what they're saying true? I hope you've come to tell me it's not."

Mullins stepped from the hallway into the living room. He pulled the nine millimeter semiautomatic pistol from his right coat pocket and leveled it at the author. "I've come to tell you it's over."

Jordan paled. First at the sight of the suppressor on the barrel and then at the sight of Mullins' gloved hand. "Rusty. You're making a terrible mistake. I didn't know anything about this. Amanda and I've hardly seen each other the past six months."

"Really? So that wasn't you in the Tahoe last night or at the bomb scene earlier today?"

"God, no. How many Tahoes are in this town? Yes, I rented one yesterday. I got in late from Paris and didn't want to disturb Amanda. Frankly, I wasn't sure what I'd find here."

"You would have found me. But surely she told you."

"You're crazy. Tell me she's sleeping with another man?"

"Who said we slept together?"

Jordan forced indignation in his voice. "Well, she didn't tell me anything, and I think you'd better leave. I'll chalk this whole episode up to the strain you must be under."

Mullins reached into his left coat pocket. "Fair enough."

Both men stood still for a moment. Then a buzzing sounded from Jordan's coat on the chair.

"You'd better get that," Mullins said. "But if anything other than a phone comes out of that coat, then you'll be permanently unavailable."

Jordan set his glass on the coffee table and pulled the cellphone from the inside pocket. "Hello."

"You lied." Mullins held Amanda's phone to his ear. "Amanda called you last night when she told me she was phoning Rudy Hauser. That was right after I revealed we'd discovered Asu purchased Cinderella's Castle and wrapping paper. That was a surprise to her, wasn't it? We were getting too close."

"I never talked to her. She must have dialed my number by mistake."

"Yeah, right. Sit down and let me tell you about the recording."

Jordan sat on his suit coat and dropped the phone on the carpet. "What recording?"

"I'm afraid your wife had a propensity to brag. She thought I would be dead soon, so as we rode from the Federal Reserve to Henry Bacon Drive she had to tell me how clever you and she were." Mullins reached back in his coat pocket and withdrew the flash drive. "It's all here thanks to the microphone and recording chip I substituted for the collar stays in your shirt. By the way, thanks for the loan. I'm sorry the bomb blast ruined the shirt but the recording is quite remarkable."

Jordan felt panic rising in his throat. "If that's true, why haven't you turned it over?"

"Because I think it's worth a lot of money. And I think you control a lot of money, an incredible amount of money."

A slight smile broke across Jordan's face. Here was something he could deal with. "What's your price?"

"We'll come to that. But first aren't you curious how your intricate plan went so awry?"

"I don't know about any plan." He leaned back in the chair. "But I love a good story."

Mullins took a step closer, the flash drive in one hand and the pistol in the other. "Actually it was my wife Laurie who set me on the right path."

Jordan looked confused. "Amanda told me your wife died. That's why you left the Secret Service."

"That's true. But when you really love someone, their voice is never extinguished. Laurie told me I was looking at Luguire's death upside down. That was so like Laurie to examine things from a different perspective."

"Upside down?"

"Yes. Amanda said she told Luguire about the unusual payment that went from the Richmond Federal Reserve's discount window to Laurel Bank. She claimed it triggered an alert she was beta-testing for the cyber-security of payment systems. Now I understand the payment system is a highly classified aspect of the overall Federal Reserve system. Any breach would be disastrous.

"But looking at it upside down, I thought what if Amanda hadn't come to Luguire, but Luguire had gone to her with a confidential request to look into it. Once I started thinking that way, I thought of another possibility. Maybe Luguire was never involved. Maybe there never was a transaction from the Federal Reserve. Then I learned Luguire never dealt with member banks. Yes, Amanda said the record was erased, but what if it never existed in the first place. The money simply came to Laurel Bank from an offshore account.

"Why? Because real money was needed. Money for Khoury's bomb materials and living expenses. Money for Asu. Money that could be tied to me. It was ingenious."

Jordan nodded, visibly acknowledging the compliment.

"Paul Luguire and Hugh Radcliffe were preparing to testify at secret congressional hearings. Some people were unhappy with the direction Radcliffe and Luguire would be recommending. The further I looked into it, the more I understood the impact the Reserve has beyond our borders. The pressure on the Federal Reserve is not a domestic issue but has international consequences. Cheap dollars at almost no interest courtesy of the Federal Reserve."

"So you're saying Amanda fabricated her story to entrap you in this conspiracy?"

"I knew Amanda had to have gained a tremendous amount of knowledge regarding the Federal Reserve payment system in order to design firewalls and protocols to protect it. Her story was believable. I wanted to believe her. But I couldn't ignore the other possibility, and I always have a contingency plan. So I set up a parallel investigation with an Arlington detective that she knew nothing about. She anticipated I'd investigate Luguire's death so she used my motivation to set a process in motion that was designed to ultimately tie me to the assassination of Chairman Radcliffe. Then the suicide of Paul Luguire would be re-opened and I would be prime suspect for that murder as well."

"And you got all this from your dead wife," Jordan said. "Excuse me, but it's pretty farfetched."

"That's true. But then there's the puzzling part about the POD."

"Print-on-demand?"

"Yeah, you're an author. You'll follow me on this."

Jordan sneered. "It's mostly used by people who self-publish. I know very little about it."

"I know." Mullins circled back around the coffee table and sat on the white sofa, keeping the gun on Jordan. "Ironic isn't it? A detail about publishing tripped you up."

"What detail?"

"POD books not only have a barcode on the back cover but also one on the last page. It's blank except for that barcode, and in some cases, the date and city of publication are also printed."

Mullins watched Jordan's face change as he began to understand the error.

"Amanda told me to pick up a book at the counter of Barnes and Noble. This was before I knew I'd be meeting her. But why do that cloak and dagger stuff when she already knew me. She could have told me to buy any book and wait in the Barnes and Noble coffee shop. The book she left at the counter was *Betrayal at Jekyll,* a very accusatory and vitriolic attack on the Federal Reserve, just the kind of book to make me look like an anti-Fed zealot when my apartment was searched. But this POD book had a print date of June twelfth of this year. It wasn't in Barnes and Noble's inventory because Amanda ordered it before her alleged conversation with Luguire even occurred. That told me a plan had already been put in place."

"Authors warehouse books all the time."

"You'd know that better than me, but odd that the June twelfth copy was the only one printed within the last six months. Not exactly a big seller like you. Or maybe like you used to be."

Anger flashed in Jordan's eyes. "I'm read across six continents and translated into fifteen languages."

"Really? I didn't realize remainders were so widely distributed. But it's not really books you're interested in, is it? I'm judging an author by his cover and you've got a terrific cover. Jetting around the world. Moving from capital to capital. Are you an errand boy or an actual player in the game?"

"Let's just say my best stories are the ones no one reads but have an impact around the world."

"Then I would have thought you'd be a better judge of character motivation."

For the first time, Jordan seemed genuinely interested in what Mullins said. "What do you mean?"

"You were right that I'd be focused on finding Paul Luguire's killer. And you and Amanda provided a path for me to pursue, a path you controlled. But that wasn't my only motivation. You didn't allow for minor characters to exert their own influence. Fares Khoury was a man in pain, a man who pleaded for my help. You had him killed, and you were ready to sacrifice his wife and daughter. I couldn't let that happen, and that motivation went beyond the bounds of your imagination. You might be a writer, but you're a hack. You have no empathy and therefore all your work will," Mullins paused, searching for the right words, "all your work will end up on the remainder table of history."

Jordan's face flushed. He leaned forward. "You don't know what I'm capable of or what I'm in line to control. Cut to the chase. What do you want for the flash drive. A million? Ten million?"

"I'd say the price is tied to how many crimes could come to light. We know Luguire was injected with ketamine. But Luguire had to let someone into his apartment. Someone he knew. There's Amanda again. But she couldn't do it alone. That's where the real mastermind of the whole scheme got involved. You went with her."

"I was in Paris."

"The next day. Amanda told me the name of your hotel. They said you checked in the afternoon after Luguire died and checked out last Thursday, in time to return to Washington for the grand finale."

Jordan said nothing.

"And that brings up the matter of Colleen."

"Who?"

"Sidney Levine's girlfriend. The woman you shot in his apartment. You see, Asu and Chuchi wouldn't have come across Sidney's postings. They were too tied up with the logistics of moving the Khoury family. But you would. Particularly during Sidney's postings overnight when Paris would be in normal waking hours. Two bloggers, Mountain View and Congressional Confessional, stand out as writers who responded with an effort to steer Sidney's inquiries in another direction. I blame myself for that. I should have realized the Internet was as dangerous a place to pry as anywhere in the real world.

"When I told Amanda about Colleen, she was genuinely shocked. That information and my news about the wrapping paper unnerved her. So, she called you while I was in the apartment. Did you tell her to try to sleep with me? To make sure I wasn't wearing a wire? Did you pimp your own wife?"

"I recruited Amanda, I married her, and I loved her. She knew the stakes we were playing for."

"And I'm sorry I had to kill her."

Jordan eyed the flash drive. "How high?"

"How high does this conspiracy go?"

"You can't imagine."

Mullins studied Jordan with all the training and experience of his years in the Secret Service. "Orca?"

Jordan's eyes widened just enough. "Tell me your price and I'll get you the money. You'd better take it because I'll never be convicted of anything. Understand we'd do it all again and there's nothing you can do to stop us."

Mullins stood and held up the flash drive. "The price for this, twenty bucks at Best Buy. The price for Craig Archer, Fares Khoury, Sidney Levine, and for my friend Paul Luguire—" He stretched out his hand offering Jordan the flash drive.

Jordan eagerly reached for it.

"Justice." Mullins put the muzzle of the suppressor against Jordan's temple and pulled the trigger.

Jordan fell back against the white chair, blood smearing across the fabric like a painter's brush sweeping over a blank canvas.

Mullins went to Jordan's study and retrieved the brown bag he used to bring Archer's envelope and Khoury's journal. Both now sat under a manuscript box on Jordan's desk. Then he stopped at the linen closet in the hall and took a plain white pillow case.

Mullins looked at Jordan's body slumped in the chair. Plausible. Jordan leaned forward, shot himself, and fell backwards. Mullins took Jordan's right hand. He'd watched him use it to pour and stir his drink. Mullins wrapped the dead man's hand around the pistol grip, pointed the gun into the pillow case, and fired.

The shot made a sharp bark and the blank cartridge spit wadding and burning powder into the pillow case. Mullins dropped the pistol on the floor at Jordan's feet. He picked up the blank's shell casing that had been ejected over the sofa. The first one lay by the chair. Investigators would find it, the gun, and the powder residue on Jordan's hand.

"What goes around comes around," Mullins said. He stuffed the pillow case in the paper bag and left.

Chapter Forty-nine

"Welcome back, Nails." The Secret Service agent stood outside the closed door to the Oval Office, his normally serious face hijacked by a broad grin. "Congratulations. Job well done."

Mullins shook his hand. "Thanks, Sam. Good to see you again. It's been a long time. It's also been a long day."

"Tell me about it. Because of you we got scrambled here from Camp David. So much for the president's holiday weekend."

"Sounds familiar. If you're not arriving, you're leaving. But I don't understand why he wants to see me. I had a debrief with Hauser."

"Tomorrow when the full story comes out, you'll be a national hero." Agent Sam Dawkins lowered his voice. "And it's an election year. Brighton could benefit from basking in your glory. Enjoy it while you can. Monday you'll be old news."

"Then here's to Monday."

The door opened and Mullins faced Daniel DeMarco, President Brighton's chief of staff. The man wore a white shirt with a maroon tie loosely knotted around his neck.

"Welcome, Mr. Mullins."

Mullins caught a whiff of Scotch on DeMarco's breath. "Thank you. Please call me Rusty."

"Certainly. I'm Danny." He pumped Mullins' hand with too much energy for ten o'clock at night. "Come in. I understand you've been here many times." DeMarco stepped aside and with a sweep of his arm, gestured for Mullins to enter.

"Thank you, Agent Dawkins." DeMarco closed the door.

Mullins swept his eyes across the Oval Office. He immediately noticed the differences, those elements that change with each new president: different pictures on the wall, different chairs and sofas in different groupings, different colored drapes for the three windows overlooking the South Lawn. Brighton had chosen royal blue and they were closed, shutting out the night and the long lenses of any photographers.

The Resolute desk given to President Hayes by Queen Victoria was still placed in front of the windows, and the oval rug with the Great Seal of the United States hadn't changed. What was missing was the president. Mullins stood for a moment, unsure what to do next.

Then the door on his right opened and President Brighton walked in from the adjacent study. He had to make an entrance, Mullins thought.

"Mr. Mullins. Or should I say Agent Mullins? Once an agent, always an agent. Outstanding work."

Like his chief of staff, Brighton wore a white shirt and loose tie. His long sleeves were rolled at the cuffs, and Mullins figured he and DeMarco decided to appear prepared for business in case they were seen coming from the helicopter to the West Wing.

"Call me Rusty, sir. And I'm too rusty to be back in the service."

Brighton laughed more than the pun called for. He clasped Mullins' hand and held on to it, a maneuver used during photo ops. Habits are hard to break.

"And modest too." Brighton pulled Mullins toward the end of one of the two sofas. "Sit, please." He released Mullins' hand.

Mullins sat on the edge while Brighton took an adjacent chair. DeMarco sat on a matching sofa opposite him. An oak coffee table was centered between them.

Brighton leaned forward. "I appreciate your coming here. I know it's been a hell of a day."

"For all of us, Mr. President."

Brighton nodded gravely. "Whenever an American institution is attacked, we are all attacked. When you served my predecessors and put your life on the line for them, you weren't simply safeguarding the president, you were defending the American people, the American way."

"Yes, sir."

"And the American people need to understand that, Rusty. I'll be addressing them again tomorrow night at seven. When I spoke from Camp David earlier today, some of my advisors wanted me to speculate which terrorists might be behind the planned attacks here and in Richmond." Brighton shot a pointed glance at DeMarco. "But I learned from Hauser and the FBI that the circumstances were still unfolding. I prefer to wait until I can assure the public of what we know and how we are proceeding."

"I agree, sir. In my opinion, that's the wisest course. There could be serious international implications if conjectures are voiced prematurely."

Brighton pursed his lips. "Such as?"

"The man we knew only as Asu is Syrian. Some will see him as proof of state-sponsored terrorism and begin calling for reprisals. I know from what transpired that Asu was a mercenary, expecting to be paid by the people running Amanda Church."

"What do you mean running?" Brighton asked.

"Well, as Hauser probably said, this operation was too complicated to have been conceived and executed by Amanda Church."

"Hauser said her husband committed suicide earlier today. They found his body when they went to check her home. You think he was involved?"

Mullins paused, as if he hadn't thought about the question. "Possibly. I never knew him, but I understand he traveled a lot. Europe mostly. A thriller writer. Why, the kind of story this turned out to be."

Brighton shook his head. "If that's the case, then the investigation could dead-end with him. Maybe there was some grudge against Chairman Radcliffe and the Federal Reserve. Amanda created the funds and her husband created the plan."

"Maybe," Mullins said. "That's for smarter people than me to figure out."

Brighton shifted in his chair, striking a more casual pose. "I understand you tried to record your abductors but there was a technical problem."

"Yes. Sidney Levine, the reporter who was killed, wasn't familiar with the equipment. I brought the data card to Hauser, but it was blank. Detective Sullivan and I reconstructed the conversation for Hauser as best we could."

"That's too bad," Brighton said. "But you did amazingly well and averted a national tragedy."

"Thank you, Mr. President."

"That's why I'd like you standing beside me tomorrow night. You and Detective Sullivan, of course."

"Thank you, sir. I only wish Sidney Levine could be there. He's the real hero."

"You have my word he won't be forgotten." Brighton slapped both hands on his knees. "Well, that's all I had. I don't want to keep you."

The president started to rise. Mullins reached over and touched his bare forearm.

"There is one thing, sir. A personal request, if I may?"

"Certainly, anything."

"I'm a little embarrassed to ask it." Mullins turned toward DeMarco. "Danny, could I have a moment alone with the president?"

Daniel DeMarco frowned. To be asked to leave the Oval Office by a civilian rankled, no matter how much the guy was the hero of the moment.

Brighton suppressed a flash of annoyance and then nodded to his chief of staff. "Why don't you start making the arrangements for Rusty, Detective Sullivan, and their families to be here tomorrow. And we should see if Mr. Levine has any relatives who can be present."

"Yes, Mr. President." DeMarco stood.

Mullins rose from the sofa and extended his hand. "Thank you, Danny. And thank you for all you do for our country."

"You're welcome." His handshake was less exuberant this time. He departed the way he and Mullins had entered, closing the door behind him.

Mullins sat down, this time a little farther away from Brighton. He paused, listening to DeMarco's footsteps fade in the hallway.

Then he took a deep breath. "Mr. President, I'm afraid I lied to you and Mr. DeMarco. And I've lied to Deputy Director Hauser."

Brighton's mouth dropped open. "What?"

"There is a recording. Sidney Levine didn't make a mistake. He captured every word from the time I was forced into the car at the Federal Reserve to when Asu ripped the microphone and transmitter from my collar."

Brighton's eyes narrowed. Instantly, his guard went up and the consummate politician grew wary. "Why would you lie about that?"

"For the good of the country. For the good of the Presidency."

Brighton's wariness transformed to unease. He didn't know where the conversation was going, and like any man of power, he didn't like losing control. "Then why did you ask Danny to leave?"

"For his protection. To give him deniability." Mullins pulled his personal cell phone from his belt. "White House security does an excellent job making sure nothing dangerous is carried in. I had to turn on my phone to demonstrate it was a working device. But fortunately no one checks content." Mullins pressed his audio player app and held the phone toward Brighton.

Mullins' voice started loud for a split-second and then the automatic gain lowered the level. *"How do you know Radcliffe will even come? The Richmond bomb has to create some kind of lockdown."*

Amanda spoke her first word in a lower volume, but the electronics boosted her voice. *"Give me some credit, Rusty. Timing is everything. Radcliffe will be here first. Even if the Richmond bomb is discovered, the Fed's confident of their D.C. security measures. Radcliffe might be convinced to skip the parade, but he'll never skip honoring his comrades. And he wants his granddaughter to see what sacrifice and courage are all about. No press or photo op. Just a private moment. And all we need is ten seconds for one little girl to give another little girl a birthday present.*" The recording stopped.

Mullins put the phone back in his pocket. "That's all I had time to excerpt. Enough to let you know it exists."

Brighton looked puzzled. "There's nothing wrong with that."

"I know. It matches the evidentiary findings and is consistent with a plot carried out by Amanda and her husband."

Mullins scooted along the sofa until he pressed against the armrest beside the president. Dropping the lie in the middle of the truth required a seamless delivery, a projection of genuine concern. "Right before Asu destroyed the transmitter, I made a plea to Amanda. I said she'd never get away with it. People wouldn't stand for the slaughter on one of our most sacred sites. She said it was the only way to protect the Federal Reserve."

"Protect it?" Brighton exclaimed.

"Yes. What better way to rally public support for an institution under fire?"

Brighton licked his lips nervously. "If it came to light that someone plotted this attack to benefit the Federal Reserve, the country would be in an uproar. Congress would revoke the legislation that established the Federal Reserve in a heartbeat."

"And they'd hear it from the lips of one of the prime conspirators," Mullins said. "Now you understand why I withheld the recording?"

Brighton nodded vigorously. "Absolutely. We need the Federal Reserve, especially in these uncertain times, but not at that price. The Reserve survived political challenges before and it would have survived this one." He grew wary again. "But why even tell me?"

"Because Amanda said there are people who will do whatever is necessary to insure the Reserve remains independently shielded from scrutiny as to where money is going."

"Who are these people?"

"She said they're outside the Reserve, operating without the Reserve's knowledge. Most are outside of this country, but the money supply from the United States is the most important asset providing their economic control. Powers behind the thrones, if you will. She said they would protect her."

"Did she name names?"

"Only one, Mr. President. Orca."

Mullins saw the fear in Brighton's eyes, not the indignant shock of a false accusation. Fear was there and then gone as quickly as it appeared. Contrived anger rose from its wake. "What the hell's that supposed to mean? Was she accusing me of conspiring with her?"

"I don't know, sir. I recognized your Secret Service code, but she didn't say president or specify you in any way. I know this town and how your political opponents would seek to use it against you."

"Those bastards would have a field day. And we're less than four months from the election."

"I wanted you to be aware of what Amanda Church said in case something surfaces elsewhere. I'm sure I was targeted to be framed and they might have manufactured something to compromise you."

Brighton gripped Mullins' arm. "Yes. They would do that. And if the investigation uncovers some lie about me, we'll be ready to refute it. Your innocence is above reproach. You and I can withstand any accusations together."

"Yes, Mr. President. Just like I'll be standing with you tomorrow evening."

"Thank you, Rusty. So, we're agreed. You'll destroy the recording."

"No, sir. I will not."

Brighton flinched like he'd been slapped. "What do you mean you won't destroy it?"

"I believe you, Mr. President," Mullins lied. "But what if I'm wrong. I have a daughter and a two-year-old grandson. You might be innocent of this accusation, but others might want to exact revenge, if there is some broader conspiracy afoot. I'm sorry, Mr. President, but it's a chance I can't take. As you know, your Secret Service agents always have a backup plan, a contingent escape option. This recording is mine."

Brighton's jaw clenched. "Are you blackmailing me?"

"I prefer to call it providing you a reality check. Something your other advisors might be reluctant to do. I've made copies of the recording. One is in a secure military classified file. Should I die under suspicious circumstances, I've made arrangements for it to be declassified. My son-in-law is in Naval Intelligence. He has access to all the necessary protocols and security clearances to protect the information, but also retrieve it. He doesn't know the content of the file, but he has his instructions. I know you are Commander in Chief, but any attempt to acquire what he secured through either a direct or indirect order will trigger its immediate release.

"The same is true for multiple copies I've encrypted and placed on secure servers that can be accessed by me and my daughter. Should anything happen to us, I've made arrangements for the information to be released, not just through my attorney but others who would be difficult for you to discover. So, innocent, which I'm sure you are, or a theoretically guilty player in Amanda's alleged financial cartel, you need not worry about any trouble from me." He paused. "Provided, of course, you make sure Sidney Levine, Craig Archer, Fares Khoury, and Paul Luguire didn't die in vain."

The color rose in the President's face. "So, it is blackmail."

Mullins shrugged. "Blackmail. Politics. I'm not going to argue semantics, Mr. President. You know how the game is played. But I'm not letting this shadow network win and derail what Paul Luguire stood for. Chairman Radcliffe will testify at the hearings and you will publicly reiterate your confidence in him and any proposals for monetary reform he puts forth. You won't exploit the public's outrage over the bombing here or the failed one in Richmond in an attempt to continue cloaking the Fed in secrecy."

Brighton stared at Mullins. He fought to control his anger as he weighed his choice between the devil in front of him and the devil lurking behind him. "All right. You have my word."

"And you have mine."

Brighton sighed and his eyes moistened. "I would never condone or be a party to the bombing of our own people."

"I know that you'd never knowingly be a party. Otherwise, I would have posted the recording on the Internet." Mullins stood, forcing the president to look up at him. "Until tomorrow, sir."

He walked out of the Oval Office without looking back.

Chapter Fifty

"Paw Paw." Josh squealed his grandfather's name and jammed a banana-coated finger into the newspaper photo.

"Yes. That's me. The handsome devil whose good looks overshadowed the President of the United States."

Kayli slid a bowl of dry Cheerios in front of her son, immediately pulling his attention away from the picture. "Sorry, Dad. You come in second compared to breakfast." She lifted the paper clear. "And I'm going to have to buy at least ten more of these."

"Why? I don't know ten people." Mullins took a sip of coffee and glanced at the photo again.

President Brighton stood behind a podium adorned with the Presidential Seal, wearing a sharp blue suit, white shirt, red tie, and U.S. flag lapel pin. The official uniform every president and candidate had to wear.

Mullins stood behind Brighton's right shoulder, also in a blue suit that probably cost nine hundred dollars less and a white shirt with a dark blue tie. Mullins had worn a red one, but a media consultant had whisked it off of him. Did she think people wouldn't be able to tell him and the president apart?

Detective Sullivan wore police dress blues. He held his cap by his side and the white gauze of his head bandage looked like a halo.

Both Mullins and Sullivan had asked not to speak, and Sidney Levine's mother was too ill to travel from New York. The president was all too happy to occupy the spotlight. All Mullins and Sullivan said was "Thank you, Mr. President," as Brighton shook their hands for the sea of photographers.

"I wasn't expecting you to give copies away," Kayli said. "I thought you'd plaster them up on each wall of your apartment."

"Hey, young lady, at my age, I avoid mirrors. All the newspapers can go in the landfill for all I care."

"Liar."

"Well, maybe keep one or two for Josh."

Kayli laughed and freshened his coffee. She brought her own cup to the table and sat across from him.

"You're something, Dad. What you did for the Khoury girl and her mom."

He shrugged. "What else could I do? You or Allen would have done the same." He stared into his cup a few seconds. "I spoke to Danny DeMarco last night after the telecast."

"Oh, so it's Danny now."

"Yeah. It pisses him off every time I say it. I gave him the suggestion to see what they could do to get Zaina and Jamila Khoury back in their home. The media has emphasized Fares was forced into his actions, and Zaina's bravery in leaving those notes is what really broke the case open."

"Did he agree?"

"Not at first. Then I said it would show the Muslim community we weren't holding them responsible. That struck a political chord. For people like Danny, it's the only music they hear."

"How many more arrests are likely?" Kayli asked.

"I'd say approximately none."

Kayli set down her cup with a clatter. "Really?"

"There's not much to go on. Chuchi got picked up a few blocks from Constitution Gardens, but he knows nothing. Asu was his only contact. I think Chuchi was hired for the convenience of the apartment. People wouldn't ask questions when they saw him coming and going. And Chuchi was supposed to die in the blast."

"More people had to be involved," Kayli argued.

"Definitely. They were probably day players brought in as needed. Somebody placed and armed the bomb in Richmond. Unlike Chuchi, they'd be well paid professionals who did what they were told without asking questions and without knowing the big picture."

Kayli shook her head. "I can't believe Curtis Jordan had all this mapped out. So many things could have gone wrong."

"I don't believe he did. He steered events more than created them." Mullins slid his cup to the side and leaned over the table. "After Luguire's murder, he had three goals. Get the bombs to Richmond and to the Vietnam Veterans Memorial, kill Radcliffe, and discredit anyone opposed to the Federal Reserve. Why Luguire was killed, we may never know for sure. Maybe he was always a threat, which is why Amanda pushed for me to be on his protection detail. She counted on me for access." Mullins thought a second. "The night he died Luguire told me he'd heard my nickname Nails that afternoon from a little bird. Amanda was the only one who could have told him that. Yet she said she hadn't spoken with him for a few days." Mullins slapped himself on the side of his head. "Hindsight's great, isn't it?"

Josh laughed and hit his own head with a handful of Cheerios.

"Monkey see, monkey do," Kayli said.

"I think Curtis Jordan turned whatever he could to their advantage. Snare me in as many webs as possible."

"And Luguire's "tough-ass" note?"

"Genuine. The shaky handwriting showed the effects of the ketamine. He slipped that by them. I think Amanda was shocked I'd already decided Luguire had been murdered. She was coming to plant that seed and start me on a trail that would be my undoing."

"But why even plant the seed? They would have gotten away with it."

"I think Amanda Church was afraid of me. She knew me too well to think I'd let Luguire's death be rubber-stamped as a suicide. Better for her to be a party to my investigation rather than be in the dark about what I was doing. Remember the real target was Chairman Radcliffe. He wasn't the thirteenth, he was always number one. Amanda's plan was to isolate me by making herself the sole contact with the federal law enforcement agencies. She knew I'd go for that because it kept me unfettered and free to pursue my leads. I did such a good job on the investigation, I moved from Khoury's backup fall guy to number one. I could be tied to Luguire, Archer, Khoury, and finally the bombings in D.C. and Richmond."

Kayli toasted him with her cup. "You can't hide talent."

"And I think Jordan also played a more hands-on role in addition to killing Luguire. He was probably Nathaniel Brown, the mystery man who contacted Archer and got him to document our meeting. Asu didn't have the skill to pull off the phone deception. And Fares Khoury told me he'd gotten some instructions from a man with a British accent. Jordan could have easily done that, as well as assembled all the technical resources for the hijacking of your phone and monitoring of Sidney's computer. I bet he also got the incriminating materials from Asu that he planted in my apartment."

"A busy man," Kayli said.

"Yes, but the timeline fits based on when we know he returned."

Beeps sounded from the microwave.

"What are you cooking?" Mullins asked.

"Nothing. That's a reminder I'm supposed to log onto Skype and talk to Allen. Would you entertain Josh? I'll call for him when his dad and I are finished."

"Certainly."

Mullins watched his grandson finish his Cheerios and then lifted him out of his booster chair.

"Ball," Josh said.

"Not inside." He set the toddler down on the kitchen floor. "Follow Paw Paw and we'll play on the rug."

Mullins sat on the carpet in front of the TV and played trucks and cars for a few minutes until Josh got bored.

"Mommy?"

Mullins didn't want to say Mommy was talking to Daddy or Josh would have bolted back to the bedroom.

"Here, I've got a new game to show you." Mullins reached into his pocket and palmed several quarters. "What's in your ears?"

Josh grabbed his ears. "Nothing, Paw Paw."

"Oh, no. I think you're wrong." He reached up, touched Josh's right ear, and brought back a quarter. "See, money?"

Josh's eyes widened and he burst out laughing. "More, Paw Paw, more money."

Mullins pulled a second quarter out of his grandson's ear.

Josh squealed even louder. "More, Paw Paw, more."

Mullins pulled a third, but when Josh grabbed for it, Mullins kept it out of reach. "No, no. Not yet. Can you repeat after Paw Paw?"

"Yes."

"Then here are the magic words that make the money appear. Say Federal Reserve."

Epilogue

Rain beat against the windows. The droning nearly drowned out the sound of Big Ben striking the hour of three.

An elderly man and woman sat in leather chairs in the center of the oak-paneled room. A third chair was empty, pushed back in a corner beside a cart holding a television and DVD player. It would stay there. Neither the man nor the woman knew how to work it.

They sat in silence, not because they didn't know each other but because they knew each other too well. They had nothing to say.

The squeal of dry hinges broke them from their thoughts. The single door to the room opened and the whir of a power wheelchair heralded the entrance of a man even older than his guests.

"Sorry to be late," he said in a voice surprisingly energetic for one so frail. "Americans do not know how to get off the phone."

"And which Americans would that be," the other man asked.

"The number one American. He needed a little hand-holding. Reassurance that we knew nothing about what happened in Washington this weekend."

"We didn't," the woman said. "At least I didn't."

The man in the wheelchair nodded. "We didn't need the details, just the results."

"A unmitigated disaster," the other man said. He looked back at the empty chair. "A gross miscalculation."

The man in the wheelchair maneuvered closer till he was facing the other two, a tight triangle of intrigue. "All wasn't lost. Yes, Brighton will cave to Radcliffe's recommendations and we will have to work harder with our congressional allies to preserve what protection we can. But the bomb attempt in D.C. and Richmond tempered the more extreme critics. The Federal Reserve itself is secure and Brighton is favored to win re-election."

"But this Mullins," the woman said. "What does he know?"

The man in the wheelchair shrugged. "More than he'll ever tell because at some level he understands. When you realize we're living in a financial house of cards, you're careful about what you disturb. Yes, this Mullins has potential leverage over Brighton, but that's all it is. Potential. Brighton will make sure Mullins never needs to use it, and once Brighton's out of office, we have nothing to fear. Besides, Mullins has his own ghosts now."

"How can you be so sure?" the woman asked.

"Jordan never committed suicide. He was too arrogant. He believed he could talk or think his way out of any predicament. That overconfidence always bothered me. As it turned out, he was wrong. We're fortunate that flaw manifested itself before Jordan was given more power. In a way, we owe Russell Mullins a debt of gratitude."

"Mullins?" the man and woman exclaimed in unison.

"Well, who else could have killed Jordan? And that's why he won't want a re-opened investigation." The old man gave a rare smile. "I have to admire him. It was nicely done."

The man in the wheelchair looked at his bewildered colleagues. "Come now. Let's put this behind us and move forward. We have an opportunity for some new blood in our little family." He rubbed his withered, ancient hand across his chin. "I was thinking it was about time we approached the Chinese."

Acknowledgments

A number of people provided information and suggestions for the background of this novel. I'd like to thank Rose Pianalto Cameron of the Public Information Office of the Federal Reserve Board of Governors in Washington, D.C., and former Secret Service agent Robert Alberi for their assistance. Any errors of fact or procedure are my responsibility. I'd also like to thank Hugh Johnston for providing a perspective of those citizens in opposition to the role and power of the Federal Reserve. Thanks to Patty and Bill Stone for coordinating the logistics of my D.C. Research, Lieutenant Liz Clarke, U.S. Navy for non-classified information on operations, Craig de Castrique for insights into banking procedures, and Reverend Bill Bigham for sharing his experience with insulin pens.

As always, the support from Poisoned Pen Press made the writing process enjoyable. Thanks to Jessica Tribble, Robert Rosenwald, Annette Rogers, and my editor, Barbara Peters, for their guidance as I ventured into new territory.

Manuscript revisions also benefitted from suggestions from my agent, Linda Allen, my wife Linda, daughters Lindsay and Melissa, and son-in-law Pete Thomson. My writing assistant, Gracie the spoiled Schnauzer, slept through everything.

The Federal Reserve System has been the subject of debate since its creation in 1913, a debate that has grown more intense in the current economic crisis. The premise of this novel, that a shadowy, international cabal benefits from the independent existence of the U.S. Federal Reserve System, is an invention for the story. However, recent court orders for disclosure of the distribution of Federal Reserve bailout funds have revealed a significant proportion of those funds went to foreign institutions.

The novel takes no side in the pro-Fed, anti-Fed debate, but I encourage readers interested in the topic of U.S. monetary policy to visit the Federal Reserve's website www.federalreserve. gov/aboutthefed and its linked sites to the twelve regional Federal Reserve Banks. Arguments against the Federal Reserve System can be found in *End the Fed* by Ron Paul (Grand Central Publishing 2009) and *The Case Against the Fed* by Murray N. Rothbard, Ph.D. (Ludwig von Mises Institute 2007).

Finally, I'd like to thank the librarians and booksellers who introduce my stories to their patrons, and you, the reader, for sharing the adventures with me.

Mark de Castrique
January 2011
Charlotte, N.C.

To receive a free catalog of Poisoned Pen Press titles, please contact us in one of the following ways:

Phone: 1-800-421-3976
Facsimile: 1-480-949-1707
Email: info@poisonedpenpress.com
Website: www.poisonedpenpress.com

Poisoned Pen Press
6962 E. First Ave. Ste 103
Scottsdale, AZ 85251